I0612832

In the Red

A Novel

LISA LIBBY

ISBN: 978-1-7341263-0-3 (paperback)
ISBN: 978-1-7341263-1-0 (eBook)
Library of Congress Control Number: 2020906067

This book is a work of fiction. Names, characters, businesses, places, events and incidents are either the products of the author's imagination or used in a fictious manner. Any resemblance to actual persons, living or dead, or actual events is purely coincidental.

Printed in the United States of America

First printing edition 2020

www.lisalibby.com

To my husband Theard and daughter Jolie,
the loves of my life.

Acknowledgements

To the unforgettable people that changed my life. They may never get the chance to read my book, but they've inspired every word on every page.

I'm eternally grateful to my Aunt Caroline and Uncle Robert for providing clothes, food, shelter, and a loving family environment. While they were rich with love and care, they didn't have the means to provide for others, but they found a way and were happy to help. Thank you for making every holiday a grand occasion for the family and for exposing me to your perfect example of unconditional love for one another and commitment to marriage. Your true love for all animals, especially horses, was beautiful to witness as a child. You have both made a tremendous impact on my life. Aunt Carol, since you left this earth, there has been a void that could never be filled. You are missed by many.

To my most creative and highly artistic friend, Diane M. Delaney, who was my greatest teacher. She taught me how to see and feel art. She honestly and openly critiqued my drawings and laughed hysterically at the strange faces I drew. Nevertheless, she shared her knowledge for anything she was passionate about, and it was everything. From flowers, to art, food, wine, history, culture, color, and interior design: you name it and we likely had a discussion about it. Thank you for being a great friend and taking the time to share your knowledge with me and so many others. I miss our after-work drinks at the bar, laughing hysterically and talking about anything that popped in our heads. I miss you every day, my dear friend and my favorite artist.

in the red idiom

Definition of *in the red*
: spending and owing more money than is being earned.

Apparently the company had been *in the red* for some time before it went out of business.

In the Red. (n.d). In Merriam-Webster. Retrieved from www.merriam-webster.com

AVA

CHAPTER 1

THE JOB

Boston is so goddamn cold in January. The snow caps the tops of trees, bending the branches so it looks like the tree is overcome by sorrow. Icicles hang from every gutter I walk past. Sand and salt canvas the icy sidewalks. The residents abandon their Christmas lights near the trash cans; the pine needles leaving a trail from their homes to where they drag their Christmas trees to the curb. Every year after the Holiday season, you can predict January, February, and even March will be the darkest, coldest, and most depressing months to live in this city. The holidays are over, cheer replaced with the miserable, long silence from the effects of the snow accumulating on the ground absorbing the city sounds and trapping them until the first thaw in Spring. The weather and atmosphere are the perfect fuel for my low mood. If I move to a new city with warm weather year-round, I just might be able to dig myself out from under my depression.

My walk home from the hospital is slow, but steady. I distract myself from the cold by searching for my drops of blood along the sidewalk, from the walk to the hospital. Feeling sickly from all the blood loss, the short walk feels daunting. I didn't meet the New Year's resolution I set for myself: suicide. I have eleven months to try again before I completely fail to reach my resolution. Maybe next time I won't pass out from the mere sight of my own blood.

Once I slit my left wrist, I didn't know I wouldn't be able to stomach the sight of the blood. I assume I lost consciousness immediately after cutting my wrist, but I don't recollect. When I awoke, the tub water was dark red. It scared me so much so, that in that moment I had a change of heart. I'm glad I didn't die today; it doesn't feel like it was meant to be.

Of course, the doctors didn't believe my story about cutting myself while attempting to debone a fish, and why should they; it was clear what my intentions were. They gave me a few stitches and some brochures about depression, the phone number for the suicide helplines, and sent me on my way. If I'd allowed the doctor to examine me further, he'd have diagnosed me with depression, anxiety, and bipolar disorder – and to top it off, a sprinkle of schizophrenia.

It's 6:30 a.m. when I get home, about the time I wake up to get ready for work. I have less than an hour to leave the house if I want to be on time. Every morning it's a struggle to get out of bed, especially on such frigid mornings. Since I've had no sleep, I don't have the problem of getting out of bed. Maybe, just maybe today I'll get to work on time.

After completing my mandatory internship credit for

graduation, Atlantic Street Financial hired me. I contemplate calling in sick to work, but I made a promise to my manager Johnny not to unless I'm really sick.

Johnny has been a shoulder to cry on ever since he found me sobbing in Atlantic's garage, while I sat in my ex-boyfriend Mac's stolen car, balling my eyes out. He went with me to return Mac's car and convinced him not to report the incident to the police. Mac's lucky I didn't return his car on fire, after catching him cheating on me with a younger, skinnier version of myself. It's only been three months since the breakup, but I still feel anger from his betrayal. Catching him cheating on me is a memory that's on replay; I can't get it out of my mind. When you're used to being with someone every day and they're suddenly absent from your life, it's tough to handle the drastic change. Since the breakup, I don't have many friends to lean on. It's awkward to keep friends that you share with your ex-boyfriend.

I feel lucky that I still have my best friend, Paul. We met our freshman year of college. I found him attractive at first, which is why I introduced myself. I admired his flawless dark skin, big brown eyes, and long lashes His tall, lean build made any girl in class watch him enter the classroom. He was easily found in any crowd of students because his curly afro towered over the others. When he didn't hit on me the first month of our friendship, I knew he was gay. He didn't tell me at first, but he didn't have to, I was just happy to have him as my friend.

By the time we graduated, Paul had become a full-time criminal hacker. He'd progressed from petty hacking to bribing politicians, corporate companies, and anyone with power and riches. If he finds dirt on anyone rich, he will hang it over their heads and bribe them for his own personal financial gain. His energy and excitement for life is what gets me out of bed most days. He keeps saying time heals all wounds, but his cliché phrase doesn't help my mind heal. Each day I care less about my appearance. I avoid mirrors, and when I must look in the mirror, I see an ugly, fat disappointment staring back at me.

I quietly open the back door and tiptoe down the hallway to the bathroom, so my roommate Samantha doesn't see the bloody bandage, but she's already in the shower. I hurry to my bedroom before I bump into her. I won't have time to take a shower, so a quick wash up is all I can do. I strip naked and use a makeup remover wipe to wash my face, neck, and armpits. I have no confidence that the perfume and deodorant will cover the alcohol smell seeping through my pores or the stench of weed. I honestly don't know why I try, because I don't care.

As usual, traffic is terrible heading into downtown Boston. The subway is the fastest mode of transportation, but sometimes its frequent delays and many cancelled trains makes me wish I could stand the cold and walk the three miles to work. I check my work emails on my mobile, all while attempting to hold onto a nearby pole on the train, but it's easier to reach for the roof of the train to brace myself each time it jerks and stops. I feel my stitches stretch and possibly break open. I don't dare to even look at the bandage for fear of seeing blood. I'm missing the 9:30 a.m. meeting. Since I'm already late, I might as well stop for coffee.

On my way to my desk, I walk quickly past the conference room, expecting the dirty looks of my co-workers, but it's empty. The entire office is quiet, which is odd. I turn the corner to see my coworkers scrambling around the office as if there's a surprise audit. I get to my cubicle section to find most of my co-workers standing around chatting.

"Johnny; what's going on? I thought we had a budget meeting today? Where's everyone?"

He leans in to whisper, "They arrested Susan this morning – everyone is panicking. The FBI have seized several boxes of documents. They told us we'll be sent home soon and instructed us not to log in or touch any computer files."

"This company must be doing some crooked shit if the FBI is digging around," I say.

I'm trying to hold my composure and not freak the fuck out because I need this job.

"What's that, are ya bleeding?" asks Johnny, grabbing the sleeve of my blazer.

Blood droplets are running down my hand. I yank my arm away from Johnny.

"It's nothing." I avoid eye contact to hide my shame. I can feel him staring at me, judging.

I excuse myself and duck into the nearest restroom to text Paul to ask for his advice. He reassures me that everything will be okay, to go home and wait to hear from him. Paul always knows just what to say to make me feel at ease.

I return to Johnny and to where most of the staff have gathered.

We continue our conversation like I never left.

"Don't jump to conclusions. Maybe it's just something Susan has done, not the company."

"Jesus Christ, Ava don't be so damn naïve."

I've never seen Johnny snap at anyone, let alone me. I didn't see that coming. Why's Johnny so stressed?

His phone rings and he disappears down the hall.

As we turn the corner, men dressed in suits walk toward us, motioning us to leave.

"Go home until you hear from your Human Resources Department," says the taller man of the group. Now my stomach's knotting. If I've learned anything in my financial courses, companies just don't get raided by the FBI for small bookkeeping mistakes. This is a serious bust. The company has given me limited access to their financial documents, so I couldn't be in any trouble. As far as I know, both Johnny and Susan have the most access, but why was only Susan arrested? Johnny could've been arrested; not sure why he wasn't. Perhaps, the FBI doesn't have enough evidence to charge him. I've always questioned his knowledge of accounting because I know more than him when analyzing the financial records. I'm amazed Atlantic even hired him because they hold a reputation as a prestigious financial institution. Even with my straight A's and advanced accounting courses, Paul still had to hack their human resources email and delete the other candidates to increase my chances of even getting the internship. Without that, Atlantic wouldn't have even read my resume.

Atlantic is the largest investment firm in Boston, MA, a multibillion-dollar company, with investments in every avenue possible. They're highly involved with the community; charities, non- profit organizations, and several state agencies. The media will be all over this story as soon as it's leaked. I may have some serious difficulty getting hired at another financial firm in Boston if I put this company on my resume. If this case goes to trial, I will likely need to stand trial because I worked in the finance department. My negative thoughts are beginning to trigger my anxiety. I'm sweating, my stomach is turning, and I feel my chest getting heavier, causing a shortness of breath.

The FBI agents force us out of the office after human resources personnel gave us a document to fill out. I want to go home to shower and sleep off the pain throbbing in my wrist, but Johnny insists we go out for a drink. I find it strange he didn't invite the others from the office. I have a gut feeling Johnny knows more about Susan's arrest than he's letting on.

We arrive outside a bar that I've walked by many times before, but never been inside, because if the inside is anything like the outside it's frightening. The two identical glass cube tile windows on either side of the black metal door don't allow light out or in. Johnny pushes the abandoned shopping cart filled with trash out of the doorway to get in the bar. There's no greeter at the door to check photo ID's. Just one bartender behind the bar and a few old men scattered throughout the bar drowning their sorrow in their drinks. The bar's counter shines with filth. I predict its counter is sticky before taking a seat on the green, ripped-seat-covered stool.

We start with beers and then move onto shots. It doesn't take long for the effects of the alcohol to set in and soon I'm comfortable with the atmosphere.

"What'dya think they arrested Susan for?" I ask searching his eyes. He looks through me for a moment then stares long into his empty beer glass.

He turned to look at me and leans in whispering, "Um, gonna tell you some things, but you gotta keep your mouth shut." He takes a deep breath before continuing. "Susan's been doing some laundry, moving large amounts of cash through the organization. I'm sort of involved, I guess."

"Wait, huh? Who're you guys working for?"

Johnny ignores my questions and waves to get the bartender's attention for another round.

"Johnny! Don't ignore me."

"The Irish," he finally responds.

I'm not shocked that Atlantic is corrupt because it's no secret Atlantic has ties to the Italians, but the Irish? I didn't think they collaborated in the criminal world.

"How the fuck do you know so much? Come on, you're full of shit," I say, raising the glass to my lips.

"Be prepared; the FBI will come to question you. It's no big deal, it's small suit and tie crime, but keep ya trap shut."

"You mean to tell me you knew about this and still hired me? How much extra are you getting paid to help Susan cover this up?"

He stares at the television above the bar.

"Ava, it's my friggin job, I work for the Irish... Mob."

I take a shot, slam the glass down on the bar.

"Go fuck yourself." I leave him sitting at the bar still staring at the television. If he's telling the truth about his involvement with the Mob, I don't want to be seen with him, I'm sure the FBI are watching us right now – or maybe I'm just drunk and paranoid. It's already noon when I stumble out of the dark bar into bright light. I'm going straight home to pack up my shit. I'm leaving the city first thing in the morning. I can sublet my room – since I own the condo, the rent would even pay the utilities and taxes. "I'm outta here in the morning!" I scream, crossing the street.

I don't pack; that was drunk Ava making plans and not following through. Instead I fall asleep on top of my empty suitcase.

I wake up confused – is it morning or night? My head is pounding hard. I can barely open one eye to check my phone. I have several missed calls and texts from Johnny. There are other missed calls and texts from numbers I don't recognize. I flick through the news channels searching for the story about Atlantic, expecting a breaking news story, but find nothing. I check my voicemails, deleting all of Johnny's slurred voicemails, but the last voicemail is from a Connor McClean, an FBI agent working the Atlantic case. He requests a meeting with him tomorrow morning at 10:30 a.m. at the police station. I return his call, but there's no answer, so I leave a message confirming the meeting.

Johnny has me paranoid. I'm afraid to call or text him from my phone. The FBI can get access to my cellphone records. I have plenty of things on my phone that may get the FBI more interested than I'd like. I roll a joint, throw on my boots and a sweatshirt, and head to the nearby liquor store, not ignoring the idling car across the street, only to discover it's just my neighbor. I try to shake off my paranoia; all I'm doing is freaking myself out. I talk to myself. *I'm a nobody, why do I think anyone would be after me? I did nothing wrong, did I? I'm fresh out of college, working my first finance job. They must know about Johnny, but how involved could he be? What if they think I'm a rat by going to the FBI? I need to know more about the investigation, so I can talk myself out of any involvement. How important is Susan?*

I grab a bottle of white rum, rolling papers, a pack of cigarettes, and a prepaid cell phone.

As soon as I get home from the store, I search my cell phone and write down all the important contacts. Then I take the sim card out of the phone and smash both the phone and the sim card with a hammer. I flush the broken pieces down the toilet. If the FBI want my phone records, they will need to ask my cell phone carrier, but they won't be getting them from me. I won't contact Johnny until after speaking to the FBI in the morning.

I wake up the next morning with the same hangover from day drinking into the night. My roommate has already left for work. I put the coffee on and hop in the shower, taking my coffee to go so I'm not late. The police station is about a twenty-minute walk. I don't own a car, so I walk when I can and when I can't, I use public transportation. When I arrive at the police station, I'm not waiting long before I'm ushered to the back offices and into an interrogation room.

"Miss, how 'bout some coffee," asks the officer. I show the officer my coffee cup. He's doesn't look amused that I'm insinuating he asked a dumb question. Sitting in the room is making me nervous; more than I should be. I wish Johnny hadn't told me anything because then I wouldn't feel so nervous.

The last time I was in a room like this, I was told my mother was dead and my stepfather, Lewis Lorcan, was in custody for her murder. I still to this day don't believe he killed her. My love for him blinded me from believing he did it. He was the only father I knew. He began dating my mother when I was two years old. After my mother's death, I spent years investigating her murder and even went to my Lewis's trial. I still don't understand why he pleaded guilty. I could see in his eyes he was lying, and my gut still says he didn't do it, but after getting nowhere, I gave up on finding her killer, and stopped visiting Lewis in prison. I tried to be selfish and focus on myself, went to college and spent my nights in bed suppressing my childhood memories to avoid deeper depression.

I just want to go home and hide under the piles of down comforters on my bed and cry. I've never felt so lonely since the day before my high school graduation, the anniversary of my mother's murder.

I hear the doorknob turn and butterflies take flight in my stomach. I grab my stomach and gulp, the air pushing acid reflux down.

"Miss Madden, I'm Officer Connor McClean. I am spearheading the investigation of your employer, Atlantic Street Financial. Thank you for coming down to the office on such short notice. I hope I am accommodating your needs by meeting at a station closer to your home. I forget that not everyone in the city owns a car."

How does he know I don't have a car?

He makes direct eye contact, putting his coffee on the table before offering a handshake. I notice a tattoo peek from under his white shirt cuff. If he wasn't wearing a suit, I'd question his occupation as an FBI Agent. His dark blue eyes smile back even without a smile. His hair has a tint of red, but mostly brown. He sits behind his coffee and notebook. It's obvious he is unprepared with his book page blank and no pen. I assume by his unshaven face he has had a long night. His stare makes me self-conscience, I regret not putting on more makeup.

"I need to ask you a few questions. If you want your lawyer present, just speak up."

Agent McClean's facial expressions change from friendly to serious as if someone turned off the lights.

"Miss Madden…"

I interrupt him, "Please ... call me Ava; Miss makes me feel old." I fail to lighten the mood.

"Okay, Ava. Do you know why your manager Susan was arrested?"

"No," I try to maintain eye contact and not swallow – advice that mother taught me at a young age. For some strange reason she wanted me to know how to lie and how spot a liar. I thought this was normal behavior for a mother, until I became an adult. Strange as it was, I'm grateful for every street smarts tactic she taught. Mother was a good liar; too good. I remember her words, "Look the other person in the eyes and don't fidget with your hands".

"It is my obligation to inform you that your manager is being investigated for altering the books at Atlantic and cleaning money through the company for the Irish Mob, and if you are in any way involved, now is the time to explain your involvement."

I pretend the news is shocking, leaving my mouth open in awe.

"Oh my Gosh! I can assure you I'm unaware of Susan's dealings, or anyone at Atlantic who is altering books," I say, the tears building.

I burst into tears not because of sadness or fear, but because I need to convince Connor of my innocence, and because my mother didn't raise a fool.

Connor nervously searches the room then until he finds me tissues.

Johnny is telling the truth. Fuck – I can't tell the FBI what I know, I'd be a rat, a dead rat.

"With all due respect, Mr. McClean, I've only worked with Atlantic for less than a year, and before that I was just an intern. I don't believe I'll be of any help with the case. I don't even have access to Susan's accounts or the company's financial statements. Susan didn't exactly like me. My excessive tardiness drove her nuts."

I'm trying to convince him but perhaps I'm piling the bullshit too high.

"What about Johnny? What do you know about his involvement?"

I gulp. "None, as far as I know. He's my immediate supervisor, so I report to him more than Susan. He assigns me a task and I do it: that sums up our work relationship."

"Listen, I can't protect you if you don't tell me what's really going on at Atlantic… I know you know something, and that's fine right now, but this is a federal case. You don't know who you're dealing with. This will not be swept under the rug. There must be rumors floating around the office?"

He's testing me, either to see how much I know or to see if I'm a rat. I can't tell who's side he is on.

"I hate to admit this, but I don't exactly associate with my co-workers. I don't fit in with the office runway models and don't share their obsession with gluten-free organic vegetarian diets. As you can imagine, I ate every lunch at my desk, alone."

He smirks at my comment.

There's a long, awkward silence. If you stay quiet for long enough, most people can't help but fill the silent void with chit chat, and will give you information they normally wouldn't, just to avoid the silence. Not me though and he seems to know how to play the same game, waiting for me to break.

"If you will excuse me, I think you've asked all the questions you need... I'll be on my way."

I stand, letting him know the conversation is over.

"Here's my card if you need to talk. I know this is a stressful situation, and perhaps you are innocent, but understand that I am just doing my job."

"I appreciate your concern, and if I think of anything, I'll call. Thank you for your time, Mr. McClean."

"Please, just Connor."

New snow covers the sidewalk and falls heavier with every stride I make. Halfway through my walk home I sense someone following me. Too frightened to turn around, I pick up the pace and so does my heartrate. Someone grabs my shoulder from behind and turns me around.

"Leave me alone!" I swing blindly at the person holding me by my shoulders.

"Ava, Jesus Christ, why haven't you fuckin' called me? I've been worried."

"Johnny, you almost gave me a fucking heart attack."

"We gotta talk, NOW!"

I steer him into the T-Bar and restaurant attached to the subway station near my house. Locals refer to the subway as the T; that's where the bar got the name, I assume. I grab a pen and paper from the bartender and write, *Turn off your phone before we talk.*

Johnny reluctantly pulls his phone from his pocket, turns it off and sets it on the top of the bar counter.

"This's why ya haven't called me back – ya outa ya fuckin' mind?"

"The Mob … the FBI, they could tap our phones, so I bought a prepaid phone."

I write the new number down and hand it to him. "I suggest you do the same."

"Ava, the guys got it unda control."

"Throw it in the river, tell them you lost the phone. Wait, what guys?"

"Not gonna happen. The guys, the Mob, they're handlin' it, fuckin' relax."

Time to bring out the tears again, hoping to tug on his heart strings, so maybe he will open up and give me more information. I'm angry at Johnny, but also pleased at his concern for me. I don't have many people I'm close to. I have issues with that kind of thing, and now, as much as I'm pissed at Johnny, maybe he's just trying to look out for me, and I should trust he knows what's best.

"Ava, everything will be fine, relax. You'll meet with my boss tomarrah. She wants to make sure you understand the seriousness of the situation and know you're on our side. Ya know the investigation and trial, just all details. We have tha best lawyers. There's no doubt the chahges against Susan will be dropped if all of us back up her story."

"I don't have a fucking choice, do I?"

He puts his hand on my leg. "Sorry, Ava – I never meant for you to be dragged into this shit, but here we are. His hand moves higher up my leg. "You were new to the company and had no ideah what wheels were already turnin'."

We sit for some time sipping our drinks, just staring at the television. His phone rings, breaking the silence. He motions he'll be right back and steps outside to take the call. It's probably his bitch of a girlfriend, Casey. I only met her once at the holiday office party. Upon meeting, we both established that we didn't like each other. At the time, she knew I was going through a breakup and maybe felt insecure, since Johnny fucks anything in the office. This was before I gained weight and let myself go. My current appearance is the polar opposite of Johnny's girlfriend Casey. She's beautiful, petite – long blonde hair with gorgeous green eyes. Although her attitude and the way she judges others when she talks at them makes her ugly. I'm still jealous of her and Johnny's relationship because they seem so close, even with all his infidelity. Not that I have any feelings for Johnny, I just wish I had someone in my life that cares for me as he does for Casey. I didn't want to break it off with my ex even after discovering the cheating. I guess in that aspect I'm like Casey. Mac broke it off with me because he wanted to be with the other woman.

I order another round of drinks before heading for the restroom. On my way I notice an old man sitting alone in a big booth. I swear I saw him at the police station, but I can't be certain. I feel him staring at me as I pass his booth. When I return to my seat, Johnny isn't there. The bartender hands me a napkin with a note on it and told me the tab was prepaid, and I can continue to order drinks and food.

The note read:

Ava,
Sorry I had to go. I'll pick you up in the morning around 9am.
Drinks and lunch are on me!!!
Johnny

I haven't eaten anything today, so I order a burger and a black coffee. I've been drinking way too much and need to sober up. I ask the bartender to send the old man in the booth a drink. I want him to know I recognize he's following me. He's either an FBI agent, a mob member or someone from Atlantic. Whatever the case, I need to find out because I'm positive he's following me. Just as my burger arrives, so does my follower. He's an overweight, balding, mustache-wearing short fucker with a mismatched suit. His appearance reminds me of a 1970s retired porn star.

"You know I've been following you, Ms. Madden, so let's just get to the point," says the old man. His breath stinks of cigarettes and cheap vodka. "I'm a private investigator hired by Atlantic Street Financial. They've opened their own internal investigation on their employees."

Hmm, Italian? I can't tell, but I know for certain he's not from Boston because he pronounces his R's; maybe New York.

"So, you follow me around, and what … what the fuck do you think you will accomplish by watching me eat a fucking cheeseburger and get piss drunk in the middle of the day?"

"Listen, Atlantic's reputation is on the line and with this case going to trial the media will run with this story. Do you think investors will trust their money with Atlantic once this story breaks? It's in your best interests to help us find the missing money and fund transfers that cover up the money laundering scheme."

"Do you think I give a shit about Atlantic's reputation and the money they will lose? I'm out of a job. I live paycheck to paycheck. I've done nothing wrong. You can contact my lawyer." I lie; I don't have a lawyer. "Maybe I should hire an investigator to follow you around."

As the words leave my mouth, I realize that's exactly what I need to do. I have people following me, but who's got my back? No one.

"Ms. Madden, if you could cooperate with us…"

I cut him off, "Not gonna happen. I'm finished talking. You can leave now, so I can enjoy my fucking burger in peace."

It makes sense why Johnny left; he was tipped off this private investigator was here. We were both being followed, and it's suddenly clear who Johnny is looking out for. It's not me.

AVA

CHAPTER 2

FIRST IMPRESSIONS

I wake up early to get ready for my meeting with the Mob boss and their lawyers. I say it out loud and laugh at the word, "Mob". I can't tell if I'm going crazy or if my nerves are getting the best of me. Last night, I left the bar before getting too shitfaced. I want to have a clear mind to prepare what I'll say at the meeting.

I choose the nicest suit jacket and matching skirt, heels and the only jewelry I own that reminds me of my mother's funeral. I want my attire to embody the seriousness of the meeting. I find it humorous to look at myself in the mirror. I look like I'm going to a funeral. Last night, after my encounter with the investigator, I realized: I no longer want to be a coward. I must play the hand that was dealt. Two outcomes can happen: win or lose. My life is a bottomless pit of depression, so I'm going into this meeting in my suicidal mindset. I haven't had this much stress in my life since my mother's murder. Again, I can't tell if it's my stress and anxiety making me feel invincible or the concoction of alcohol and weed. I'm rolling with the feeling. It's a new day that could be my last if I don't choose my words wisely.

I take one last look in the mirror before I wait outside on my porch. I haven't felt this good in a long time. Wearing a suit always gives off a fake confidence and power. I can tell by Johnny's face he's surprised to see me dressed up.

"What's the occasion?"

"Funeral," I smile.

The drive to South Boston feels long. I upset my stomach from not eating breakfast, but at least my stomach feels flatter. I can tell I've lost some weight because sitting in the car, my skirt doesn't feel as tight. If I knew losing a job and a boyfriend was a weight loss remedy, I would've signed up a long time ago.

"Ya all right?" asks Johnny, avoiding eye contact by looking out the car window

"Sure, why?"

"It's just ya look … different that's all."

"I feel different."

We pull up to a rundown corner store. There're a few intimidating men standing out front, watching as we exit the car. They see Johnny and let their guard down. I follow Johnny through the poorly fluorescent-lit store. The floor is in rough condition. The dirty yellow linoleum is torn in several places exposing a moldy, decrepit wood floor. I'm watching for a rat to crawl out from under the bare food shelves. It's obvious the store is a front for other business ventures; any officer could sniff this out. We walk through the back door and up a narrow set of stairs. The ceilings are so low, I almost hit my head several times. We go through one more door before we're in a reception area. Shockingly enough, the place has a clean sterile look, resembling a doctor's office, the opposite of the rundown store I just walked though. Everything is white; floors, ceilings, walls, but the furniture is shiny black with accents of glass.

"We're heah for the 10 a.m. meeting," says Johnny.

The receptionist doesn't speak, just nods and picks up the phone. We aren't sitting in the waiting area long before a muscular, heavy looking man approaches. He's dressed all in black, even his tie is black. We follow him into a large room with an oversized dark mahogany oval table. There are two men in suits sitting with briefcases, obviously the lawyers. At the head of the table sits an older woman wearing dark sunglasses. Her red, shoulder-length hair is neatly parted in the middle. She's a petite woman who looks to be the same age as my mother if she were still alive. I can't see if she's looking at me, but I sense she is. There are two identical looking men standing on each side of her. Seems like the uniform is black head to toe. It's obvious she's the boss. Johnny follows me in but doesn't pull up a chair. Instead he leaves, closing the door behind him. I swallow, but nothing goes down. I can hear my heart pounding, my throat is dry, and I'm feeling dizzy. I expected Johnny would be at my side to support me. The voice in my head is saying, *You got this, be confident, be strong, and don't let her intimidate you.*

"Ms. Madden, we are the lawyers representing your former boss, Susan O'Daire," says one lawyer. Both lawyers' hand me their business cards in sequence. The Lawyer Offices of Dillon & Associates, LLC. The man doing all the speaking is Terry and I presume the other lawyer is his brother. Both have a serious expression and look almost identical except one is younger than the other. Terry looks like the older of the two. The business card lists an address just a short distance from Atlantic. Terry discusses the importance of my cooperation with the case. I stare straight ahead and keep my eye contact switching between brothers and nodding I understand. I can feel her stare at me, it's burning into my skin.

"Where are your manners?" the woman in the dark glasses looks in the direction of the lawyers.

"My apologies, Claire," stutters Terry.

"Ava, this is Claire Spillane... She is in charge of the Irish Business Association that Susan holds a membership with," explains Terry.

"Terry, the girl knows I'm the Mob boss, save your nonsense explanation for someone else," says Claire in a humorous tone.

She finally speaks to me. "Ava Madden... Your last name is familiar to that of a close family friend. Is your father from Boston?"

"I never met my father."

"How can you be so certain?"

"I think I would remember meeting my father."

"Do you remember the first day you were born?"

"No, of course not."

"So, how can you be so certain?"

"I don't remember meeting my father, so *no*, I can't be certain."

She's trying to get under my skin.

"Ah, much better. I assume Johnny has run off at the mouth and filled you in on our situation, who we are, and what we do here."

"Yes."

"Then you understand what you need to do for us."

"I do, but I have a request, if I may… I would like to look over the accounting books the FBI is using in the case against Susan. I think it would benefit the case if I could understand how the FBI caught Susan. Perhaps it would help to explain a few accounting mishaps.

"Ava ... how can you be certain there was an error and it wasn't just an enemy trying to take us down?"

She doesn't let me answer her question and continues talking.

"We don't need your help in that way, we need you to say what we tell you to say while you are testifying. Let me be clear; we are demanding your help, or we will make you and everyone you know vanish, poof, into thin air."

She stands up, takes off her sunglasses and pushes her way between the two lawyers. Leaning on the table, she stares me in the eyes.

"I'm insulted that you think we don't have the means to handle Atlantic, the IRS and FBI. For you to think we'll depend on a fucking intern. You are a special kind of stupid, aren't you?"

I can feel the tension in the room shift and the air thicken.

I stand up and lean on the table, so our eyes are at the same level.

"I'm not a fucking intern, Susan hired me."

She cocks her head to the side, like an animal does before they attack their prey.

I take a deep breath. "I apologize, I didn't mean to offend your business practices. I will cooperate, you have my word."

"The lawyers will be in touch; you are free to leave." She

signals me to leave by waving her hand as if to push me out of the room like I'm a stray dog begging for her to feed me.

I walk out and exhale like I've been holding my breath under water.

This meeting proves my mother wasn't lying and everything is starting to make sense. My anxiety is higher than ever before. I'm continuing with my own plans of protecting myself. I won't be able to do this alone, so I'll need to ask a few favors along the way.

When Johnny and I get in the car, he's acting anxious and asking too many questions, not waiting for me to answer one before interrupting with another.

"Johnny, relax. I agreed to their request, all set."

"Good, good. How 'bout some lunch, my treat?"

"I have a lot of stuff to do, laundry, groceries, that type of stuff," I lie.

"Oh, alright then, we'll drop ya at home."

I obviously don't want Johnny to know what I'm up to. I'm really going to visit my ex-boyfriend, Mac. I sent him a text late last night and told him I was in trouble and needed his help. He agreed to leave work to meet me at his apartment. I'm hoping to guilt trip him into a large cash loan, to pay for illegal items and services, cash only transactions. I would refinance my condo, but it takes too long to process, plus the FBI may find it suspicious. My accounts aren't frozen, but I'm sure they're being scrutinized. If I take out a large loan, they'll know something is up. I have plenty of money on my credit cards, but criminals don't exactly accept credit cards, plus it would just leave a trail back to me.

We pull up to my house. Johnny leans in to hug me and I awkwardly tense my body. He never hugs me; this is new.

"I'll be ova later."

"Johnny, I don't know if I feel like company tonight. Call me first."

This is strange behavior; I can't tell if he's hitting on me or was told to keep an eye on me.

I get to Mac's apartment earlier than he's expecting me, so I smoke the rest of my joint from this morning. It helps with my nerves and clears my mind. He still hasn't arrived, so I sit in the lobby of his apartment building waiting. He lives in a brand-new luxury mid-rise building. I know the building amenities and layout of the apartments from the many nights spent stalking him and his new girlfriend. I'm exhausted, so I close my eyes just for a moment.

"Ava … Ava."

I'm woken by Mac shaking me by my shoulders. I must've fallen asleep.

"I'm sorry, that's embarrassing."

I give him a hug. We exchange small talk on the way to the elevator.

"You look great, Ava."

His eyes look me up and down. It's uncomfortable.

"Thank you, you do as well. How do you like this building?"

"It's okay for now."

I follow him into his apartment, even though I already know what apartment number is his. I'm paranoid that people are following me, so I look around before entering. I don't want Mac pulled into my mess. Even though our breakup was messy, I still love him very much. He's the only man I've ever loved besides my stepfather.

We enter his home – it's enormous, bright and spotless. The decor has a modern feel. The colors are various tones of beige, brown and gray. He grabs me a glass of wine and we sit awkwardly across from each other in the living room. He smiles at me through each sip of wine. I mirror his behavior and facial expressions.

"Why are you all dressed up? Is today a special occasion?"

"I had an interview," I lie.

"You look great."

I catch him admiring my legs.

"Where was the interview?"

"With Liberty Financial."

The lies continue.

"Oh, a great company, I hope you get it."

Sitting in his apartment is making me self-conscious. I'm jealous of his girlfriend and the amazing, spotless apartment they share.

I decide to get to the point. "Listen, I don't want to take more of your time than I need. Can I borrow $50,000?"

He looks stunned.

"Ava, that's a lot of money; is everything okay."

"No, not really, I need to hire lawyers and a private investigator."

I fill him in on the Atlantic situation. I don't go into detail, but I let him know Atlantic is being investigated and shut down, so he knows the seriousness of my situation.

"Ava… that's terrible. I'm so sorry to hear about it. I can get you the money by tomorrow afternoon."

That was too easy, I'm sure he's being overly nice because he feels guilty for breaking my heart.

"Do you need a recommendation for a lawyer?"

I lie again, "No, I already have someone in mind. I'll pay you back as soon as I can."

"Don't worry about it. I'm just glad I can help."

He seductively looks me up and down, from my legs up to my chest.

"Would you like another glass of wine?"

"Sure."

I walk around the room checking out the artwork, while he fetches more wine. I can't help but peek at their open mail on the dining room table. Looks like they're trying to have a baby, and by the letters and doctors' bills, it looks like they're unlucky bastards.

I wish he wanted me again, but I know he would probably only want sex, never a relationship. It would still be nice to be able to make Mac's girlfriend jealous. She'd know how it feels to wait up for him at night wondering if he's really working overtime. Pretending to be sleeping when he arrives late. Hearing the shower run, knowing he's washing off the smell of sex.

"So, are you seeing anyone now?"

I freeze.

It's as though he's read my mind.

"There's someone I like, but he's in a relationship."

"Oh, do I know him?"

He points to himself, thinking I'm talking about him.

"No," I tease him, knowing I'm making all this up.

He motions me to the terrace for a smoke. The panoramic view of the Charles River and the city skyline as the backdrop is stunning.

"Have you had lunch?" he asks.

"Nope."

"Let's go eat; I know a great place a few blocks from here."

We reach the Charles River Hotel. I wonder if lunch is code for sex, but apparently, it's not because we walk straight to the restaurant and grab seats at the bar instead of a room key from the check-in counter. I can't help feeling giddy inside. I pretend we are on a date like old times. All the reasons I first fell in love with him are flooding back. His confidence, wide smile, fit body, dark brown neatly parted hair, clean-shaven face and that charm. What's different about these feelings is I wouldn't want to be back in a relationship. He's proved that he's no good. I can forgive the cheating, but the abandonment of our relationship will never allow me to forgive. I believe a choice is never a mistake. Right now, I want to enjoy my freedom. I'm free to do whatever the fuck I want. But I could do with some sex. Perhaps this lunch will lead to a spontaneous night of sex if we rent a room at the hotel. Maybe it's all in my head, but I feel like he's coming onto me. If he wants to have sex with me, all he has do is ask. I no longer want to be the good girl Mac once dated. I mean, I just met the Irish Mob boss; that's badass. I can't shake the comment she made about my father – maybe I did meet my real father. Perhaps all the digging into my mother's past was the wrong hole to dig. I have my father's name; he may be able to piece together the information and help shed light on who would want my mother dead. I'll need Paul's help finding him, but I must start looking right away.

My phone vibrates in my pocket, breaking my train of thought. It's Johnny calling.

"I gotta take this, I'll be right back," I say to Mac, heading outside.

"Hey, Johnny."

"Checking on ya."

"Oh, why is that? Is that your new job, to keep track of me?"

"You pick up on bullshit quick, don't ya."

"Heck, yeah."

"I'm gonna come ova if that's okay."

I think about it for a moment. I'm curious, he has my attention.

"Why?"

He's silent.

"Cause… I need a drink."

What an idiot, he's so obvious.

"Ok, sure. Can you pick me up at the Charles River Hotel?"

"Ok, be there in twenty."

It won't hurt to make Mac a little jealous. Maybe it will make him want me.

I head back to the table.

"I'm sorry, I have to leave."

He leans in close to my ear and whispers, "I want you."

I melt right there, smiling back at him. His hand is now under my shirt, running up my back. He used to do this all the time when we were dating.

I push his hand away.

"Well, you know my number, call me, and perhaps we can make that happen."

"I thought for sure you would smack me for even suggesting it."

He grabs the back of my head and pulls me in for a kiss. His tongue is cold as I remember and glides around my tongue. I'm turned on and don't want it to end.

My phone beeps with a text from Johnny; he's outside. I hug Mac goodbye and tell him to call me tomorrow when he has the money.

JIMMY

C H A P T E R   3

HOME

I didn't need a reason to return to Beantown but hearing the news that my daughter's been asked to testify for the Irish, I'm scared for her safety. When I heard someone was digging around trying to find me, it was either the Pigs or Italians. One of my enemies may know that Ava is my daughter. Anyone with this information could manipulate me. Sure, it was possible Mary, her adoptive mother told her about me, maybe even gave my name and my role with the Irish Mob. I just wonder what things she's told Ava. I warned Mary when Ava was just a baby, to never speak my name or say anything about the Irish Mob. Mary's empathy, love and her belief in God was stronger than I anticipated. She knew Ava would be at risk and could be killed by any of my enemies if they found out about Ava. Mary was aware of our agreement and the terms of the adoption, but she didn't take my advice.

I admire Mary for wanting Ava to know her biological family, but to sacrifice her own life was foolish. Nice people make stupid mistakes, they're easy prey for any killer. What could Ava want with me, a relationship? Or is she in a heap of shit? If she's anything like me, she's in trouble.

Returning to Boston after almost twenty years is the strangest feeling. The City looks the same, except for a few new landscape changes, new high-rise buildings, and the Zakim Bridge, a large white cable-stayed bridge that lights up blue at night. A nice additional to the city skyline. Various underground tunnels have replaced the dark green metal stacked highway roads. It's easy to get lost in the highway's underground tunnels if you don't pay attention. Ending up in the wrong lane can cause anyone to be spit out on an entirely new direction and highway. The Big Dig, the largest and most expensive construction project in the world, turned into the longest running political scam in Boston history. Many of my criminal pals were killed contributing to funneling money through the construction project. Many friends that worked those construction jobs are serving time for getting busted dealing drugs to other construction workers. There're rumors that there's an uncounted amount of bodies buried deep under the cement foundation holding up the bridge.

Besides the Boston skyline changing, the same family names run the same neighborhoods. The cops, politicians and the media will make you think they're making headway decreasing crime, but they're paid to cover up homicides, drug deals gone wrong and filthy politicians using mobsters' contributions to win elections. The Irish spend most of their profits and resources on controlling the local media, and the politicians do the same to keep crime out of the news. They want Boston to seem like a safe place to visit, raise a family and open a business. Crime flows underground, like the traffic in the tunnels. Boston hides the horrible congested traffic under the city, so the rich don't see it from their high-rise condos.

I've always compared organized crime to rivers because rivers never stop flowing and the water is ever changing. This is how the criminal world runs: the water in the river is the money, a constant flow. The debris and trash gathered on the riverbanks disturb the wildlife and changes the flow of the river. The same goes for the organized crime world, constantly changing its atmosphere when a mobster dies or is imprisoned. If there is too much debris, the river will back up and the water flow will slow down. Cops will put the criminals in jail, temporarily stopping the flow of money. People who think they'll change the world may change the course and lives of some, but the change is really just an exchange. For every bad guy locked up or murdered, they're replaced before the jail doors slam shut. Cops are heroes for many, but when it comes to organized crime, they're wasting their time, and the smart cops know this, so what do you think they do? They become the dirty cops. They want a piece of the action.

It was my freedom to choose to work with the Irish as a hitman. My father didn't force me, but I was never given another choice. My family ran the Irish Mob in Boston for decades, so it was natural for me to continue my father's legacy. My first hit was at thirteen years old. A bible was the first object I used for a murder weapon. The victim was an easy target. I broke into his home to find him kneeling by his bedside during prayer. His facial expression told me he was expecting death. I jumped on the bed above him, yanked the bible from his hands and beat him in the head, over and over. He fell backwards, hitting his head on the floor and knocking himself unconscious. I didn't know how to tell he was dead, so I didn't stop hitting him with the Bible until his face was no longer recognizable. I gripped the book so tight for so long that my hands and wrists became numb. Against my father's advice to never take anything from the dead, I couldn't help but take the man's rosary beads as a souvenir. The next day at school, my hands were so sore it hurt just to hold a pencil.

The Mob never told me why I had to kill him. All I know is they pinned my first killing on the manager of a bank who wouldn't collaborate with them. The banker was charged a life sentence but was paroled after fifteen years. No one would give him a job, so he sold weed to make money. Someone killed him six months after he got out of jail. He was found sitting in his idling car at a liquor store parking lot with a knife sticking out of his neck. I've never regretted my first killing or any of them after that and had no remorse for the man that served a jail term because of my doing. If I had empathy, I would've been dead already. A hitman must be able to turn their emotions on and off. It's just a job that needs to get done.

I left Boston when Ava was about four years old. It was clear Ava was in good hands with Mary; she treated Ava like her own daughter. I would spy on her and Ava at parks, out at the stores, and sometimes at night when she would lay her down to sleep. I never wanted to give my daughter up, but I loved her so much it scared me. My first plan was to stay in Ireland after her mother gave birth. Then Ava's mother changed her mind about keeping her and wanted nothing to do with her. I wanted to stay in Ireland, find a small town and cottage to raise my daughter, but this was impossible. I would've been murdered by my boss had I not returned to my job has a hitman. Sadly, Ava would've faced the same fate, so I took her back to Boston. I believed that fate would help me figure out the next step.

I hid Ava from my enemies, right under their noses. I rented an apartment across the river from the Irish in the city of Cambridge. If you want to hide from your enemies, move next door. I hired a babysitter at night to be able to continue my work with the Mob. I needed to maintain some normalcy so nobody would ask questions. One morning, I was stopping at the store to pick up some formula and diapers when I bumped into Mary. Growing up, Mary lived down the street from me and when I did go to school, I'd see her in class. She was a nerd, and her parents were strict. She wasn't allowed to play outside. Even with her thick tonic bottle glasses, she was a pretty girl, but far out of my league.

"Jimmy… Jimmy Coonan?"

"Mary, ya parents know you outta tha house?"

"My parents are dead."

"Oh, Jesus, I'm sorry, I was just … just makin'… never mind, how the heck ah ya?"

"Okay, I guess. I just lost my job, so things are tough."

Her eyes begin to water.

"Hey, ya gonna be fine."

I give her a hug, holding her tight. She peeks in my shopping cart.

"Jimmy, you have a baby?"

"Nah, I mean ya. Mary, come over for super and a few beahs. You can meet my little girl."

"Really? That would be great."

At that very moment, I knew I'd found my fate; it was Mary.

Being home reminds me how dark Boston can be. The Irish are now battling each other to take control of all South Boston, Charlestown, Dorchester. Somerville has always been controlled by the Irish, but the Hispanics are slowing taking ground. The Irish rally against the Italians, but not our group, we have long-standing deals with the Italians, from the North End to East Boston. We haven't always established standing relationships with them, but with the African Americans and Hispanics it's becoming difficult to share business without them taking over our neighborhoods. The Irish and Italians working together, an unlikely duo; we kept control over a lot of businesses and kept our footing in neighborhoods that were African American or Hispanic. At first, both sides refused to unite, but in one last attempt, Claire, my boss, made a deal with the Italians. Together, the other groups stuck to controlling their own neighborhoods. There were constant, unnecessary turf wars against each other. The Irish and Italian didn't work like that in the beginning. Everyone worked together in the best way, but these are criminals and criminals are difficult to predict. We have mighty Irish egos, and kill over stupid shit like women, cars, drugs and money. I've had more than my share of friends dying over spilling whiskey on the wrong man. When you get drunk in one of our bars, you better be on your best behavior because you don't know who's who sometimes. We get powerful people pop up in our bars to do business all the time. If you see a new face in the bar, they're either a big boss or an informant. That's why you never see me walking through a bar with a drink in my hand. If I'm killed, it better be for a goddamn good reason.

PAUL

CHAPTER 4

HACK THAT JACK

I read an article today declaring less than forty-four percent of the American population purchase newspapers and magazines. This number is way off; I envision only a quarter of people in the world buy newspapers, based on the difficulty of finding a store that sells them. Some days I need to take the subway to Harvard Square just to find a newspaper. If I wake up early, I can grab a paper from the small corner store near my apartment. I would have the paper delivered to my house, but that leaves me susceptible to people knowing where I live. A simple thing like newspaper subscription is a window of opportunity for hackers; I should know. Although nothing in the apartment's under my real name, I still wouldn't take the risk.

Paul isn't my birth name; I think the name sounds like an old man, rather than a young man of my generation. Criminals don't take to a request from specific names, so I simply changed it.

I wasn't always a criminal, or, as I prefer to call myself, a hacker. Once, I lived a regular life. Before my sophomore year of High School, I was accepted to several prestigious universities all over the world. I chose to stay close to home. Harvard University and MIT were both options. However, I chose Suffolk University because they gave me a full ride including housing and food. My parents set up a college fund, but I didn't want to use their hard-earned money on college when I could go for free. Plus, having that money for the future was appealing, but eventually the money in the bank burned a hole in my pocket. I had to spend it or invest it. I decided on investing the money in the stock market. I thought I had a bulletproof plan and saw rapid returns in the first quarter, until, Bush, 9/11, the recession and housing market crash sent the market spiraling out of control. This happened my first year at Suffolk. It was devastating to lose so much money so fast. Around this time, I met Ava in my advanced accounting class. Her beauty caught my eye first, then her intelligence. It was difficult not to notice her since she annoyingly asked the professor so many questions in class. Most of her questions were what if's? Everyone in class sighed every time she opened her mouth, everyone but me. The student who asks the most questions is not the dumbest. She was just trying to learn the angles of accounting. I found her questions were rather criminal, but the innocence of her face made the questions seem sinless. I never asked questions in my classes because I already knew the answers. Suffolk turned out to be an easy master's degree. I should have challenged myself, but laziness got the best of me.

Ava and I grew close those six years. She doesn't know this, but her thesis paper about investments gave me the idea to hack my way through the stock market. Her paper was inspiring and helped dissect the errors made by some of the largest US money market scandals. There was one other inspirational mutual friend of ours: Thomas Kennedy. The best way to describe Thomas is an over-privileged rich boy. His family provided him with money to stay invisible in their political involvement; he was an embarrassment to the family name. Thomas was a trouble-maker, instigator, and would argue with anyone just for the joy of arguing. He was studying to be a lawyer, but he was unmotivated and lazy. He dropped out his second year, but still came to visit me at the dorms. He liked the college atmosphere without the being a student aspect. He wasn't always troublesome, but after his younger sister drowned in the Bahamas on a family vacation trip. His family blamed him because he didn't protect her, and it was his idea to go cliff diving. Plus, the parents needed someone to blame besides God. They were jumping off cliffs, and when his sister didn't resurface after a jump, he dived in after her. He almost drowned himself looking for her. The water was rough, but he found her and pulled her to shore. He did CPR until the lifeguard arrived. Thomas could never get to the rest of the story. He always stopped at the bit where the lifeguard arrived. Thomas drank, and smoked weed daily and would always talk about his sister. The stories would always start cheery and turn dark when he would go back to the day she died.

He was my closest friend until we both admitted we were gay. Then we secretly started dating. Thomas could never come out as gay; his family would make sure of that.

He was there in my dorm the first night I hacked. It was a rush;

an exciting night – we didn't sleep the entire night and spent most of the next day hacking. We started off small, hacking a local credit union, skimming one cent from every bank account and transferring it into a new account. Then we stole credit card numbers, but the real fun was when we started sharing corporation's secrets to investors and sharing politician's secrets with corporations. I hacked the secrets and Thomas took these secrets to bribe politicians and businessman. He was the face of the business, a rather adept salesman; the most confident, narcissist manipulator I've ever known. He built a relationship with his political empire of a family just to make more connections and make money from the unsuspecting rich family members, friends and business partners.

All didn't end well when his family found about what he was doing. That's when the darkness took over our operation, making it risky, but it got darker when I found Thomas dead in his home. Investigators confirmed that he died by suicide, but I know otherwise. He was making a mockery of his family's name by being labeled as a criminal. I alone know of more than a few associates we did business with who could've wanted him dead. Someone did want him dead, and with a snap of their finger, Thomas was gone. I was terrified to go to his funeral for fear of being the next victim. Most murderers show up at the funeral and if it was a family member that had him killed, they would certainly be there so not to raise suspicion. Also, I couldn't bear to see my lover and best friend in a casket.

His death temporarily ended my greedy hacking practices, but I slowly returned to hacking, much like an addict saying they'll only do drugs on the weekends. We all know it will turn into being every day. I told myself the same thing when I started hacking again. I can't help it; I'm addicted to scamming people and hacking into private accounts. I love finding out secrets and bribing others. Your secret is safe with me, but only if you pay the bribe. Soon as you miss a payment, that's it – my victims are exposed.

I still have the dirty money Thomas and I made in college. The last I counted it was over a billion dollars' worth on the dark net, but exchange it into usable cash, it amounts to about a quarter of that. I'm one of the top twenty wealthiest men in Boston, but it's no bragging right, since I can't tell anyone, and I can't spend the money in the real world, only in the criminal world. I could shop all day on the dark web. Instead of buying stuff from a store, I buy political influence, police protection, entrance to hacking highways one can only dream of. I can buy any drug, in any amount I want. The money is dirty, and I never want to clean it, because when you clean money—that amount of money—you're most susceptible to getting caught. The way I clean the money is when someone pays me for a job or a bribe, I only accept cash unless my services are requested from other hackers in the dark web. Wiring funds from my accounts to another hacker is our own currency; we call it H-SAC; the H is silent. One H-SAC dollar equals about $0.10 US clean money. It fluctuates depending on the dark web market. There are membership fees and transaction fees just like corporate banks. An anonymous hacker oversees the H-SAC accounts. You need a lot of money and credibility to get an H-SAC account. With the account comes other perks, like protection and alerts when the FBI or others catch on to the criminal activity. Having someone with the ability to wipe out my account is risky, but it's the same risk normal law-abiding citizens take when they put their hard-earned money into the stock markets, real estate and banks.

Ava, like everyone else in my life, knows only a little about my criminal acts and my financial wellbeing. The only reason Ava knows anything at all is because Thomas was a blabbermouth. We both trusted Ava, but some business deals shouldn't be discussed. I believe being paranoid all these years has kept me alive and out of jail.

I never would have thought she'd put herself in this situation, and in the same breath, I'm shocked to hear her deny any wrongdoing. I know the level of intelligence she has and it's bullshit she didn't know Atlantic was laundering money for the Irish. She's devious and a fantastic liar who always needs to understand everything. If there was one number off in the accounting sheets, she would backtrack until she found the accounting blunder. Either way, I'm in no situation to judge my friend and will support her in any way possible. I will not allow a friend of mine go to jail over such a minor crime, and especially not over an underhanded tycoon like Atlantic Street Financial. They're messing with the wrong girl.

When Ava sent me the email about hacking into Atlantic, I was excited, and felt excitement again, like I did when Thomas was still alive. Having Ava work at Atlantic is every hacker's dream. I gave her my customized hacking software with a USB, so all she had to do was install it to her computer, and the lines would open, like a vein when heroine is injected. I was riding the money highway. We achieved pilfering the original target.

We'd still be embezzling if Atlantic didn't get caught laundering money with the Irish. I'm waiting patiently for Ava to come because she claims she has additional information about the case with Atlantic.

AVA

CHAPTER 5

TO DO

I'm awoken by heavy banging on my bedroom door.

"Ava, someone's car is parked behind me in the driveway," yells Samantha.

Am I dreaming or did my roommate just ask me who's parked behind her? How the hell should I know? I don't have a car, maybe it's the neighbors.

I look to my left. Fuck, it must be Johnny's car. He's naked in my bed.

"Um, give me a minute," I say, pulling the sheets back. *What the fuck happened last night?* I'm tripping over my feet and all the clutter on my floor. I think I'm still drunk. I throw last night's clothes on and grab Johnny's keys from the nightstand. I don't want Samantha to know Johnny's in my bed. She's a nosy little bitch who loves to run her mouth. Samantha is from South Boston, so she likely knows someone who knows Casey.

"Hold on, I'll move the car, give me a sec," I yell through the door.

When I get out of my bedroom, I see Samantha nosily searching my face for answers.

"Who's that?" she asks trying to see past me. I close the door fast and stand guarded.

"It's an old friend I met at the bar last night," I lie.

"Ooh, I want all the details, text me later. If I'm late, my boss will have my ass."

I hurry out the door behind her to move Johnny's car. It's a real badass car, a white Mercedes; not sure what type, but it looks and smells new.

I brew a pot of coffee and peek in my room at Johnny, who's sound asleep. I hop in the shower, grabbing clothes, trying not to wake him. I see a condom in the trash can, so that answers the most important question, did we sleep together? I'm both flattered and puzzled that Johnny and I ended up in bed; I never thought he was the least bit attracted to me. I'm sure it's just a drunken mistake for him.

I hear a knock on the bathroom door.

"Ava, I'm comin' in."

What the fuck? Oh my God, does he not understand privacy?

I ignore him and stay quiet.

The bathroom door opens. I peek from behind the shower curtain. Johnny's naked, taking a piss, one hand above his head leaning against the wall for balance, the other hand gripping his large, erect penis. I'm not complaining; while the notion of him pissing is awkward, his body from this angle is nicely sculpted. His back and arms are covered in tattoos: crosses, roses and skeletons. Not a fluffy bunny tattoo kind of guy. I didn't know he had so many tattoos because he always wore suits to work but lately it's jeans, hoodies, and his dirty, ripped up Red Sox ball cap. He has let his facial hair grow out, giving him a disheveled appearance. His thick brown hair is now long enough to pull back into a ponytail. I can't decide if he looks better in a suit and tie or casually dressed.

"I have extra toothbrushes in the top left drawer near the sink, and clean towels on the top shelf."

He doesn't answer me; instead he steps behind me in the shower and grabs the bar of soap from me. I swear he's still drunk, or just an inconsiderate jackass.

"Rememba last night?" he says with a smirk.

"No, but I think I can figure it out." I rinse off and leave the shower without washing my hair.

"Ava, come on, we were drunk, it happens; we've all been in this situation, there's nothin' to be ashamed about."

If a psychic told me a year ago, I'd be here while Johnny is taking a shower after a night of sex, I would've asked for a refund.

"This wasn't a good idea. I want us to remain just friends, and I need you on my side."

He steps out of the shower and he gives me a long wet naked hug, kisses my forehead. "You're over thinkin' this." He grabs my face, leans his forehead against mine, looks me in my eyes and lies to my face. "Everything will be all right."

He leaves after a cup of coffee and sharing a smoke. I'm relieved; I have so much to do. First, I'm going to pay a visit to my friend Paul, a genius tech junky, who works from home part-time for a local college. He's always home so I can pop in whenever, but he still makes me schedule an appointment.

I hop on the redline train, a few stops to Central Square where Paul lives, and just a short walk from the station. His small crummy apartment is next to the housing projects. I know he can afford to live in a better part of Cambridge, but I think he just likes the location. Paul buzzes me in. Five flights up with no elevator in the building; the last door on the left. The hallway is scarcely lit. I knock a few times before he comes to the door.

"Come in, quick." He's wearing a ridiculous gaming headset and looks down the hall, paranoid.

I push past stacked computers, books and newspapers cluttered in the barely passible hallway; it's impossible to get from room to room without stumbling.

"Can you get me a computer and cellphone that can't be traced by the FBI, or anyone?" I say, taking a seat in an old brown recliner.

He's back to focusing on his video game.

"Yeah, you already know I can, but why?"

"Yesterday, I met with both the FBI and the head of the Irish Mob."

Paul rips the headphones off his head and shuts off the game.

"Shh, don't say another word."

He nervously logs into his computer and turns on the radio, loud. He rolls his computer chair over to me.

I lean in closer so he can hear me over the music. "Why the loud music?"

"You can never be too careful. They can hear us."

"Who exactly?!"

He gets up from his chair and paces from the kitchen to the living room, removing boxes from his windowsill, his makeshift curtains, and peeking outside. Taking a seat back in his chair, he sighs. "Tell me everything."

"A private investigator hired by Atlantic is following me. The FBI interviewed me asking about my job at Atlantic, my relationship with my boss Susan, and Johnny. Something was off about the FBI agent. It gets worse. Johnny works for the Irish Mob; he told me, then he brought me to visit Claire Spillane."

Paul stared at me confused. "Who's that?"

"Oh, right, she's the Mob boss. Paul, she threatened to harm me, my family and friends if I don't go to trial to defend Susan."

"Did anyone mention the Mafia?"

"No."

"Good. Be cautious around Johnny, but keep him around for now, so the Irish know you're cooperating with the investigation and trial. Don't say nothing to the FBI, and if they request to see you again, make sure Johnny is aware. It's important you hire a private investigator, a second set of eyes. I'm turning off the music, but no more talk about this; you can never be too cautious."

"Okay. How much for the phone and computer?"

"$15,000 for everything and I can have it to you by the end of the week."

"Come on, that's a lot of cash to come up with. Can you give me a break?"

"$12,000, that's as low as I can go."

"I'll drop off the cash tonight. I have another favor." I hand him a paper with my biological father's name on it. "I need to find this person and any information you have on him and please don't ask me why."

He smirks. "Why?"

I pull out a bag of weed for Paul. A bonus for helping me out. "Just what I need," he smiles.

I get up to leave. "I don't mean to rush, but I need to go find money to borrow – I'll be back tonight," I lie, an excuse to leave.

Paul's behavior gets stranger with every visit. He's always been socially awkward and doesn't talk unless it's about money, technology, or government conspiracy theories, but lately he has become increasingly paranoid.

My next stop is hiring a private investigator. I hop back on the redline. Johnny has texted a few times. He wants to have drinks tonight if I'm interested. I respond with a maybe. I can't tell if he genuinely likes me or if he's just hanging around because he was ordered to by the Mob.

I reach my second destination, a private investigator's office in Boston's Beacon Hill, one of the more beautiful neighborhoods in Boston and richest. The snaking alleys are lined with brick homes with matching brick sidewalks, and even some of the streets still have the original cobblestone. Some of the roads were a part of the underground railroad, which has been preserved and organized as the Black Heritage Trail.

I'd made an appointment with a small private investigator; I presume he's Jewish with a company name like Alterman Investigations. I'm early for my appointment so the receptionist asks that I have a seat.

"Mr. Alterman will be back from lunch shortly."

The receptionist is an elderly lady with a permanent scowl, likely doesn't take shit from anybody. Our phone conversation the other day was more pleasant, I pictured her very differently.

A man enters the office—I assume this is Mr. Alterman—holding his take-out lunch in hand.

"You must be Ava, my apologies for keeping you waiting." He motions me to follow him into his office.

I sit in one of the two comfy chairs in front of his desk. His office is filled with oversized dark furniture, with matching built-in bookshelves. It's a nice office, which translates to he charges a lot for his services.

"How can I help?" he says, opening his lunch container. *Is he going to eat his lunch while we talk?* It's distracting, since I haven't eaten anything today.

"I have someone following me, and I need to know why and who they are."

"Why do you think they're following you?" He stuffs a handful of french fries in his mouth.

"I worked for Atlantic Street Financial as an accountant. They're under investigation by the FBI, for allegedly laundering money."

He looks interested with this new information. He closes his lunch container and cleans his greasy hands. "Go on," he says with a pen and pad in front of him.

"I was approached by a private investigator, hired by Atlantic. I'm pretty sure he's been following me."

"Did he give his business card?"

"No, sorry. I just told him to fuck off and to stop following me."

Mr. Alterman doesn't look amused. "Can you tell me more about Atlantic's troubles? I haven't seen anything in the news."

"That's the strange part. I was even interviewed by an FBI agent, Connor McClean."

I stop myself, leaving out the details about the mob shit.

"I'm scared, and I need someone looking out for my best interests."

He looks through me, staring, not immediately answering my question. I look back to see if there is someone behind me.

"I think I can help you. My secretary will write up an agreement and call you when it's ready."

"Okay, sounds good." I get up to walk out.

"Ava, wait. Are you positive there is nothing else concerning you?"

"Nope," I lie and exit his office.

The last errand on my list is to visit my roommate's ex-boyfriend, Jose Ramirez. He can get me a new identity in case things don't go as planned. My hope is Johnny will somehow save me from the Mob cutting my fucking head off and dumping me in the river.

I'm late to meet Jose. He isn't happy to see me; I can tell by his body language.

We meet at his restaurant, Pollo Centro. The place looks like a shithole – I can't believe people eat here. Hopefully it's just a front to launder money. Last I knew, Jose was a small-time drug dealer, but from what I can see he could be running a bigger operation.

"Hey mama, how's it goin'? You lookin' good…" he says.

We hug, but he holds on longer than appropriate.

"I'm sorry for being late, I got lost."

"No problem."

He grabs two beers from behind the counter.

"Sit, sit, make yourself at home."

I take a seat in the white bamboo chair.

He drinks the beer, looking at me past the bottle. I forgot how intimidating he can be.

"How's Slutmantha."

"You mean Samantha; she's fine."

He's such an asshole, and he wonders why they broke up. I hate that I need to ask him for a favor, but he's the only person I know who can get me a new identity.

"I'm here for a favor. I need a new identity, preferably a US passport."

He sucks his teeth like he has food stuck between them.

"I got you, but you need a lot of dinero."

"How much?"

"First, you must tell me why a good girl like you needs this."

"I can't tell you."

"Wow, like that huh."

He's looking at me like he wants more than money. It's got to be the reason he's stalling.

"I'm sensing you want a favor in return."

"Bingo," he laughs.

"I need you to pick up a package in the Dominican and bring it to me," he explains.

"Jose, I can't leave the country, not now."

I don't want him to know any details about the FBI and the Mob.

"My employer is under investigation, and I'll need to go to court soon."

"Tell 'em you're going on vacation for a few days to relieve some stress."

"If I agree, what's the package?"

"It's better you don't know."

"No, I'm not doing that, it's crazy. Please let me pay you and we'll be even."

"Okay, fine, $10,000. It will be ready in two days."

"Thank you, thank you."

I finish my beer, give him a hug goodbye. There's sense of unfinished business, and I'm sure I've made a mistake by saying no.

When I get home, Mac is sitting on my steps waiting for me. I notice a black SUV parked a few feet from my house. I'm being watched again.

"Thanks for meeting me at my house. Come in."

"You look exhausted, Ava."

"I am exhausted, and I haven't eaten all day. I'm gonna heat up some leftover Chinese food, you want some?"

"No, I'm good, but how about a drink?"

"Sure, I'll get you your favorite," I say.

I shovel food down while Mac watches.

"Here's the loan." He hands me a thick envelope.

"Thank you. I'll pay you back when I can."

Now that I have the money, I want him to leave, but I can't help feel he's hanging around for something more.

My phone beeps; it's a text from Johnny – he's outside. So that's the black SUV, that's him. The door buzzer goes off.

Is that him? What the fuck?

I peek through the door; it's Johnny all right.

"Johnny, I wasn't expecting you."

He smiles that cheesy smile of his. Looks like he's up to no good.

He walks in like he owns the place and walks right up to Mac.

"Hey," he says to Mac.

They shake hands.

This is all entertaining, but I need to make sure they don't start fighting. Johnny can be a real asshole and Mac is hardheaded.

"I wasn't expecting you. You want a beer or food?" I ask.

"Ya, sure." He takes a seat next to Mac in the dining room.

From the kitchen I can't hear what they are talking about, but there's no yelling so they must be playing nice. I'm more worried about Johnny than Mac. Johnny is unpredictable and Mac, well he's calm, with better manners.

Just as I bring Johnny a plate and a beer, Mac gets up from the table and grabs his coat.

"I got to get home for dinner – my wife was cooking when I left."

I didn't know they were married. He says that intentionally because he knows it hurts me. We were supposed to get married at one point.

He shakes Johnny's hand and says goodnight. I follow him out the door and to his car.

"Thanks again for the loan, I'll pay you back as soon as possible," I promise.

"My wife doesn't know I lent you the money, so please make sure you keep that promise."

"Is everything okay with you? You seem upset. I'm sorry, I

didn't expect Johnny to come over."

He looks down at the ground.

"I just wish I never cheated on you, and seeing another man interested in you makes me jealous. I know it sounds like bullshit, but I think of what we could have been."

I've been waiting for this day since he broke it off with me. Waiting for him to admit he was wrong and admit his regret.

"We can't change the past. I honestly don't see us ever getting back to the place we once were."

His expression changes from poor me to arrogant asshole. He walks towards me and, pushing the loose hair behind my ear, goes in for a kiss.

"No, Mac. Not here."

I turn my head, looking in the direction of my kitchen window. Johnny is standing in the window eating from his plate. He doesn't look happy.

"Okay, I get it. Johnny is my replacement."

He gets in his car and drives off before I can respond.

I go back into the house. I'm pissed off, the nerve of this cocksucker to just show up at my house. He's so disrespectful.

"Who the hell do you think you are, showing up here unannounced?"

"I texted."

"Yeah, then knocked on the fucking door. Jesus Christ! Humor me, why are you always around?"

I walk away from Johnny to the refrigerator to grab another beer.

"What was ya ex doing ovah here?"

"None of your damn business. What the hell are you doing here while Casey is home alone? You should be worrying about your own relationship."

Johnny stays quiet and continues to eat in silence. The longer he stays silent the more aggravated I get.

He takes his last bite of food.

"Ava, you know who I work for, don't make me say it."

"I want the fucking truth."

"They were gonna have someone else keep an eye on you, but I offered. I like you a lot. I don't want nothin' to happen to ya. I feel guilty because I sort of brought you into this situation. There's more I want to tell ya, but my hands are tied."

He looks sincere and appears to be telling me the truth. I guess I just needed to hear him admit that he's following me. I would like to know more, but I won't push it. I wonder if he knows why Mac was here, and if he followed me to visit Jose. I hope not because I don't want him to know what I'm planning. Shit, I forgot about Paul; I promised to deliver the cash to him tonight.

"I don't want to argue, I understand the situation, I'm just stressed."

"I know."

I send Paul a text to tell him I can't make it right now. He says if I can't make it tonight to come first thing in the morning. He tells me the stuff isn't ready, so it buys me some time. The money's still on the table. I take the opportunity to put the cash in my safe while Johnny is using the bathroom.

"Can I ask you a personal question?"

He nods yes.

"What do you tell Casey when you don't come home, like the other night?"

"She's used to it, comes with tha job."

Casey must know he cheats and works for the Mob. Still, it doesn't make it right for us to have slept together, but if I'm being honest with myself, I don't care that it's wrong.

We continue drinking through the night. The more drinks we have, the more the sexual tension builds.

I climb on top of him, straddling him and pull off my shirt. In this moment I feel in control and in charge. The first night we slept together I don't remember all of it because I was drunk, but as time passed, I start to remember how we ended up in bed. He pushed himself on top of me while we were sitting on the couch. We fucked right there while my roommate was in her bedroom down the hall. After that, he carried me to the bedroom, and we fucked again. This second time he was rougher. I remember waking up the next morning with a sore mouth because of him biting me, and my hip bones felt bruised.

This time he's letting me be in control. I ride him slow and gentle in the beginning and move faster when I feel his excitement. I find it more thrilling because it's teasing him. I do like it rough; hair pulling and biting, but it's better to build to the rough stuff. I kiss him from his mouth to his neck, as my hands play with his nipples and chest. He's getting excited and moving his hand up my back, grabbing my ass, pushing himself deeper inside. In this moment, I know I've caught feelings. I want him – maybe because he's already taken, or maybe because he's a bad boy. There's no denying I'm attracted to him. He can never know because that would give him power. He already has too much. I must remember this could all be a distraction from my reality, the dangerousness of dealing with the Mob. They could kill me with a snap of their fingers, but could Johnny kill me? I believe yes, yes, he could, because he knows it would be me or him.

AVA

CHAPTER 6

KING PAUL

I wake up, open one eye to peek at Johnny sleeping, but he's gone. I'm relieved I'm alone. I lay staring at the ceiling reminiscing about my mother. I miss her so much. On my nightstand is a coffee, a breakfast sandwich, bottle of water, and two Tylenol. The Tylenol is a nice touch. The taste of weed and cigarettes are still fresh on my breath. I take a sip of the coffee. There's whiskey in the coffee – an Irish Coffee. I wash down the Tylenol, eat breakfast in bed and scroll through my phone messages. Several text messages are from Paul. One reads: *Both are ready, come over when you wake up.*

That's fast; he told me it would take a week.

I respond: *See you in an hour.*

On the way to Paul's, I smile when I think about Johnny. I hate that I'm even thinking about him. I'm also thinking about Mac and feel conflicted. I thought I would want Mac back in my life but now it doesn't seem so appealing. I knew borrowing the money from Mac would have strings attached. They're both a distraction.

I purposely take a different route to Paul's apartment just in case I'm being followed. It's easier to take the train, but too many people to watch. The bus late morning will be easier. If I sit at the back of the bus, I can see all the passengers. The bus windows let me watch for cars that could be following me. The bus passengers consist of a handful of seniors, a few mothers or nannies with children, and some lone passengers. I watch everyone, no matter their age or look of innocence. I don't want to bring unnecessary people into Paul's world. I'm sure he has enough to worry about.

I get a text from an unknown phone number with a country code in front. It reads: *Smash your phone, you've been hacked.*

This must be Paul. Shit. I get off the bus a few bus stops away from Paul's. I look around to double check no one is following me. I find a large rock, duck into an alley, and smash my phone until it's dust. My blood is boiling because I know who the fucker was that put a tracker in my phone. Johnny!!

After I grab my shit from Paul, I'm staying at a hotel room for a few nights. I need no interruptions while I plan my next move.

I'm still shaking with anger when I ring Paul's doorbell. I hear him come to the door, peeking through the peephole, opening the door just a crack.

"Did you get rid of your phone?" he asks.

"Yeah."

"Do you have any other electronic devices on you?

"No!"

I push through the door past Paul.

"What the fuck kind of shenanigans have you gotten yourself into?"

"Oh, you mean besides helping you hack Atlantic and steal their funds?"

"Shh, we don't talk about that, not here. Sit; let's talk for a moment cause there's a lot to discuss."

I move the stack of newspapers from the chair before taking a seat.

"Will you ever trust me?"

"I... I'm trying. You know trust is an issue since my mother's death. It has nothing to do with you."

"We thought we were stealing from Atlantic, but really it was the Italian Mafia, and it's not the Irish's accounts."

"We need to find out for sure who, if anyone, knows we stole the money."

"Yes, I know and I'm working on that right now. Likely, someone will eventually find out if we don't fix it right now."

"Fuck, it's getting too complicated and dangerous."

Paul lights a joint, takes a few hits and passes it to me.

"Why no loud music like the last time. Are you not worried about being bugged?"

"No; I installed a device in my apartment that blocks radio and Wi-Fi signals, and if they are detected they scramble the recordings. It's a prototype I bought from the dark web. It's actually quite interesting..."

I interrupt Paul. I have no interest in hearing about his high-tech toys.

"I'm sleeping with Johnny. I know for sure he's the one that put the tracking device in my phone."

"Come on Ava, really? I ran your prepaid phone number through several pieces of tracking software and noticed a lot of activity. It's possible Johnny inserted the tracking chip or installed it remotely by using just your phone number. Whoever installed it isn't too bright because they didn't rename the app or block it from being discovered."

"It's a prepaid phone; I thought those were untraceable?"

"That's a myth. Phone companies use it as a marketing scheme, to get people to buy the phones. The FBI has always been able to track them."

"Can you tell who hacked my phone?"

"It's not the FBI, they aren't amateurs. Here's my solution to the phone situation."

He hands me two phones.

"The black phone no one can hack, except me of course. The phone has no registered number and the location is blocked, so internet searches are allowed, but I would suggest no downloading applications and refrain from checking emails even though they can't be traced – we don't want to make you susceptible to even the possibility of being hacked. You can make calls, but the phone number comes up unknown. The only calls you should receive are my calls. Now, the white phone is the decoy. Let Johnny or whoever hack the phone, but only take this phone with you when you don't care about being followed. Leave it at home if you don't want to be tracked. What you don't want is to be untraceable; this will raise red flags. Do not search anything on this phone that you want to keep a secret, even from me."

"Paul, you're a fucking genius," I say, hugging him.

"I know. Now for the laptop. This is bulletproof against any hackers. Even if they hack you, they won't be able to trace it to anywhere. The serial number and manufacturing numbers are brand new and unregistered. I've disconnected the USB power; the sockets are all there but if you plug in anything, there's no power. The battery and any component that can be opened on this computer has been glued shut, and has an alarm attached if someone attempts to open it. With that said, I still wouldn't leave the computer with anyone for a long period of time, just to be cautious. Now, you can search whatever illegal things you like: how to kill someone, buy drugs, illegal guns, hire a hitman…" he went on and on.

"Paul, I think I get it."

I hand over the cash for the devices.

He slowly and carefully counts it to ensure it's all there.

We sit for some time bullshitting and smoking joints. When you smoke weed with Paul, be ready to listen because he loves to hear himself talk and he knows everything. His conspiracy theories make him come off as a lunatic, but if you listen long enough, he will almost convince you that it's true, or at least leave you questioning your knowledge. He is convincing because he can back up his topics with facts from his in-depth research. He hasn't admitted it, but I assume he has a photographic memory. He writes down nothing, unless it's for publication. He is a published writer and has spoken at several events about various technology topics, most of which are about advancements in technology and how they affect the economy. From what he claims, he makes a lot of money from speaking engagements, but you wouldn't think so from the look of this apartment.

"Paul, one last favor: can you book me a hotel for a few nights?"

"To get some distance from your new boyfriend? Do you think it's a good idea, with what's going on?"

"He's not my… Yes, I need a few nights away to clear my head."

Paul is a millionaire in dark web currency, but actual cash in hand, probably not much if he is charging me outrageous prices for the phones and computer. From what he has told me, the internet funds cannot be cashed out, unless he steals from actual accounts, like we did with Atlantic. I am still waiting for my portion from the Atlantic job, but he claims it takes time before it can be put into an account to be used in the market. He opens credit cards online under other people's names and transfers the money to them, but he can't do big sums without the credit card companies being alerted. The credit cards expire in days, not years, which makes them difficult to use.

"What city?"

"Boston."

He makes a hotel reservation for two nights at the most expensive hotel in the city.

"They have the best security since only the very wealthy and elite stay here."

"Paul, I could just kiss you. Thank you."

Before I head to the hotel, I stop to pick up my new passport from Jose. My fake identity is Sherry Conley. The picture in my passport is a fat version of myself. I should've given Jose a more recent photo since I have lost weight.

I stop by my apartment to grab a few things for the hotel and text Johnny my new phone number from the white phone, leaving the phone on and charging, hidden under my bed with the ringer on silent.

It's just turned dark outside when I get to the hotel. I pinch myself; I'm staying at The Plaza Hotel in the Back-Bay area of Boston, one of the most luxurious hotels in the city. When professional athletes come to our city, their players stay here, as do celebrities and the wealthy.

My room is larger than I need, but Paul claims this room is in a more secure part of the hotel.

I drop my stuff in my oversized suite and head down to the bar to eat. I'm dressed like a slob, with my hair tucked under my green baseball hat. I'm sure the bartender thinks I'm homeless, but I don't give a shit. After dinner and cocktails, I head up to my room for the night. I feel relief to be the only one in the elevator; my paranoia has reached a new level. I would have taken the stairs if I wasn't on the twelfth floor, but there's no way with the amount I smoke I'd walk up that many flights without having a heart attack. I get off the elevator, and see a man waiting outside my room. His shape looks familiar, but I can't tell because he's too far away. *Fuck: what should I do?* I should've planned ahead. I have no gun, but even if I did, I don't know anything about guns. I could've at least invested in a taser or knife, but it's too late. I need to know who is near my room door.

"Hey dickhead, why the fuck are you standing near my door?!"

I begin walking towards my door, facing my fear head on.

I realize the man coming my way is a familiar face. It's Mr. Alterman. Last we spoke he was supposed to send a contract for me to sign. My phone number changed, so maybe he was trying to get in contact with me. I didn't see anyone following me; boy is he good, but it's concerning because this could mean someone else knows I'm at this hotel.

"I tried calling you, but your phone keeps going directly to voicemail. It's urgent we talk," he says.

"Come in. How the heck did you find me here?"

"I'm a good private investigator."

I open the minibar, searching the selection.

"Whiskey?" I ask.

"Yes, dry."

Mr. Alterman takes a seat in the oversized chair. I hand him a glass of whiskey.

"Cheers."

We clink our glasses together. I sit on the couch.

"You didn't mention the Mob are following you. It's seems you are in deeper shit than you led on."

I give him a dirty look.

"Mr. Alterman, can I trust you?" I search for eye contact.

"Well, that all depends. Can you be honest?"

"Okay… Atlantic is involved with the Mob."

"Before you set foot in my office, I already knew everything about you, from where you live, down to the very brand of toilet paper you buy. I don't need to tell you the pile of shit you're in, but I'll help you shovel it for a reasonable fee."

He stands up and helps himself to the minibar.

"I've lived in Boston my entire life, and as you can see, I'm an old man, with old values. With my years of experience, I've familiarized myself with the Mafia, Mob, the various gangs from here to there. I know who's trustworthy at the FBI and which cops can be paid off. This of course makes me a target, so my services are pricey."

"What I need from you is simple. I just need to know who's following me, and why."

"I think you will need more than just that from me, but that's a good start. You already know why and who, don't you? You'll need me to keep them from torturing and then murdering you. I don't know many survivors that worked with the Mob. Usually, when they're finished using you, they chop you up and throw you in the river."

He's trying to scare me. It's not working, but he's right, I need him as a lookout.

"My fee is $10,000, cash only. This is a deposit for current and future services. We will see how things go, and additional fees are to be determined. I suggest you purchase a gun and learn how to shoot it," he says before standing up to leave.

"Will you tell me how you found me?"

"Boston's a small city."

"Give me two days to get you the money," I say before closing the door behind him.

I lean against the door, sliding to a sitting position on the floor. I close my eyes, listening to my breath, talking myself down from my anxiety. I'm having a panic attack; my chest is heavy. I've never felt such shortness of breath and pressure on my chest. It's stress, just so much stress. There's been so much change in the last month. My emotions are on a rollercoaster, and my body is waiting in line for the ride.

I pull myself together enough to take a hot shower. I jam a chair underneath the doorknob, just an additional obstacle if someone tries to break in. I don't bother getting dressed after my shower, but instead throw on a robe and wrap my wet hair in a towel. Off to bed with my laptop and a list of people to search and things to do. My first search is my biological father. My mother told me horror stories about him, and how he worked for the Mob. I don't want to find him for a relationship, I want him to help me out of the mess I've created.

Paul gave me a few websites and installed several illegal search engines used by the FBI, including access to their database. It's doesn't take but a few minutes to find my father. His arrest history is over fifteen pages. Most is petty crap, like drugs, assault and license violations. There're a few dismissed robberies and a murder charge. He must still be alive because I can't find a death certificate or a missing person report. I dig deeper to see who he's been arrested with and who visited him during his time in jail. I jot down the names to research later.

There may be a link to Susan's family or associates, but I hit a wall. I search Claire Spillane, the Mob boss. I need to know who's connected to her. The Irish Mob tree gets larger the more I search. There's the ugly old bitch I met. She married Billy Coonan, my uncle. My father is Jimmy Coonan, his brother. Holy shit, a better connection than I thought I'd find. I've got to find my father.

AVA

CHAPTER 7

WHITE MOUNTAINS

I fall asleep with the computer on my lap. The hotel room phone ringing wakes me. It's a courtesy call, asking if I would like breakfast delivered to my room. I order breakfast and get dressed. I call Mr. Alterman.

"Good morning, Adam Alterman speaking," he answers.

"Adam, what a lovely name," I snicker.

"Who is this?"

"It's me, Ava. This is my new phone number."

"You sound like you are in a glorious mood."

"Is this a safe line to talk?"

"Let me call you back."

He hangs up and seconds later my phone rings; it's an unknown number.

"Yes, go ahead."

"Write this name down: Jimmy Coonan. I need you to find

this guy."

"May I ask why?"

"It's my father, he has a connection with the Irish Mob in Boston. He may get me out of this mess."

"I see. Consider it done."

We both hang up.

My breakfast arrives and I eat quickly, then call the concierge to reserve a car rental before checking my phone messages.

Paul gave me access to both my cell phones through the computer. I can see Johnny has been blowing up my phone with text messages and phone calls. I couldn't care less – let him freak out a little. I see a text that tells me to get in touch with the lawyers on Susan's case. I'll call the lawyers on my terms.

I make a quick stop at home to pick up my fake passport and cash. Then I'm heading to New Hampshire to visit a shooting range, to purchase a gun and learn how to shoot. Mr. Alterman was right – I should have thought about protecting myself a long time ago. The FBI had the shooting range under surveillance during my father's murder trial that was dismissed for the lack of evidence. I read that the gun used was bought from this location. I figure I can knock two things off my to-do list with one visit.

My drive to New Hampshire is relaxing. Once I enter the White Mountains region, I spark a joint. It's a calming feeling being surrounded by mountains. There are piles of snow along the sides of the road, making the streets narrow, so I drive under the speed limit. The roads are icy, and the temperature has dropped fifteen degrees since Boston. I have always liked the winter. The constant struggle to keep warm is pleasing.

I get to the shooting range. The place looks like it was once a farm. I sit in the car for a minute to finish my cigarette. I'm nervous because I've never shot a gun or even held one. I get up the nerve to go into the gun shop. I'm looking for a man named Robert. He sounded old with a heavy smoker's voice. I don't think I will mistake that voice for anyone else.

Entering the shop, I see two older men sitting behind gun-filled glass counters. The small room is lit with fluorescent lights, half of which are not on or flickering. The walls are made of wood paneling almost matching the color of the wood floors. There's a smell of cigar and a musty combination odor. There is a thick lingering cloud of smoke throughout the room. When I inhale, my nose burns.

"How can we help you today, young lady?" the old white bearded man says. I recognize his voice; that's Robert all right. He can't finish a sentence without the last syllable sounding like a whisper, like he's run out of air.

"I called earlier and spoke with Robert…" I hesitate.

"Yes; Sherry, right?"

I nod. I didn't give them my real name because I don't want the gun traced back to me.

"I'm Robert, we spoke on the phone."

I pictured him in a wheelchair with an oxygen tank.

The American Indian looking man puts down his wood carving and stands up, looking at me. "My name is Koda; follow me."

He's very tall, over 6-foot, intimidating features, with dark, grey-streaked long black hair tied back into a ponytail. Around his head is a suede string headband.

These guys are real gun handlers. I have all the faith in the world they know how to handle any gun. I feel like I'm playing out a scene in an old cowboys and Indians film. Growing up, I've heard tales about Indians owning land throughout New England, and most history books mention tribes in this area, but I have never met a true American Indian. Lewis used to tell me Indian stories at bedtime. How they keep themselves hidden deep in the mountains, hidden from society for fear of getting their land taken by the government. He told me stories about his ancestors crossing the US border through Canada. He convinced me that if I ever did his family tree, I would find American Indian ancestry.

We enter a transformed barn with columns with half walls, shooting stalls – a sort of setup like the police target practices you see on crime and drama TV shows. I'm no longer nervous, but more excited to hold a gun and shoot it.

"Try these guns, then you choose what you like," instructed Koda.

My plan is to get a handgun that is easily concealable, but I would like to shoot a shotgun because they are so intimidating.

After some general safety instructions, and learning how to load the gun, I am ready for target practice. I feel the blood rush to my head. Sweat is seeping from under my safety glasses. The power of holding a gun turns me on. I stare for a few minutes at the target sheet, then shoot until I'm out of bullets; I reload and keep shooting. I can't remember how many times I reload the gun. I imagine it's more than the Indian expected, but he doesn't interrupt me. I black out at one point from the adrenaline.

"First time?" He pulls the paper target towards us to see how well my shots landed.

"Practice more," he says as he loads a shotgun.

The shotgun is heavy. I almost break my shoulder when it kicks back. I only shoot it once because I'm too afraid I'll shoot myself by accident. The Indian can tell I don't like the shotgun.

"I like this handgun – I'll take it."

"Go see the White Man."

While the paperwork is being processed for the gun purchase my phone rings. It's Mr. Alterman.

"I found him, he lives in Jackman, Maine, near the Canadian border."

"Text me the address."

"I'll go check out the location first. He's hiding for a good reason. It's a bad idea to go looking for him."

The phone went dead. That bastard hung up on me.

I'm finished at the gun shop now. It's dark out, and the mountains don't look as friendly as they did on the drive up here. I should've rented a room for the night at a nearby inn because I'm too tired to drive back.

I notice boot tracks leading to my car. As usual, I'm freaking myself out over nothing. I'm afraid to get in my car, so I peek through the window to make sure no one is in the back seat. It's empty, nothing to worry about. I get in the car, start the engine. Just as I go to hit the *lock all doors* button, the passenger side door opens. I'm punched straight in the face. The driver's side door opens, and I am dragged out of the car backwards with someone's large hand covering my mouth. My face is throbbing. I feel a warm sensation dripping down my face. I try to breathe through my nose, but I suck in blood. My nose feels so numb, it must be broken. I'm tossed in the trunk of their car like trash. I slam my head on something hard, then everything goes black.

JOHNNY

CHAPTER 8

THE INTERN

Three Months Ago

Ava is the latest intern to join our office. My boss insists I train every intern, and they shadow me. Out of all the interns I've trained, Ava is different. She understands our accounting software with ease, never hovers over my shoulder throughout the workday like the other interns. She's smarter than me in terms of accounting, but I would never let her, or my boss Susan know that. She should've been hired as an employee, not an intern, even with her tendency to act like a girl straight out of college. For one, she wears her headphones through most of the workday and always leaves early. She's working for free, so I won't be a dickhead about it. She gets her projects completed before I have the chance to ask her for them. Her appearance doesn't fit in with the other girls in the office. They're supermodel skinny, always eating organic and gluten-free foods, or whatever is the newest diet trend, and they do their hair and makeup. Ava has fast food delivered every day and always eats at her desk, then disappears for about thirty minutes. Her behavior is predictable.

Ava is pretty for a heavier young lady. When she first started, she wasn't as unattractive, but now her belly hangs over her skirt. Still, if you're desperate, you'll find beauty in her full face. Her long thick red hair has tints of blonde, a tiny patch of freckles covers her nose, and her full lips are pink even without lipstick. Her fading hourglass figure is most unattractive. I would never sleep with anyone of that size. I don't think my dick could even get hard if I saw her naked. I would need to focus on her face.

Ava is the only girl to enter the office I didn't screw in the first week. Sure, I have a girlfriend, but that's never stopped me. My girlfriend Casey is fucking crazy, that's why I never want her at the office. She'd make a scene, as she has in the past. She fully knows of my cheating habits, but it only bothers her when she sees the other woman. She throws tantrums like a three-year-old. I blame myself for her craziness. She won't leave me no matter what I do wrong, and I won't give up the other women; it's part of my lifestyle. I want Casey, but she has never been woman enough to hold me down. She's just not confident enough and depends on me too much. I've broken up with her so often, I've lost count. I even treat her like shit sometimes to see how far I can push her away. I tear her down only to build her back up. It's a cycle I can only break with an apology. Then we start all over again. She does the same – she's far from perfect. She has games and plays them well. She's cheated on me. We both promise we will change, but neither of us ever do. I do love

Casey, but I won't leave because I'm comfortable. I'm bad for her and I know that'll never change. I don't want to be the good guy; I want to be the bad guy.

I met Casey over ten years ago at the bar down the street from my grandmother's house. It was Thanksgiving night. All the women were in the kitchen cleaning up. My uncles and cousins walked to the neighborhood bar for a few drinks and to play a couple games of pool. Casey was out with her friends having drinks at the same bar. They were the only attractive women in the bar; but there were other women there, barstool whores – that's what we call women who're always in the bars, who're likely turning tricks. Casey and her friends were the typical Irish loudmouth girls from Southie, that only hung out in Dorchester because they didn't want their dads or uncles to see them hooking up with guys or out with their boyfriends.

"What are you ladies drinking?" I said, walking up to Casey and her friends.

"Jack and coke," replied Casey.

I bought the entire bottle of Jack and a couple pitchers of coke. We spent the night at the bar, drinking and laughing until the sun came up. She reminded me of my mother. Easy to read, strong willed, but gullible. She trusted me too soon, a hopeful romantic, like my mother. I would be lying if I didn't admit that I felt a connection.

Unlike Casey and I, my parents met in a church in the 1960s. My mother, Irene Diorio, tall, slender with long thick brown hair, Italian. My grandparents owned a bakery in the North End. My father knew of the Diorio's, since his family's restaurant was a few streets over from the bakery. One of the few Irish run restaurants in the North End, also known as Little Italy. Every restaurant was Italian, but my grandparents. In the beginning they refused to migrate to South Boston like the other Irish families. Instead my grandparents made the best of the situation. Their restaurant was unique to the North End because we served American diner dishes: burgers, fries, shakes and always fresh pie and coffee. My grandparents eventually moved from their apartment above the restaurant to Dorchester, but kept the restaurant open, until my father took over and turned it into a deli/market.

My mother was nineteen when my father took her out on their first date. Her father was okay with them dating, but her mother couldn't get over my father being Irish. The Italians and Irish didn't get along then, or today. The Irish migrated to South Boston when the Italians showed up in boats to settle in the US, the North End. My father was a smart business owner, always hanging around politicians, but also mingling with the mobsters. He found both parties important: one party made the laws, the other broke them. My father could manipulate the laws he wanted passed and if they didn't get passed, he broke them anyway, expanding his many business ventures. They go hand in hand then and today. You own a business, so if you're smart you get to know the politicians for tax cuts, city contracts and permits for breaking ground on new business ventures. My father owned several fishing boats, a few restaurants in the North End, and invested money into several bars in the South End. He expanded his companies so fast, that he told me at one time he'd lost track of which business he'd invested with. The mobsters were difficult to avoid if you owned a business.

You either worked with them or paid them a fee; there wasn't a good choice.

My father, Sean Cormick, is a short, stocky guy, blue eyed with light brown hair which he always wears slicked back, even today with the hair he has left; he just slicks it over the bald spot. He always sports a thick mustache. He's the most patient man and always speaks softly; I've never heard him raise his voice around me. Because of his demeanor, his friends and colleagues call him Cool Cormick. He's a sneaky man and good at keeping secrets. He tried to take my mother for a fool, but she's always known about the women and the dirty business dealings. She's a loyal woman and would never even consider divorcing him. She loves him too much. This is why Casey reminds me of my mother, except she'll confront me and the other women. They're so similar in the way they're vain and brag to their friends about lavish trips and purchases.

Ava is graduating next month, which means her internship will soon be over. I've noticed a change in her, she's tense, quiet, and withdrawn. She dresses sloppier and sometimes I swear I smell weed on her clothes. I try not to get too friendly with the interns, since we never hire interns.

We're getting audited today, meaning I will be stuck in meetings all day. Before this hell begins, I sneak out to my car to get some whiskey for my coffee. We get audited often because we are a financial investment organization. My father got me this job for a few reasons: one, he was sick of paying my bills and two, he was embarrassed to have a jobless son.

Walking through the parking lot I can smell a strong stench of weed coming from a car. I see in the distance Ava sitting in a smoke-filled car, crying. It's a strange sight; her makeup is running down her face. I feel uncomfortable and should pretend I don't see her, but I feel sorry for her. As I approach her, we make eye contact. She attempts to hide she's smoking and scrambles around in the car. I tap on her car window. She rolls it down only a few inches.

"Ava, I didn't know you had a car."

"I don't, it's my ex-boyfriend's."

I lean closer to the gap in the window.

"I'll assume that's why you're smoking a joint, crying."

Embarrassed, she finds a tissue, flips down the visor mirror to fix her face. She looks sad, not at all mad, but just sad. I've never seen a woman so upset before and trust me; I've made plenty of women cry.

"I'm sorry, I shouldn't be getting high on company time, I'm just having such a bad week. I caught him cheating, and he's moving out of my house today, or, well … he tried to – I stole his car before he could leave. Shit, shit I fucked up, I've lost a boyfriend, now my internship and I'm going to jail for stealing his car."

"Don't worry, I won't tell tha boss. Anyway, I came out to get some whiskey from my car to spice up my coffee."

We both laugh. I see my intern is a bad girl underneath. I knew there was something fascinating about her. Her anger unleashes a more attractive Ava.

"I know this is a lot to ask, but do you think you can follow me to my ex's house to drop the car off?"

"Whoa, why ya want me to go?"

"Maybe you can help me persuade him from not pressing

charges, if he hasn't already."

"I see, ya want me to make him jealous or threaten him."

"Yes, to all."

We both chuckle.

"Come have a seat. We can finish this joint and you can enjoy your coffee."

As promised, I went with her to return the car. The guy's a goddamn pussy. He didn't press charges and didn't even make eye contact with me. If I were in his shoes, I would've been wicked pissed at the man that shows up with my ex and my car. It's clear he doesn't care for her anymore.

Present

I've lost track of how long it's been since I heard from Ava. I'm afraid my boss has decided to kill her and has left me out of the plan. I haven't been home in days, haven't slept, just been racking my brains trying to find her. I have no choice but to accuse my boss and demand to know what she's done with Ava. I would lie if I wasn't paranoid that my boss has also put out a hit on me, but deep down I know that I wouldn't have had this much time to contemplate.

It's 5 a.m. and I'm just leaving the strip club. I stumble to my car, drunk and tired, unsure which problem is creating a greater challenge of walking a straight line. My car is parked so far from the club because the parking lot was already full when I arrived. I stop halfway to my car to rest, light a cigarette before continuing the struggle to walk. I think to myself, *I'm too old for this shit. Partying all night and chasing women.*

I get close to my car and notice a paper folded under one of the windshield wipers. I'm scared to pick up the note for fear of the car exploding. I cautiously pick up the note and read.

AVA

CHAPTER 9

MOTEL

Is this how I die? In a motel room, with a grand mixture of 70s and 80s décor? Wood paneling, floral curtains with matching bedspreads, yellow smoke colored walls, mirrors on the closet doors, pink tiled bathroom with mold in every corner. A thick square television with brown paneling, and two big knobs for changing channels. The carpet doesn't match the rest of the room; it looks and smells new. All the furniture is a cheap walnut color. The lamps are bolted to the headboards of both beds.

I try to think positive considering my circumstances; I haven't been raped. I think they would have done it already. I'm tied to a chair with wheels. My hands are tied in the front and another rope tight around my chest. The duct tape around my mouth is sliding off from my sweat, so I push the tape that was originally wrapped around my eyes up to my forehead. I'm nervous they're allowing me to see them because this means they plan to kill me.

I'm so tired, but I'm afraid to sleep. I need to think of a plan, something to get me out of this situation. I have run several escape scenarios through my mind. The chair's on wheels, so I could roll to the door, but they've tied my hands in such a way I can't reach the doorknob to turn it or unchain the lock. I suppose I could stand up, but for fear of falling I could fail the escape.

I move my chair to get the fat one's attention. I motion my eyes to the bathroom.

"What?" The fat bastard stands up from the edge of the bed.

I motion my head towards the bathroom.

"You need the bathroom, too fucking bad."

I notice a large mole on his neck when he cocks his head to one side staring in my direction. His black hair is slicked back and greasy, his eyes are small and beady, there's stubble on his face. His stomach protrudes over his jeans. His worn-out brown leather jacket is too small to zip over his enormous stomach.

He breaks his stare when his phone rings but returns his glare after the phone is to his ear. I can't make out the conversation since he just keeps agreeing with person on the other line. Before he hangs up, he says, "I understand."

At that moment, panic sinks in, sweat begins to drip past my eyebrows down my face and off from my chin. I am trying to control my body from shaking from fear of being murdered. The skinnier of the two kidnappers walks behind the fat one when he ends the call. I feel my head get heavy, and I see black and white dots floating in front of me. The last thing I see before I blackout is the shadow of my kidnapper on the wall.

MR. ALTERMAN

CHAPTER 10

TROUBLE

I knew first meeting Ava, she was untruthful about her situation. I research all my potential clients before I even agree to meet them at my office. Then after the initial meeting, I do more exploring. I read about the upcoming trial in the Newspaper, so I had some insight about what was going on. I have lived in Boston my entire life; I know everyone and recognize the last name of her ex-boss at Atlantic Street.

I didn't take on Ava as a client for bankroll but more for the thrill. I knew it would be a challenge and could be dangerous with the Mob involved. This was the client I'd been searching for. If I had to take one more case from a scorned wife who wanted to drain her husband's bank account, I would give up on life.

I'm an old man with a growing alcohol problem, and I think my urge for drinking increases during times of boredom or investigating monotonous clients. If I don't keep myself busy with something that is interesting, I will drink the day away. In fact, when Ava came into my office that day, I had a terrible hangover. Ava looked just as hungover. A pretty girl, but she needs to take better care of her hygiene.

Last time I spoke with Ava, I told her I found her father. She wanted the information of her father's location, but I like to withhold information from my clients, it's my way of maintaining control. I want to keep information close, because that's my business. If I gave all the information away, my clients wouldn't need me any longer and that means no steady income.

Ava's father is not a person you seek. Most people are running or hiding from him, considering his occupation. I won't be visiting him in Maine; I may as well put a gun to my head and pull the trigger. I find it hard to believe that she doesn't know her father and his lifestyle. And that it's a coincidence she works for a company that has such a close relationship with the Mob.

Two days ago, I received the handwritten letter from Ava. Angie Palo, my receptionist, barely had her key in the office door when Ava approached her with a note addressed to me. At first, Angie, didn't recognize Ava; she was wearing a wig, hat, and sunglasses. Angie says that she looked ridiculous; a really terrible disguise. We both had a good chuckle. Ava made Angie promise she would give me the letter.

I read her note again, contemplating if I should help her.

Mr. Alterman,
It is important that you know where I am, since you may be one of the few people I can trust. I'm stopping at Guns and Roads,

a shooting range in Lincoln, NH. If I don't phone you by day 5 at 5:00am, please send Johnny to help me. I know you know who Johnny is because you've been tailing him when he leaves my house. He will know what to do.
Ava

I'm impressed that she knows I have been following Johnny. I know Johnny won't figure it out, he isn't a smart young man, and to think he works for the Mob. He will most likely be dead or in jail in no time.

As I sit staring at the note, something isn't right. Why would Ava be afraid of going to a gun range? I can't shake the bad feeling in my gut. I open the app to the tracking device on Johnny's car. His cars at a local strip club—shocking—he frequents this location almost daily. I'll leave an anonymous note on his car. In the meantime, I will try to call Ava again.

JOHNNY

CHAPTER 11

STAN

I'm driving erratically on Highway 93 heading South bound, to visit the boss. What did those fuckers do with Ava? I know she has something to do with Ava going missing. They wouldn't send me to do the job or tell me because they know I like her and may feel the need to warn her. Perhaps Atlantic has something to do with it. I still don't understand how Ava's acquaintance knew where to find me. My head is pounding from all the thoughts mashed with the hangover.

No sooner do I pull up to my father's house than my phone rings. She's called a meeting. Just the sons of bitches I was looking to talk with. I don't get out of the car. I see my father sitting in the kitchen window. Looking back at me, he waves. He knew about the meeting before it was even called. He was once in my shoes at his age. He says he retired, but no one retires from the 'Family' business.

I walk into the meeting, ready to pounce on my boss asking about Ava's whereabouts. I decide this is not the best time. Perhaps a better approach would be to admit that I lost track of Ava and somehow, she slipped out of my sight. Then my boss will break a few of my fingers, if I'm that lucky. I think it's best to be calm and listen at the meeting before putting my foot in my mouth.

I chickened out at the meeting, I didn't mention Ava and neither did my boss. As soon as it was over, I headed North to find Ava with a trunk full of guns and my right-hand man, Stan.

Stan and I grew up together in Southie. My parents took him in after his father went to jail. His mother was a whore working out of the combat zone in Chinatown, at the time the most dangerous intersection in downtown Boston. On occasion, she would show up at our home uninvited with her pimp boyfriends. My father promised Stan's father he would take care of him while he served a life sentence. Every time his mother showed up, it took Stan weeks to shake the anger she brought out of him. He would lock himself in the attic for hours and would skip family dinners. My father hated to see Stan go through this time and time again.

When Stan and I turned 16 years old, our birthdays just a few months apart, my father bought us both a car. They were the shittiest cars on the block, but we loved them. We would tinker with them every day after school and every weekend. We replaced the radios, toyed with the engines, cleaned, painted, buffed out minor dings and dents. The car was just another thing my father bought me, but to Stan this was everything to him. His car ended up being nicer, cleaner, and just overall ran better. My car was never finished; I lost interest. He had a father figure who he respected and who showed care, and admiration.

The last time I saw Stan's mother was when Stan blurted out that his mother molested him as a child. His father didn't know what was happening when he was at work. I will never forget the day – we were all eating dinner after a stressful day of having his whore mother show up. My father convinced Stan to have dinner with us. Stan didn't eat, he just stared at his plate, moving his food from one side to the other and taking occasional sips of his drink. Then be blurted it out, like he was telling us the weather for the week. My mother ran from the table in tears. My father stayed silent, gripping his fork and knife so tight his knuckles were white, then ordered us to go sit in the living room. He joined my mother upstairs, only returning downstairs when someone knocked at the door. I didn't dare move from the living room; my father scared us. That time in the living room I didn't know what to say or do. I thought of hugging him, but we were not allowed to show affection.

The priest sat in the kitchen with my mother and father and prayed together before he came to the living room. My mother, clenching her rosaries, motioned me into the kitchen. I followed her outside to the backyard, and the memory just ends.

Till this day, I still hold a deep secret from Stan. I know why Stan's mother stopped showing up. My father took care of his mother – either he killed her or instructed someone else to. I couldn't tell Stan this; he thought the world of my father, thought he could do no harm, even to this day. Stan is the son my father wanted all along. In my mind, my father never stated that, but Stan worked for my father, took over the stores and restaurants.

I didn't do jack shit, sitting on my ass, enjoying my father's money and spending too much time with the ladies. My father wanted me to focus on money, the business and socializing. I didn't envy Stan; I was happy that someone else could take my father's attention away from me.

So, who better to take along to find this crazy bitch Ava than Stan?

"I'll assume that the boss doesn't know you're on this trip to find your Cinderella," says Stan with a wide grin.

I throw him the 'shut the fuck' look. I don't have to answer; he knows I make moves with barely thinking things through.

"There's a lot of shit you know nothing about, my old friend. Like my ass is on the line if this girl doesn't return to Boston to testify."

"Don't worry about it, we'll find her and if someone has taken her or hurt her, we'll find them. It's been a few weeks since I've given someone a good ass whooping, outside the boxing classes."

"Oh, please, your boxing classes are full of skinny females and old men wearing diapers."

"I could kick your ass with one hand behind my back."

"Just because I used to sit behind a desk most weeks, doesn't mean I don't get my hands dirty."

We fight like brothers. He knows I am only playing with him; Stan could kill me with his pinky.

The rest of the ride to New Hampshire we are quiet. The snow falls heavier the closer to the mountains we get. The GPS is cutting in and out, keeps saying we are thirty minutes away and then saying recalculating route. Goddamn the ride is long to this shooting range.

AVA

CHAPTER 12

RESCUED

I don't know how long I was unconscious, but I wake with the feeling of something heavy sitting on my chest. I can't breathe, I feel wetness on my legs. I pull my chin up to see what is heavy on my legs. I see the fat kidnapper lying on top of me. My arm is pinned between the floor and the chair. It hurts so bad I'm doing everything to hold back my tears and screaming from the pain. I play dead, when I hear heavy footsteps approaching. It must be the other kidnapper, but how was the fat kidnapper killed? Then I hear a familiar voice calling me. It's the Indian from the shooting range.

Holy shit! How did he find me, and is he here with the kidnappers or here to save me?

"I will help you up," he says.

He pushes the fat one off me and lifts the chair. I feel immediate relief in my wrists. The Indian sits me on the edge of the bed and cuts away the tape from my wrist and feet. I look down around my feet at the blood and two bodies. He's shot the skinny one between the eyes and the fat one looks like he got a shotgun to the back of the head.

The Indian leans down to pull the tape off my mouth. It's caught in my hair, but he pulls it down enough for me to speak.

"Are you okay?" he asks.

"I... I... I'm fine," the words come out. It's as if I've forgotten how to speak. I've been talking to myself inside my head for so long, it feels strange to hear myself.

"Do we call the cops now; how does this work?" I hesitate to keep asking questions.

The Indian roars with laughter. I feel uncomfortable by the insane look in his eyes matched with his deep laughter.

"We don't call police. We take care of it."

The White Man from the shooting range appears in the doorway with a bucket and what appears to be cleaning supplies.

"Get up girl, it's time to clean up the mess you dragged into our motel." He hands me blue latex gloves.

I stare at the blue gloves, still in shock. The Indian and White Man wrap the bodies in plastic and tarp and throw them in the kidnappers' car. Then just like that, I'm an accessory to murder. I begin to scrub the evidence from the motel room walls and ceiling. A shotgun is messy to clean up, the blood and brain matter splattered everywhere. I throw everything not nailed down into trash bags: beddings, pillows, curtains, and even lampshades. The blood on the carpet isn't as easy, it won't disappear, no matter how much I scrub. I scrub and spray and pat with paper towels, soaking up the blood. I repeat this process for what feels like hours, before it finally disappears. Whatever chemical is in this bottle worked. All evidence has faded from the room, but the smell of death lingers.

I'm not sure where they're going with the bodies or car, but I don't care. I'm tired, hungry, dirty, and just want to get back to Boston.

The Indian enters the room with a cat carrier.

"Skunks – they will piss everywhere, giving us reason to clean the room without suspicion," he says, unlatching the cage.

"You cleaned good, come," he motions me out the door.

An old woman in a bathrobe and slippers walks out of her motel room waving down the Indian.

"Indian, skunks again? I heard a lot of shooting in that room next door. The boys you rented to scared off the bears near the trash," she says, speaking with a lit cigarette hanging out of her mouth.

"Yup, skunk piss everywhere."

The Indian helps me into his beat-up pickup truck and drives me back to the shooting range.

"Do you have clean clothes?" he asks me.

I nod yes.

In the Indian's bathroom I stare back at the reflection in the mirror trying to figure out who this new person is looking back at me. My face is much skinnier than I remember, making my eyes appear larger. There is duct tape tangled in my hair. I smile; not sure why, but I smile. I break out in a quiet laugh. I look a goddamn mess. I'm filled with adrenaline – I feel powerful, all because I survived, I guess. I cheated death today. How many people can say that? Few. I'm excited to be alive for once and to continue my journey finding my father. I can't help but think if I find my father, he'll also be able to help me figure out who would want my mother dead. I undress and shower, all the time thinking about what I can offer the Indian and the White Man. Money; I have little right now. I could offer my bookkeeping services to repay the debt to them for saving my life – or should I be so eager to offer? Playing the victim sometimes works; they were trying to rape and kill me, yeah, that's it.

I've never felt so satisfied to shower in all my life. I feel better, except for the hunger pains. I approach the kitchen where I see fresh biscuits sitting in the middle of the table. My mouth waters.

"Sit," the Indian motions me to a chair. He returns with a steamy bowl of chicken soup.

We sit in silence eating. I eat more than my share of food and drink two cups of coffee before I speak.

"Those men would have killed me. Thank you for saving me."

"I know."

He cleans off the table and starts the dishes, while I sit chain smoking cigarettes. I watch his back muscles rotate with every hand movement from washing each dish. I wonder if this was his first time killing. I mean, they own a gun shooting range. I can only guess the amount of acreage they own, if they own the gun range and the motel. They could own the entire mountain. Both the White Man and the Indian seemed to instinctively know how to clean up the murders of my kidnappers. They had to have done this before. I feel great pressure on my chest, a panic attack approaching. My debt to these crazy mountain men. I can never repay them.

The door opens, breaking my train of thought and pausing my panic attack, like someone turned down the loud music at my panic attack party. It's the White Man. He hangs his hat and coat near the door and leans his rifle against the door before sitting at the table. The Indian grabs three glasses and an unmarked bottle of caramel colored liquid. He pours three glasses and pushes one towards each of us, keeping one for himself.

"Let's toast to new friends, old friends and phony friends," the White Man says.

I go along with the toast and wait for someone to speak because I don't know what to say.

The White Man pushes back his chair and leans his body on the table, his elbow propped on the table, holding the half-drunk glass of liquor.

"Explain to us why you brought all this trouble to our mountain?" he asks.

"Honestly, I saw no one following me and I don't know those guys."

"Try again."

I need more time to think; I can't tell them the truth, they won't believe me – they won't believe it. The mess I'm in sounds so fake, like a movie scene, but if I don't tell them some truth, I may not walk out that door.

"I was on my way to find my father. I'm in trouble and I think he's the only one who can save me. This was all a stupid, stupid fucking mistake. I should have never tried to find him."

"Who knows you came here ... besides maybe your father?"

"No one."

"What's your father's name," the Indian asks.

"Jimmy Coonan."

"Bullshit!" the White Man chimes in.

The Indian raises his hand for the White Man to stop talking.

"You are free to leave; return in two weeks with $20,000 in cash," he demands.

I don't even blink, just nod my head yes. They both stand up and I walk to the door, all the time thinking I won't make it out alive.

"Hey!" the White Man yells.

My heart is in my throat, pounding so hard I can't speak. I don't want to turn around and face the gun pointed at me. I prefer to be shot in the back.

"Yes," I say without turning around.

"Drive safe."

I drive for an hour before stopping to use the restroom, get gas, cigarettes and rolling papers. I sit on a picnic table to smoke a joint and check my phone messages. I have over fifty voicemails. I don't bother listening to them before deleting them all. I forgot about one major detail in my planned trip. I asked Mr. Alterman to reach out to Johnny if he doesn't hear from me in a few days.

I call Johnny's phone.

He picks up after one ring.

"AVA, WHERE THE FUCK ARE YOU?"

"I'm at a rest area in New Hampshire. Look, I'm okay, my phone went dead, and I had to find another charger. I'm sorry if I worried you."

"Where are you? You're a pissy liar, you know that. I'm

you're okay. I'll meet you. Text me the address."

"Okay."

I roll a series of joints and smoke another while waiting for Johnny. I'm tired and can't be bothered to drive anymore. I search the internet for nearby hotels. There's a hotel about twenty minutes from the rest area, just over the border into Massachusetts. I text Paul the information, asking him to book a room for one night. If he doesn't respond in time, I'll have Johnny pay.

Just when I almost lose my patience and leave, I see a black Mustang pull up. Johnny's driving and there's a muscular young man in the passenger seat. He looks disgusted to see me. I wonder what Johnny's told him about me. Johnny gets out and his passenger heads into the store, not acknowledging me at all.

I roll down the window to talk to Johnny. He stops me by opening the door and pulls me out of my car.

He presses his body against me, grabs my face and kisses me hard. His lips are soft and cold. I have missed him, and I question why I didn't just tell him where I was going.

Johnny holds me until his passenger interrupts, climbing into the driver seat of Johnny's car. He rolls down the passenger window and leans over.

"Johnny, I'll see you back in Boston."

Johnny leans into the window and whispers; I can't hear what he says. He drives off, squealing the car tires as he exits the parking lot.

"What the hell happened to your nose?"

"I slipped on some ice."

Johnny takes a closer look at my nose. I can tell he doesn't believe me.

"Who's that?" I ask.

"A friend."

I leave it at that; I can tell Johnny isn't interested in explaining who his friend is. We drive to the hotel in silence. He doesn't ask where we are going, and when we get to the hotel, he doesn't question it.

I check my phone to see if Paul has responded. He has – our reservation is confirmed and paid.

As soon as we get into the room, he pushes me onto the bed, undoes my pants and pulls them down around my shoes. He kisses my stomach, moving up under my shirt. I lean up to unhook my bra. To my surprise, he goes down on me. He has never done this for me before. It feels amazing; I can't remember the last time I was pleasured. I let my worries melt away and put my mind at ease. He lets me come and doesn't stop pleasuring me. It's so sensitive I push his head away. Johnny love's teasing me during sex, and I wonder if this is how he is with Casey. The thought of her never bothers me, but I do think of how he pleasures her. She will keep Johnny no matter what he does, and he will never leave her side. It will be me who decides when we are done. Johnny and I both agree that this is temporary.

Johnny rolls me over on my stomach, spreads my legs, grabs my hair and pushes himself inside me. It was sex like we have never had; I can tell he isn't happy with me. He's aggressive during sex when he's angry. This time he takes it too far. He is hurting my insides and I feel like my neck will break. I am vulnerable – if he wanted to kill me, he could do it now. I let my guard down when I am around him, and I don't know why I am so trusting of him. I shouldn't be. Before he finishes, he smacks my backside hard.

We both lie for a few minutes before cleaning up. He tells me not to bother getting dressed because he wants me again. Ignoring his wants, I get dressed anyway.

Lying on the bed smoking a joint, I text Mr. Alterman. I want him to know I'm alive.

His response comes quickly.

Ava, what the hell is wrong with you? I want to see you in my office first thing tomorrow.

I reset my phone, deleting all my voicemails and text messages.

INDIAN

CHAPTER 13

RITUAL

During one of my weekly tribe rituals I dreamt of a little girl running through cornfields. Her hair was blonde with tints of red and a tiny freckled nose. She reminded me of someone, but I couldn't figure out who. I felt I've known her for years and we were friends. The smoke-filled room and sound of the drums pushes one's mind open and allows spirits to enter your world. Her innocence and happiness mesmerized me, running through the field. I watched on, sitting high on a rock; the grass was knee high, itchy on my legs. A man was behind me, whispering, "She's coming to visit you. Protect her, keep her away from me." I was never so confused during or after a ritual. I didn't understand who these spirits were, so the message was unclear. After the ceremony, the child's face remained etched in my head. I never saw her or heard the male spirit again.

A year later, I connected with that little girl spirit, Jimmy Coonan's daughter. She came to my gun shop to buy a gun and learn how to shoot. I knew the moment I saw her, she was the spirit, but I didn't know she was Jimmy's daughter, or know he had a daughter. I only found out because she told me, and when I confronted him, he confirmed it was true. It infuriated him she'd come to our shop, but he was relieved when I told him we saved her life from the kidnappers. The kidnappers were identified as Italian Mafia members, based on their tattoos. I don't know why they were after Ava, but I left that for Jimmy to figure out. If anyone sought revenge against Jimmy, they'd take great pleasure in killing his daughter. I can't tell if that would bother him because in all the years, we have been friends, he has never once mentioned Ava. If I was a father, I'm sure I would talk about them from time to time.

The spirits have never guided me or my tribe wrong, so I will protect Ava, but the male spirit that whispered in my ear was not Jimmy. I would know if it was him. We've been in each other's minds in other rituals.

When my father, Arawak Tzibatl, was Chief of our Abenaki tribe, he taught me the rituals and the business of the white men. Sadly, by the time I was Chief our tribe had shrunk to just a few dozen. This was the result of the poor leadership of my father. When my great grandfather, Chwewamink (pronounced Wyoming) was Chief, there were over a hundred tribesmen and women. After his death, families began to leave the tribe seeking domestication: healthier living conditions, employment for money, access to medical care, education for their children and to get welfare services provided by the government. We were starving, getting sick, and many were addicted to drugs under my father's control. It didn't help that the government offered free services as trickery to get us off our land so they could take over. Chief Chwewamink didn't believe in domestication, even when our tribe was dying from simple diseases that could've been prevented. We were lacking resources that the land once provided. Still, he refused to believe we could co-exist with the white man and keep our many Indian traditions alive. Chief Chwewamink envisioned the tribe's future would lay in skeleton fields. He was right; my father turned greedy, made deals with the white man, sold most of our mountains in return for more money. He even allowed to be called Chief Tob, in replacement of his tribal name, to please the white man. I used the money gained from the sale of our land to build a more modernized village and homes for the tribe. He had the motel built to produce a regular income flow, built larger farms to harvest food for the tribe and for trading for other resources and the gun shop to protect our people. He believed the gun shop would not only generate income but would also send a message to his enemies. My father's spirits guided him to the same skeleton fields, the same fields my great grandfather visited. We know this because my great grandfather brought us to skeleton fields during many rituals. My grandfather died young, so the tribe raised my father. Out of everyone in the tribe, he was the last Indian anyone would expect to turn his back on the spirits and not follow his true path. Instead, he chose drugs, whores and money. I didn't want to believe the stories about my father told by my elders, but I had to come to terms with the reality.

I believe my father did the best he could during the changing times. He left me as Chief with a business but a diminished tribe. Although there are only a handful of us left, we continue our journey, following the spirits. Thanks to my father's drug problem and lifestyle, I had no choice but to continue in his footsteps and continue allowing the criminal transactions. This was the only way for the tribe to survive. I had no choice but to use the knowledge I was left with, and I know more than my share of drug dealers, mobsters and money-fueled politicians.

When my father was murdered, he left this world with many enemies and debts. I don't own the shooting range and motel because he sold percentages of the them to pay for various debts. They have told me that his business was set up like a pyramid scheme. I've never been to school; everything I learned was from the elders in the tribe. I didn't need school to figure out what a pyramid scheme was: borrowing money to pay off one debt, then borrowing money from someone else to pay off another debt, and so on. I wasn't my father, so I ended most contracts by murdering the men he owed. The ones that could not be killed, I had to work with and renegotiate to avoid being killed. It took several years of allowing my father's business partners to smuggle drugs from Canada using the motel as a drop-off point. The motel used to be mainly a whore house, but now it's common for felons, drug addicts and criminals to rent rooms at the motel. The sign outside the motel always says, 'no vacancy'. I try to keep the tourists away, and if they arrive at the motel, I lie and tell them we have no rooms. This policy is in place to protect the innocent and has been this way since a little girl by the name of Kate was kidnapped, sexually assaulted and murdered. She was just six years old, on a road trip with her family, driving across the country all the way from New Mexico. They were only planning to stay one night at the motel but ended up staying for weeks while the police invested her disappearance.

When Kate turned up missing, I didn't know where to start. My motel was full of filthy criminals, but when Joe disappeared the same night and never returned, I had a feeling he had something to do with it. He was a frequent renter of the motel, a small petty crook who was in and out of jail for violating probation. I didn't give the police any information about Joe because I wanted to make sure I found him before the police. The next evening, I waited until darkness fell, took my hunting dogs through Joe's apartment until they got his scent. I grabbed a few clothes of his, to keep the dogs on his trail. I hiked all night and only rested in the morning. The ritual was conducted on my own; it's unusual for Indians to do this because it is more difficult for one's mind to open for the spirits to enter. A red cardinal landed on my arm and spoke using the wind. The wind sounded from the cardinal, *follow me*. It was almost impossible to hear, but I heard him, and he flew from tree to tree, looking back to make sure I was close behind. Just beyond the end of the trees was a wide meadow, and one large tree in the middle. The tree looked out of place. The bird flew to the tree waiting for me, but concentration broke from the loud flock of ducks flying overhead. I knew where the meadow was, but I don't recall a tree being in the middle. Still, I decided the meadow is where I should go.

After hours of hiking through the mountain valley, I came to the meadow. There was no tree, as I remembered, but beyond the meadow, tucked away in the trees was a small one-person makeshift tent. The blue tarp peeked from under the branches and bushes piled on top. I knew this must be Joe's tent. I took the bullets out of my gun to prevent myself from killing him at first sight.

I unhooked the dogs from their leash, and they took no time, bolting straight towards the tent. I walked slowly through the meadow yielding my knife. The dogs positioned themselves outside the tent, but didn't bark, so I knew he wasn't in the tent. I removed the tarp, searching for any sign of a little girl, dead or alive, but found only a sleeping bag, boots and a small pile of clothes. There was a small fire smoldering, so I knew he couldn't be far. I grabbed a shirt from the pile and let the dogs sniff it. I instructed them to hunt. They took off through the dense forest towards a stream that ran nearby. I heard the dogs barking, so I knew if that scent from the shirt is Joe then the dogs had found him.

"Go on, get, you darn dogs," yelled a man flailing in the water.

I walked to the edge of the water and called to the dogs to sit and be quiet.

It was Joe.

"Where's the girl?"

"Indian, I don't know what you talkin' 'bout."

I took his clothes hanging on the branch and threw them in the water.

"Now why the fuck did you do that for?"

"Put 'em on, come."

"Like fuck I'll come with you!"

I stood in silence, looking him in the eyes without breaking my stare.

"Jesus, can I at least get some dry clothes?"

"Was Kate warm when you took her?"

"Who's Kate?"

"The little girl you took, raped and killed."

"Now Indian, you done lost your mind."

I ran out of patience and sent my dogs to attack him, chasing him out of the water, biting at his limbs. I jumped on his back and turned him around, bound his hands together in front of his body with zip ties.

I tied both leashes around his hands. He wouldn't dare run; the dogs would chew him apart.

"Where is Kate?"

"I told you, Indian, I don't know what ya talkin' 'bout."

I took my handkerchief out and tied it as tight as I could around his mouth to stop him from speaking. I was tired of his lies.

Kate's family would choose his destiny, just as he chose Kate's.

I walked through the meadow with Joe in tow. We weren't walking for that long when a cardinal landed on a nearby bush, looked in our direction, then flew to another bush. This was a sign to follow the cardinal. He flew from branch to branch, leading us south to the where the stream bends into the river. The closer we got to the river, the more muffled sounds came from Joe. He was trying to get my attention and say something. I looked back at him, his eyes full of fear. I knew we were getting close to Kate.

On the edge of the riverbank was freshly dug soil. The Cardinal perched high above on a tree nearby and did not fly away. *She's here, under this pile of dirt.*

With no shovel, I walked to the river to find a flat rock.

"Dig," I said, handing the flat rock to Joe.

Joe was kneeling on the ground, his head in his hands, sobbing.

"Dig," I said again in a louder voice.

He took the rock and crawled to the soil and dug. I sat on a rock nearby watching him dig. I needed to see the girl before I could bring him to the parents. I didn't want to give such devastating news if it was untrue.

Joe stopped digging and laid next to the hole in a fetal position.

I hesitated before walking over to the hole. I knew whatever I was about to see would be in my mind forever. I didn't want to see it, but I felt an obligation to the family. Allowing them to stay at my no-good motel full of criminals and danger. I owed them the closure.

I peeked over the hole to see the little girl, Kate. Her eyes were wide open, pale, blood around her mouth, a rope wrapped around her tiny neck. Fear frozen in her facial expression. Her blue dress was filthy, her underwear pulled down around her ankles. He could have wrapped her in a blanket.

"Bury her," I said to Joe. He didn't move, just cried.

I motioned to the dogs to attack. They growled and moved towards Joe. He rose to his knees and pushed the dirt back into the grave all the while sobbing, not for Kate, but for himself; he knew death or jail was waiting for him beyond the mountain.

I would have carried Kate to her parents, but I didn't want to tamper with the evidence. I didn't want my DNA or fingerprints on a dead child's body.

We walked all day and through the night without stopping too much. Joe remained naked with bare feet. I didn't offer food, water, or warm clothes. Likely, the same way he treated Kate, but worse. When we made our way to the motel, I left Joe in the woods with the dogs. I wanted to make sure Kate's family got to see him first.

I knocked on the door. The father answered. I asked him to step outside and come with me. He followed me to the edge of the motel parking lot but was reluctant to follow me into the woods. Joe was sitting, still naked, leaning against the tree. My dogs sat staring at him. I cut off the bandana from around his mouth.

I turned to Kate's father.

"This is the man that took your daughter," I said.

"How do you know?" asked the father.

"I was out hunting with my dogs and stumbled upon his camp. My dogs sniffed out Kate's body buried near the river," I said.

"I haven't called the police. You can do what you want with him," I said.

The father stared at Joe until Joe made eye contact.

"WHY, WHY, did you take my daughter from us?" Kate's father begged with rage.

Joe sat still cowering, avoiding eye contact with Kate's father.

Kate's father just stood there looking at Joe.

"Leave him with me. Call the police in fifteen minutes, no sooner, no later," Kate's father requested.

I cut my dogs loose from Joe and handed the knife to Kate's father.

I did as he requested and called the police.

Kate's father walked from out of the woods with his shirt bloodied. I thought for sure he'd killed Joe, but later saw Joe sitting up in the stretcher, bleeding from the waist down. They handcuffed Kate's father while I gave the police my statement. I told them Joe insisted on confessing to Kate's father. The police were confused why Joe was naked; I told them I didn't know. I explained where they could find Kate. After this incident, I never allowed anyone to stay at my motel that wasn't a known criminal. People find my motel only by word of mouth. There is no advertising. I promised myself and Kate that I would never again risk the lives of an innocent traveler for money.

The news stations were all over this story, since nothing like this ever happens in our town. People were obsessed with Kate's murder, because her father sliced and diced Joe's private parts. He would never use a bathroom the same and never have sex for sure. Kate's father got off on most of the charges, some small-time, and fines for stabbing Joe. He pleaded insanity and most of his sentence was served in a mental facility. I never placed my hands-on Joe, so I paid a few of his jail mates to beat him up occasionally. I still regret not shooting him myself but am glad Kate's father got some of his anger out. Occasionally, I head to the spot on the river to talk to Kate. I made a wooden rocking chair and carved a Cardinal in the back. I go there and sit and tell her stories of my ancestors. I can feel her presence in the trees and wind and every so often, a butterfly will land on my shoulder as if listening to the stories I tell. I have no children, so Kate is my daughter in the spirit world.

Kate's family has never been back to the motel, and I don't blame them for not returning to a place that reminds them of hell. I got a letter and a gift from Kate's father some years later. His letter read:

Dear Koda,

I never thanked you for finding Kate. God put you the right place at the right time. Our family needed closure and without your help we may have left your motel without ever finding her. I have had more than my share of dreams about Kate and nightmares of her murderer. When Kate comes to me in my dreams, she tells me to thank the Indian. In my dreams she says, "Daddy, he was looking for me and made Joe dig me up, and he visits me at the river. He tells me stories about his family."

Our world will never be the same without Kate, but we are forever grateful for all you have done.

Enclosed is a hunting knife I had custom made for you as a token of our appreciation.

Take care,
Yours Truly,
David Dawson

I unwrapped the neatly wrapped knife. It was encased in a brown reddish leather holster with a strap attachment for my belt. The knife was sharpened on both sides, with a large grip carved wood handle. I turned the handle over to find a Cardinal carved in the handle, with the words, *With love, Kate.*

I don't cry often, but this gift tugged at my heart for several reasons. This confirms the spirits are still guiding us. Kate's father could've known about the Cardinal without Kate visiting her father in his dreams.

Just as Ava came as a spirit, we should dismiss no message. The signs were there, I just needed to dissect the spirit's message.

The men who booked a room at my motel take on various jobs for the Italian Mafia and are small-time crooks. They have never stayed at the motel, but other members of their family were frequent visitors. I wouldn't have known they were staying here to kill Ava. They're idiots for even trying to murder anyone at my motel thinking I wouldn't know. They made so many mistakes it was obvious this was their first kidnapping and attempted murder. Their first mistake was leaving Ava's car at the shooting range. The second mistake was kidnapping someone during a snowstorm. The fresh snow left clues of the struggle and footprints, and it was easy enough to track them to the motel by following their tire tracks. Their third mistake was trying to make a kill at my motel without proper permission. I killed them to send a message to anyone who thinks they can get away with doing crime at my motel without permission or proper payment. I wasn't there to save Ava; I was there to figure out why her car was still at my gun shop. She's lucky to be alive. Once she told me who her father was, I'm glad I was able to save her. Jimmy would have killed everyone and burned the entire place down to find out who killed his flesh and blood. The family is always used as leverage or a tool of revenge. Now I know, I must make sure Jimmy knows I am on his side and will make sure his daughter is safe whenever in my presence.

MR. ALTERMAN

CHAPTER 14

VISITOR

A loud bang wakes me. I grab my gun from the nightstand, but before my feet hit the floor, something's pressed hard against my forehead. I know this feeling; it's too common with my lifestyle, but one is never prepared to be awoken this way. The moonlight reflects off the barrel of a gun. The streetlight peeking through the window allows me only to see a tall figure towering over me. No movement or sound is made by me or of the unknown figure. My bedroom light is switched on by someone. Standing in my small bedroom are five, maybe six men; I can't count fast enough. I haven't a clue who these men are and certainly not the man dressed as an Indian holding the gun to my head. I have many clients, enemies, enemies of clients – it would be impossible to guess who they are.

"Mr. Alterman, it seems we got ah problem." The rather tall, muscular graying man speaks. His face is concealed by unkempt facial hair, gray with hints of red.

"New friend, I've heard you've been lookin' for me on behalf of Ava. And this has disturbed me in my retirement," he says in a serious tone.

"If you haven't figured it out, I'm Ava's fathah. I need you to tell me everything that's goin' on with her. If you lie, leave out any minah detail, my friends will take turns breakin' every frickin' bone in ya body. This is my one warning." He pulls up a chair in front of me.

When I searched for Ava's father, I stumbled upon more information than I needed. Searching his name doesn't show a great deal of information, but I used facial recognition with specialized software that the FBI and other agencies use and found his nickname. Searching using his nickname was overwhelming. I don't think Ava knows who her father is or what his previous job was or still is. I always withhold information from my clients. If I gave them everything up front, I wouldn't make a living. What Ava doesn't know is her father has been hiding out since a few years after she was born. Her father was a hitman for the Irish. He left Boston before the FBI opened an investigation on the Irish Mob. Coincidence, maybe. I have no reason to hide anything from Ava's father about her upcoming trial. If I had to guess, he must see a gain in his daughter's new troubles. I can't imagine he will put himself on the line for the sake of a daughter he barely knows. This may be an excuse to return to the Irish or financial gain. Why he's here, I do not understand?

AVA

CHAPTER 15

SOUTHERN HOSPITALITY

I sneak out of the hotel room without waking Johnny. My body is sore from a long night of rough sex. My nose is visibly swollen, dark shadows under my eyes. I'm eager to swim in the indoor pool and soak in the hot tub. Last night, Johnny's anger never subsided. He spoke to me like a man who's in love. I recognize his expression of feelings and they're suffocating me. The need he feels for me is becoming an unattractive quality. While I know a little about Johnny's upbringing, I can only imagine he was spoiled rotten and has a doting mother. Johnny sometimes acts like he's trying to be my boyfriend. In our world we created, Casey doesn't exist. I don't want to digest their relationship; I couldn't care less about her and Johnny. I need Johnny on my side. If that means we need to play part-time house, then so be it.

The indoor pool is supposed to be heated, but when I jump in, it is no warmer than maybe sixty degrees. After a lap around the pool I warm up. There're only a few people sitting around the pool. I notice a handsome, young dark-skinned man soaking in the large hot tub. I hate getting in a hot tub with other people, but with an attractive man, that's a different story.

I'm embarrassed to get out of the pool wearing my makeshift swimsuit: a black tank top over my bra and gray jersey shorts. I have lost so much weight these last few months that the shorts are baggy, so I roll the waist band over twice to keep them from falling off. I almost slip on the steps getting into the hot tub, attracting unwanted attention. I laugh it off. The attractive man bursts out in deep laughter and I can't help but laugh with him.

"Ya sure lucky I wasn't recording dat." He smiles.

"You're so lucky because I would've thrown your cellphone in the pool," I fire back, smirking.

"I'm sorry, dat was rude, honey. Ya okay?"

"My ego or my foot?"

"I'm more concerned about ya ego."

He smiles a wide, gorgeous smile. I think to myself, *this guy is beautiful, but so young; I mean, he can't be older than 21.*

"My name is Ava, and you?"

"Ruben."

"Like the sandwich?"

"Yes, ha ha; I never heard dat before."

He has a deep southern accent. It makes him even more attractive.

"I can tell by your accent you're not from Massachusetts, so what brings you to this cold, miserable state?"

"Corporate Training, I can't wait ta get back ta New Orleans. I've neva drunk so much coffee in ma life."

"Have you tried the clam chowder yet?"

"Nah, I haven't. Do ya recommend a restaurant?"

"Fuck no, I'm not from this area. There isn't shit to do in this part of the state. Your company was smart to have training classes in this boring suburb."

"Maybe I can take ya out for some dinner and drinks. Are ya stayin' at da hotel for a while?"

"I don't know; I was supposed to check out this morning."

He laughs and licks his lips. I think to myself, *Fuck, I'm stuck here with Johnny, and should get back to Boston.*

"Why don't you drive down to Boston later tonight, so I can show you a good time."

"Dat sounds amazing."

I give him my cell phone number and sneak away before Johnny comes to break up the fun. I grab two coffees from the lobby before heading back up to the room. I want breakfast, but I missed the free breakfast provided by the hotel, and there's no restaurant. When I get to the room, Johnny has already showered.

I hand him a coffee and sit on the floor across from him, my legs crossed in front of me.

"Good Morning," I say after an uncomfortable silence. Johnny won't look me in the eyes. My blood is boiling. His silence is pissing me off.

"What the fuck is your problem?" I say, lighting a cigarette.

"There's no smoking in this room," he says.

"There's no smoking…" I repeat, mocking him. I can't stand to even look at his face. I just want him to leave.

"Whatever you're hiding from me and whatever happened in New Hampshire, I'll find out," he says.

"It's my business, it's personal and none of your concern."

"Then why was there a note left on my car?"

He's now standing over me. I think for a minute that he'll throw his coffee at me.

"You're the only person I can trust right now, and I hope you feel you can trust me."

"Trust … trust… You don't trust me, Ava. You're a shitty liar, you know that. I want you to know I'm not your fucking personal bodyguard, superman. I have a job to do and you're making it real difficult. You got me out here looking like a bitch."

"What do you mean? Oh, no, I know what you're saying."

Now I'm standing too, and we're face to face.

"Your old lady Mob boss bitch put you in charge of keeping me in check, but poor little Johnny, can't keep his tiny dick in his pants," I yell. Then motion my hands like I'm crying like a child.

Johnny raises his hand high and smacks me in the face. The smack is so hard I fall back, hitting my head against the wall. My ear is ringing, my face stinging, and shock pours over me. I retaliate by punching him, missing his face and connecting with his head. He falls back on the bed and I am straddling him, slamming and swinging my fist, hitting his chest and face. He is trying to grab my wrists, but I've lost control. I want to kill him. I roll off him and lock myself in the bathroom and yell through the door.

"Leave now, before I hurt you."

"No problem, you fucking whore."

The hotel door slams shut.

I leave the bathroom and latch the door just in case he still has a door key. I shove a chair under the doorknob. I call down to the lobby and book another night but request a different room. Soon after, the concierge brings me my new key and room number. He is staring at the brand-new red mark on my face, the cut on my nose and slight bruising under my eyes.

I just need to find some food and clear my head. There is a restaurant across the street from the hotel. My rental car is gone; that explains the missing keys. Johnny must have taken it when he left.

The diner has a 50s vibe with oversized vinyl booths and a small bar. I order so much food that the waitress asks more than once if someone will be joining me. I respond with a dirty look. While I'm enjoying my food, my phone vibrates loudly on top of the table. It's Johnny. I can't believe he is calling me already.

"Hello," I mumble.

"Ava, don't hang up," he begs.

I stay silent for a moment.

"I'm listening."

"I'm sorry, I don't know what I was thinkin'."

"I'm not Casey, I won't take your shit. So, I suggest you go home and take your anger out on someone else."

"I just want you to know I'm sorry."

"If you ever put your hands on me again, I will kill you! I... Will... Fucking...Kill...You! Do you understand me JOHNNY?"

The entire restaurant is looking at me. I'm changing; something in my mind snaps. The thought of killing him is giving me pleasure. He's disposable to me, trash; I could just throw his dead body in the garbage. I decide that I'll be the one in control. I, ME, I'M in control, not Johnny.

"Goodbye, Johnny." I don't let him respond. I just hang up.

My mind shifts to my view across the street just outside the window. I see my new friend Ruben leaving the hotel with a group of suited men. I assume they are off for their full day of seminars and training. He's beautiful, even from this distance. To say a man is beautiful is unconventional, but gosh, he looks like he was molded by God's hands. A body of perfection, the sweetest southern accent, large, dark brown eyes framed with long black eyelashes and a quiet, reserved poker face. I gave him my number expecting him to call or text me his number, but he never did. I hope I can see him tonight. I continue to daydream about Ruben and sip my coffee. The waitress startles me.

"More coffee?"

"Yes, please. Is there a bar nearby that plays live music?"

"Wheels Sports Bar is where my daughter goes. I'd say she's around your age."

I pay the bill and go back to the hotel where I wait for Ruben to call. I completely forgot to call Mr. Alterman to let him know I won't make it to his office today. I'm sure he's figured it out already. I boot up my laptop and email him. I'm in no mood to talk over the phone, to anyone, so email will do for now. Mr. Alterman responds immediately. He writes the strangest thing. He says my father has reached out to him. I don't understand how that's possible. How does he know Mr. Alterman? This new information puts me in an even worse mood. I'm not sure if I believe Mr. Alterman, since he was the one who found my father. I don't respond – how do I even know that Mr. Alterman sent that email?

I email Paul and ask him to dig up any information about Mr.

Alterman. Maybe I misjudged him. He has no problem digging into a criminal's backgrounds; maybe there's something there that he's hiding.

I count in my head how much cash I have left. I haven't touched my credit cards or bank accounts. I use them only to pay my bills. I promised to pay back my ex, but the way it's going, it doesn't look like that will happen, since I now owe the Indian. There must be a way to make some fast cash. Just as I finish the thought, I get a text message from an unknown number. All it says is…

Did ya trip over ya own feet anymore today?
I reply. *Only in the hot tub*
What ya plans for da night?
You are my plans
Lol
How 'bout ya come to da casino?
Hmmm, I'm not much of a gambler
I am, I'll show ya da ropes
What time?
7?
Come to my room at 6
There's a pause before he responds. Perhaps I came on too strong.
I think we need more than an hour, how's 5:30
Room 510, see you soon

I lie on my bed fantasizing about Ruben. The thought of Johnny's face if he saw me out with Ruben. It turns me on to know what Johnny would do to Ruben. Sometimes during sex with Johnny, he whispers threats in my ear while nibbling on my earlobes. He's threatened to kill me and any man he catches me with. I brush it off, but when he acts controlling, it turns me on. I've never had a man want me like Johnny does. Him slapping me today wasn't shocking. Ever since we started a sexual relationship, I knew he was capable. I was more shocked at being slapped at that very moment. I've seen that look before, like he could easily kill me. Still, for some reason or another, I feel invincible.

I wake up to a knock on my door. Fuck, it must be Ruben, it's 5:45. I clearly fell asleep in the middle of smoking a joint. The linens have a burn hole near my head.

"Coming," I yell from the bathroom, getting a quick look at myself. I don't look too bad.

I check the peephole; it's Ruben, as I expected. He looks unbelievable. He is wearing a navy blue fitted suit, with a light purple collared shirt. I open the door.

"Did ya just wake up?" he asks.

"Can you tell?" I respond sarcastically.

As I walk towards the bed, he grabs my hips from behind and pushes his body into mine. He is breathing on my neck.

"I thought 'bout ya all day," he whispers.

I turn around to get a better look at him. We lock lips and kiss passionately. His lips are consuming mine and his tongue is everywhere in my mouth. He lifts my legs so that I am straddling him. We both waste no time getting undressed. I lie on the bed naked with one hand under my head. He is in just his underwear when he climbs on top of me. We continue to kiss. I reach down to grab his penis. It's completely soft, so I try touching and rubbing it to get it hard. It's still soft. Suddenly, I am no longer interested.

"Is everything okay?" I ask.

"It sometimes happens, please don't think it's you."

"That's exactly what I was thinking," I reply.

He gets off the bed and reaches into his pant pocket and pulls out a bag of white powder.

"You want some?" he asks, holding up the bag. I've never tried heavy drugs and promised myself I'd stick to weed. Before now I've also never been kidnapped, cleaned up a murder scene or screwed around with a man working for the Mob; times have changed.

"Sure, I've never done it, so maybe just a little."

He takes my makeup mirror, room key, and rolls a hundred-dollar bill.

"Ladies first." He hands me the mirror and rolled dollar bill. My hand is shaking while I snort one line in each nostril. Immediately I feel awake; my thoughts are clearer. I start to think about everything at once. I'm overwhelmed, my heart's racing, but I'm happy, so happy. I can't stop moving my mouth and my eyes are blinking uncontrollably. My eyes feel large and dry, but I'm so happy, nothing matters in this moment.

Ruben slowly lays me on my back and pushes against me. I feel his hardness on my leg, and this excites me.

We fuck three times on the bed and once in the shower. Finally, we pull ourselves out of the sex cycle to take a shower and dress. I'm wearing a tight black long-sleeved sweater dress with black over the knee boots. I look in the mirror and am shocked to see how much weight I've lost. I still have plenty of hips and a tiny noticeable tummy, but other than that I look great. I did my makeup heavy; a smoky eye look and red lipstick. It's clear Ruben likes what he sees. I'm wearing a heavy suede black jacket, belted at the waist. We look damn good walking together to the lobby.

There's a black Lincoln SUV waiting out front of the hotel. On the way to the casino, we continue to snort more coke. I'm so hyper that I feel the urge to jump out of the moving vehicle. We arrive at the casino and head straight to the betting booth. There's a fight Ruben wants to place a bet on. I thought I heard $100,000 on Gonzalez, but I'm so high, it must have been $1,000. I stuffed about $5,000 in my boots, so as not to leave it stashed in the hotel. I'm hoping not to spend my own money, but I did put a few hundred dollars in my purse just in case Ruben is a cheap date. It's $100 just to play one game at most tables.

"Poker's my game, and ya ma lucky lady," he says, pulling out a chair for me to sit at the nearest poker table. He bragged the entire drive about how great he is at playing poker.

"I start out with poker and if ma luck runs dry, I move to craps or 21."

"What? Yeah, okay, I don't really know much about this," I say licking my teeth clean. Must be a side effect from the coke because I can't stop doing it.

Ruben loses the first two hands, but wins three times in a row, then loses; this cycle goes on and on. I'm getting so drunk because the free drinks keep coming and they are strong. Watching someone gamble is boring, especially when you don't understand the game. I have been counting in my head what he's bet, gained and loss. Being an accountant, I can easily count numbers in my head, and large numbers are no problem. If I've counted right, he has more than doubled $10,000 in an hour. We move from poker to the craps table. This is when he really starts to shine. Adding and subtracting his winnings and losses, he is up about $38,000. Time seems to stand still, and I'm drunker than I'd like to be. I check my phone for the time, it's 4 a.m. I think my cell phone time is wrong. I was planning on checking out tomorrow and driving back to Boston by noon. That's clearly not going to happen. Finally, Ruben seems satisfied and goes to cash out and collect his winnings from his boxing bet.

He hugs me tight and kisses on my neck while we wait in the cashier line. I immediately feel a tingling sensation. I can't get over how attractive I find him.

"Let's get a room at the casino and order room service," he practically begs me. I'm so drunk and tired that I just go along with whatever he wants. Luckily the front desk has rooms, but they make him pay for two nights because of the early check in. He gets us a suite on the eighth floor. When we get to the room, it's unnecessarily large and has a jacuzzi in the living room. There are walk-in closets, a wet bar, a bedroom with a large sitting area and an oversized king bed. I lay back on the bed, exhausted, I just want to go to sleep. Ruben stands over me, unbuttoning his shirt. He takes my boots off and my money falls on the floor. He isn't fazed by the money in my boot, and why should he be, he won over $200,000 when combining the boxing match and table games. He bragged about it walking to the room. I think to myself, *Somehow, I need to get my hands on some of that money*. I still owe the Indian and haven't really stopped thinking about my kidnapping since I left New Hampshire. I still can't figure out who the kidnappers were and what they wanted. I've had several nightmares about that night and have begun sleeping with the light on. I don't feel the least fazed by the murders of the two men. Why would I feel remorse for anyone who was trying to kill me? My concerns are the police finding out about the murders or the Indian killing me. Right now, my focus is on Ruben; I need him for a few good reasons. Sex with him will do for now, but first, a little coke to wake me up; and Ruben's better half.

There's blood and makeup smudged all over my pillow. Last night was amazing, but this headache I have is relentless. I check my phone for the time, it's 1:15 p.m. I was supposed to check out of my room at 11 a.m. I call the hotel and inform the front desk I will be staying another night. I wish it wasn't so late; I need to get back to Boston. Everyone is blowing up my phone. There are several text messages from my roommate and Johnny, and a shit load of missed calls from unknown numbers and a few voicemails. I can't be bothered responding right now with this headache.

I hear the hotel door open and in walks Ruben. I didn't even notice he was gone because the rooms are over the top big. He has coffee for us and shopping bags.

"Good Morning, pretty lady."

"Oh, yeah, you like the bloody nose, running mascara look."

"I've seen worse."

He hands me a coffee and a shopping bag.

"What's all this?"

"I bought ya a change of clothes. No lady of mine is goin' to do dat walk of shame leaving a casino."

I laugh. There's a beige sweater and black skinny jeans, underwear, bra and socks. Also, a cute black winter pom pom hat and black leather fitted gloves. No denying he has expensive taste.

"Ruben, thank you, this all so sweet."

He brushes off the thank you and gives me a kiss on the forehead.

"Let's go take a shower, I will help soap you up."

In the shower, he lathers my body with soap, even between my legs, my butt and breasts. I can't help but be turned on by his touch. I offer to do the same and he declines. Instead he lifts me and positions me on the shower seat as if to have sex, but instead he goes down on me. It feels amazing and I orgasm in minutes. He doesn't want any favors in return, which I think is strange. He certainly looks like he wants sex by his erection.

We don't waste any time leaving the casino and starting our journey back to the hotel. Ruben texts someone on his phone the entire drive back. I see why he prefers to be driven rather than just renting a car.

"When are you flying home?" I ask.

"I was supposed to leave dis mornin', but I missed my flight," he explains.

"Well, that's irresponsible of you," I wink. "I'm driving to Boston tonight," I add.

"I had an amazing time. Can I see ya again? Perhaps in a month you can fly out to visit me."

"I would like that a lot,"

I lay my head in his lap and he rubs my head. He makes me feel relaxed and comforted by his presence.

Back at the hotel, he sits on my bed, carefully watching me pack.

"I want you to have some money for a plane ticket and a hotel room, fa when you visit me," he says.

"Okay. When should I come visit?"

He hands me a large stack of money. It's mostly hundreds, but I couldn't even try to guess how much is here.

"That's too much."

"Not for first class and five-star hotels," he smiles.

"That's true. Then are you sure this is enough?" I joke with him.

We kiss and hug a few times before he walks me down to the lobby. I'm a little sad to leave, but at the same time too much affection makes me uncomfortable. It was getting a bit creepy. I catch him staring at me a lot, which is strange. I look out the cab window at him. He's the most handsome man I've ever been with. I give him a small wave and he smiles wide back at me. I'm anxious to get home. I've missed the city. Even with all the stress it brings me, there really is no better city than Boston.

AVA

CHAPTER 16

FRIENDS

After being kidnapped, and on a cocaine binge casino night with Ruben, it feels good to be back home and taking a shower. I love and hate having a roommate in the same breath. It's not that Samantha isn't the ideal roommate, it's just that I have never gotten along with other women. She's working a double shift at the restaurant, so I can unwind without her up my ass, asking where I have been. Having a roommate, I never feel one hundred percent relaxed in my home, but it makes me feel less lonely. I take advantage of her absence by walking around in my bra and underwear, eating junk food on the couch and drinking white wine straight from the bottle. I've missed Cambridge with its endless city sounds. I'm half a bottle down before I boot up my computer to check for any correspondence from Paul or Mr. Alterman. They are the only two people I kind of trust right now.

Mr. Alterman has emailed me a second time about my father

visiting him. He says it's urgent I come to his office. I respond, *I'll be at your office tomorrow at noon.*

I choose noon because I know both of us will be nursing a hangover tomorrow.

I move on to Paul's several emails with documents attached. Before I read his emails, I draft an email explaining to him what happened in New Hampshire. I don't go into too much detail because I would rather tell him in person. I assure him I am okay and ask him to brainstorm some theories of who these people could have been.

I then open the documents and start reading them. I can't believe the bullshit I am reading. I grab a notebook to write some names, so I can go back and find a connection. I wouldn't have even been able to piece this all together without Paul.

I spend over three hours reading and taking notes. I just can't believe some of the connections to my father. This confirms it: my father is a hitman for the Irish Mob. Well, that explains why I was put up for adoption. I'm still not one hundred percent sure who my biological mother is, but I have a few ideas. I'm doubtful my father will be so open as to tell me this information. The mother that raised me even claimed she didn't know who my biological mother was.

If my father is still working for or has worked for the Mob, Claire is or was his boss. If they are in good standing, I can get the Mob off my back about testifying and move on with my life. Seems like I need to have a conversation with my father, in hopes he will help me.

If convicted, Susan is facing ten plus years in prison. Right now, I don't see how my testimony will help keep her out of prison, so if my theory is correct, their plan could be to pin it all on me. I need to make sure I have a plan in place if this theory plays out. Even Johnny isn't safe, although I can't imagine Johnny's parents will let their precious son go to jail, with their connections. It connects Johnny's father to the Irish and he's a respected businessman in Boston.

I have uncovered nothing more regarding Susan's rank in the Mob. She must be important to someone, but until I can figure that out, I can't use that as leverage.

Paul confirms that the Italians and Irish both don't know we were skimming money off the top of the money laundered through Atlantic. I'm not surprised; Paul has been stealing money from corporations for many years. I have all the faith in the world in Paul's hacking abilities. If they knew, they would've killed us both. I'm not all innocent, I know this could be a reason for someone to kidnap and attempt to kill me. Anyone could've followed me to the shooting range in New Hampshire; I wasn't paying attention on the drive up. My father visiting Mr. Alterman is similar timing to my kidnapping but why would he have me murdered, when he was the one who put me up for adoption? I have a lot of information to sift through and right now is not a good time, since I am down my second bottle of wine. Before I close my laptop, an email from Paul pops up.

Ava -
I am concerned for your safety. I'm coming over. Be there in a couple hours.
Paul

There's a knock at the door. Paul said he would be here in a few hours. I'm so drunk the time must have slipped away. I guess I should put on clothes. I throw on a t-shirt. I'm so intoxicated that the room is spinning. If I had cocaine I wouldn't have drank so much.

I walk sideways to the door and try a few times to turn the doorknob. Eventually I get the door open.

"Mac! What are you doing here?"

"Ava, are you drunk? And where are your pants?"

I look down, shocking myself. I thought I'd put on underwear.

"Oh, no, Ava has been a bad girl, she needs a spanking." I put my hand to my mouth and bend over pushing my naked bottom in his face.

He just stares at me.

I grab the joints from the kitchen table, and hand them to him.

Mac ignores the joints. "Let me get you to bed."

"I don't want to go to bed."

He grabs my waist and walks me to my room.

He lies me on the bed. The room is spinning.

I feel my shirt pushed up over my breast.

I sit up. "What the fuck are you doing? I don't want you!" I yell.

He doesn't listen and grabs my wrists, climbing on top of me. Holding my hands above my head he bites my nipples.

"Get off me, no, no."

I twist my body and get on my knees, trying to climb off the bed.

He grabs me from behind.

"It's mine, I paid a lot of money. I can fuck you whenever I want, and you will never have to pay me back."

"Fuck you, get off me."

He pulls my hair back and climbs behind, trying to put his dick inside.

I squirm the best I can, but I'm drunk and tired. I give into Mac and let him rape me.

I turn my face looking at the picture of me and my mother. Happier times. I don't cry because that would give him pleasure. I don't fight back because that turns him on.

He slams into my backside for what feels like a lifetime. When he's done, he rolls off me.

Too scared to move, I lie there quietly, waiting for him to make the first move.

"Go to the bathroom and clean yourself up," he demands.

It hurts to walk, and I can feel the cum run down my leg. He didn't even have the consideration to use a condom. I lock the bathroom door once I'm inside. I just stare at myself in the mirror, trying to understand what just happened. *Was I just raped? Is this rape if it's an ex? What is the definition of rape?* Who am I kidding? He raped me, that bastard raped me.

I cry washing his cum off. I put my robe on and wash my face. I grab my gun from underneath the hidden compartment under my sink. I put in in my robe pocket.

"Ava, you in your room? You shouldn't leave your front door unlocked," yells Paul.

Never have I felt so relieved to hear Paul's voice.

I listen from the bathroom.

"Woah, Mac I wasn't expecting you here. Ava didn't tell me she would have company," says Paul.

"Well, I'm leaving anyway," Mac responds

A part of me thinks I should just stay in the bathroom until he leaves, but that's the voice of reasoning the old Ava would use.

"You raped me, you pig," I say walking out from the bathroom.

Paul backs up from Mac.

"I didn't do anything you didn't want," he says arrogantly.

"Really, let's see what the police say when my rape test kit results are done."

"You're a fucking whore, who's going to believe you? If you try me, I will tell your dirty little secret to Paul," he threatens.

I freeze. He wouldn't dare, would he? I put my hand in my robe pocket and turn off the safety on my gun.

"Ava, is this true? Did Mac rape you?" asks Paul walking towards me.

"Yes. Get back, Paul."

I pull out the gun and point it at Mac.

"Ava, put the gun down," says Paul.

"Don't listen to her, she ain't got the balls. You've graduated from poisoning people to just shooting them," says Mac, walking closer to me.

"Shut up, shut up," I yell.

"You're drunk, put the gun down," begs Paul.

Mac is now just a few feet from my face.

"If you go to the police, I will tell Paul your secret. You owe me; I'll be back for more until you've paid your debt."

I don't break my eye contact with Mac.

"I don't ever want to see you ever again. Get out of my house."

"Then pay me the money you owe me."

"I will."

"I don't trust you and neither should Paul. I mean, you killed his best friend or lover, whatever Thomas was to him."

The gun goes off but misses Mac. He lunges at me, trying to wrestle the gun out of my hands. Paul jumps on Mac's back, distracting him long enough for me to gain control of the gun.

"Get off me," yells Mac.

Paul is thrown off Mac's shoulders. Mac gets back on his feet. With two hands gripping the gun I pull the trigger. Mac drops to his knees. I see Paul looking at me through the hole in Mac's head before Mac's lifeless body falls on top of me.

"Ahh, Paul, get him off me," I cry.

Paul comes to my rescue, pushing Mac's body off me. There's blood and chunks of flesh splattered on Paul's face and clothing. I can feel Mac's blood dripping around my mouth.

"Paul, we have to clean this up, get rid of the body. Go to the kitchen under the sink, grab trash bags, cleaning supplies … oh and gloves."

He doesn't respond; instead, he goes into my bathroom.

I throw a blanket over Mac's lifeless body. I can't look at him. I run into the kitchen and grab a trash bag and fill it with all the cleaning supplies I will need to get rid of the evidence. I have flashbacks from cleaning up after my kidnappers were murdered.

"What am I going to do with his car and body?" I whisper to Paul through the bathroom door where I hear the sink faucet running.

Paul opens the door.

"You killed Thomas?" he asks.

"No, no, Mac doesn't know what he's talking about."

Paul is now crying.

I grab his shoulders, but he pushes me away.

"We were in love. Thomas was my lover. Why would you kill him?"

"I didn't," I lie.

"You're lying," he yells.

He walks out of my room. He's leaving me.

"Paul, no, please don't leave. I love you; I would never do that to you."

He looks back at me still crying before he walks out the door.

I panic and all my thoughts rush in at once. *When is my roommate getting home?* I check her work schedule on the refrigerator. She's working a double tonight, but I must call her to confirm.

The phone rings and rings.

"Come on Samantha, pick up the damn phone," I talk to myself.

"Hello."

"What time are you coming home, because I have a hot date and he's parked in your spot?"

"Jesus, Ava, no hi, how are you doing," Samantha responds.

"I'm sorry, I'm just nervous about this guy. I really like him."

I cover my mouth to hide my sobbing.

"OH, Ava is in love. What's his name?"

"Um, Mike."

"Is it Mike that works at the bookstore in Harvard Square?"

I'm pacing the living room.

"Jesus Christ, Samantha, what fucking time are you coming home?"

I lose my temper.

"Jeez, chill out. I'm not coming home tonight."

"I'm sorry. I'm just a little stressed tonight. I'll see you tomorrow."

I hang up.

I check both doors to make sure they are locked. Close all the drapes and shades.

First thing I need to do is clean up all the blood and brain matter. I dilute bleach and water and scrub for hours and throw all I can in trash bags. After I finish cleaning around Mac, I go in the bathroom and clean any blood Paul left behind while he cleaned himself. I throw everything out in the bathroom that isn't tacked down.

I strip everything off and shower, scrubbing my skin roughly and washing my hair three times.

I get dressed and put all the bloody items in suitcases, dragging them outside and throwing them into the trunk of Mac's car. I didn't want to throw trash bags in his car; I figured that may look slightly more suspicious.

The only thing left is getting rid of Mac's body. I'm going to need help. I should call Johnny; I can manipulate Johnny better. He was at my house the day Mac was at my house. He knows Mac was trying to get back with me. He will believe me when I tell him Mac raped me and I was defending myself.

I call Johnny.

"What's up?" he asks.

"Can you come over?" I ask.

"Now?"

I start crying uncontrollably.

"What's wrong?"

I can't speak, I just keep crying.

"I'll be right there," he says.

I'm scared Johnny will look at me differently when he sees Mac dead on my bedroom floor.

I chain smoke and drink straight vodka from the bottle. Not my first choice, but it's the only liquor in the house. I jump when I hear Johnny knock on the door.

"Are you okay?" he asks offering me a hug.

I hide my head in his chest and cry.

He pulls back, holding my face in his hands.

"What's wrong?" he asks.

I pull him to my bedroom without speaking. He looks back at me confused, but slowly walks inside my room.

"I don't see anything." He looks confused.

"The floor, under the blanket."

"What the fuck! Who the fuck is that … who did this … you?" Johnny asks in a frightened tone.

He runs out of my bedroom like he's scared.

"He … he was raping me, and I shot him. It was an accident. I was just trying to scare him so he would leave, but he wouldn't leave."

"Jesus, oh Jesus, Ava. You're nuts. Where's the gun?"

I point outside.

"I cleaned up everything and put it all in the trunk of his car including the gun."

He keeps running his fingers through his hair. He does this when he's stressed.

"Have you ever got rid of a body?" I ask.

He just looks at the floor.

"Ya, sorta," he responds.

"Tell me what to do."

"We're gonna wrap him in your rug and get him in ya cah."

"What about my neighbors?"

"Ava, we have no goddamn choice. Unless you prefer to cut him up in ya bathtub."

I follow Johnny into my room, and we wrap Mac in my bedroom rug; a rug my mother helped me pick out. I will miss the rug more than Mac.

We struggle dragging Mac's heavy body to his car. I try not to look paranoid, but I can't help but worry one of my nosy neighbors will peek out their window. It's late enough that most people are asleep.

"Thank you. I couldn't do this without you," I say giving him a big hug and kiss.

"You owe me big time. I'll be back in a few hours. Do me a favor and make breakfast?"

"Of course."

And here it begins; the favors he will ask will be for an eternity.

AVA

CHAPTER 17

D.R.

I haven't seen Johnny in a few days, and he hasn't reached out to me. He must be giving me some alone time since the incident with Mac. To be honest I'm relieved; it's been difficult dealing with the rape. I feel no remorse for killing Mac. If he spoke anymore about Thomas, I would never be able to convince Paul it wasn't true.

I did poison Thomas, but it was all for Paul. Thomas was no good for him. He was an emotional mess and they were in a toxic relationship. Anyway, if I never did it, someone else would have.

If I lose Paul's friendship, I'll have an impossible time avoiding going to trial to defend the Mob. He's my only connection to the money we stole from Atlantic.

I try to convince myself Johnny's isn't keeping tabs on me only because his boss orders him to but instead enjoys being with me. Sometimes he's difficult to read and sometimes he's an open book. I'm still confused if I have real feelings for him or if I am just using him and have no clear plan. I need more time to piece it all together. One thing is for sure: I will not rot in jail while the Irish, Susan and Johnny walk free. I'm not enjoying their financial gain and power, so why should I lie on the stand and possibly do time for their stupid accounting mistakes.

In the meantime, I'll need to find money to continue to protect myself. The FBI hasn't frozen my accounts and nor should they, according to the detailed letter I received. I have plenty to continue to pay my bills and living expenses, but nowhere near enough to pay the Indian and Mr. Alterman. Paul told me I'd be expecting my cut from the Atlantic account, but it's taking time, and I don't have more time. Even with the remaining funds borrowed from Mac and the cash from Ruben, it's still not enough. The most important thing right now is to find the money to pay my debts. I know just the person to visit: Jose.

Jose's excited to see me and even more thrilled to use me as his mule. According to him, white American women are less likely to be targeted by the TSA. It sounds like a crock of shit. The mule job is lacking details and there're several holes with his plan. All the information I have is that I'm traveling to the Dominican Republic with two suitcases full of medical supplies for a charity organization: bandages, antiseptic and ointments. I'll have a carry-on bag containing just my belongings. I'm excited to wear a two-piece swimsuit on a beach for the first time in over a year. I'm traveling under my alias, Sherry, and Jose has given me what look like fake papers showing I'm registered with the non-profit to whom I'm bringing the supplies. Jose stresses the fact I should return with the same number of bags I arrived with. Therefore, the drugs are hiding in art supplies and crafts made by the children from the charity. I don't want to know how much or what type of drugs I'm transporting because it will make me more nervous. US customs tracks several details of all travelers. I asked Jose if he has connections with customs and the TSA; he claims he does, but his eyes tell a different story. When I ask him the question, he avoids eye contact and itches his neck. This tells me he's lying. This concerns me, but not enough to back out of the job. Jose is paying me $80,000 for this trip and is covering all my traveling needs. It is a decent amount, but not for the risks I'm taking. A few weeks ago, when Jose asked me, I said I would never do it, but here I am, desperate for cash. I should just ask Johnny or Ruben for a loan, but my ego won't let me. I feel they'd find me less attractive.

My plane lands in Punta Cana, Dominican Republic just after 4 p.m. I step out of the plane onto the tarmac. The heat and humidity consume me, and I immediately take off my sweat-shirt. It was thirty degrees when the plane took off in Boston. I'm frightened to go through customs because I'm using my fake passport for the first time. I keep repeating in my head my alias name, date of birth, address, and social security number. I don't want to misspeak in front of immigration.

The lines are long and confusing going through customs. It's very disorganized and doesn't feel secure. I see how easily people can sneak by customs, but you can't avoid it if you need to return to the US. Relieved after passing through customs and out the door to find my arranged ride, I see a man holding a sign reading Sherry Conley. I almost walk by the sign, forgetting my new name.

The taxi driver doesn't speak English at all or does a great job pretending. I speak some Spanish. I studied it in high school and took a few college courses. It's difficult to remember some words, but I know the basics. I plan on practicing some while I'm on vacation.

After a forty-minute ride we arrive at Princess Beach Resort. Since Jose arranged everything, I had no idea what to expect. This place is amazing: steps to the beach, all inclusive – all the food and alcohol I can drink and eat. My room is on the fourth floor; a corner, ocean front suite with two balconies. The room is oversized for one person, with two full bathrooms, a living room and a king bedroom with a sectional sofa. I see what Jose is doing; he is trying to make this job more appealing and thinks I will continue to do this. I told him this was a one-time thing and to not expect it again.

I spend the next few days lounging on the beach or poolside, drinking cocktails and reading. I packed books for my trip with subjects about how to start a non-profit business: *Top 10 Ponzi and money laundering schemes, Obvious Accounting Errors, Whistleblower 101*. One story caught my attention. It was about a businessman that opened several banks on the Island of Antigua. He was given permission by the President of the banks of Antigua with bribes. He was selling fake stocks and bonds. He made a lot of money for several years and only got caught because he wasn't paying out to his investors. I feel this is always the same ending to every financial scammer who gets caught; they don't keep their promise. The major issue is the promise was too enormous to ever be kept or the fact that greed or the pure excitement of scamming people is the rush in itself. There are many cases you'll never hear about because they never get caught. I read all my books in three days and am restless, longing to explore the island.

The hotel is selling many excursions. I choose the air-conditioned option that includes lunch and drinks. It's all day, so I get picked up at 8 a.m. The bus is filled with older couples and couples with small children. The tour guide is a happy, tall, slender middle-aged man. He's wearing a polo shirt with the tour company logo, khaki shorts, and a generic pair of black shoes. He has the friendliest, trusting smile. We wind through the narrow roads of the Dominican Republic visiting museums, churches, shops, stopping to have a buffet style lunch and even visiting a beautiful public beach with water so clear you can see schools of fish swimming at your feet. The tour is coming to an end and we stop to visit a school for children from five years of age to their early teens. They give us a brief tour of the school. The cramped school is made of concrete and lacks an appropriate number of windows, the reason for the dark and depressing halls. The glassless windows that exist are too high from the floor to lookout. I notice right away that there is no kitchen to make lunch for the kids, but a small area to sit to eat lunch. I try not to feel depressed for the children who study at this school. The children I see look rather happy. However, I can't help but think there could be a greater happiness at this school with some donations.

I ask the tour guide if I can speak to the principal about how to donate. He claims he'll go find the principal and hurries off down the hall.

The tour guide returns in less than fifteen minutes with a short, heavy-set woman with a smile reaching from ear to ear. She's wearing a bright colored floral dress that falls past her knees with brown wedge sandals. Casually dressed for a principal, but appropriate considering the tropical climate. In almost perfect English she introduces herself as Mrs. Sanchez. My first impression is that she's a caring and trusting women. Her eyes smile even when she's not smiling. She guides me to her office, so we can talk in private about my donation.

"Thank you for offering a donation – as you can see, we need any help you're offering."

"I'll get straight to the point so as not to hold up the others on the tour," I explain. "I've lived a selfish life and have never given money or donations to those who need it. I want to make this change and visiting this school today has inspired me to get involved. I'd like to donate $30,000 US dollars to your school. Your students should have a kitchen where meals are cooked and provided at no cost to the children. Is this enough money to at least start this project?" I ask.

Mrs. Sanchez presses her hands against her cheeks in shock. She stares and says nothing. The tears roll down her cheeks and she jumps up and goes around her desk to hug me. She doesn't need to say anything; I can already tell she's thankful.

"Ava, you're an angel from above. You don't know how much this will mean for my students and my teachers to have lunch … provided," she says, sobbing.

"Research the cost to get the kitchen and all you need, send me the estimates and I'll write the check to cover the cost," I explain.

She agrees, and we exchange personal information.

I take a few pictures of the school before leaving. When I arrive at my resort, I hardly get through the door before bursting into tears. I'm sobbing and can't gather myself. I don't know why this overwhelming emotion comes over me, but I can only think how lucky I am, even with all my problems; there are others worse off. I have been thinking of only myself in every aspect of my life. This is why my last relationship failed. I feel I can do something good out of all the bad I do. Maybe heaven can still be an option, if I can offset my bad with some good. I laugh at the thought.

I don't feel like leaving my room, so I order room service.

I'm missing Johnny so I text him:

I miss you

Waiting for his response, I boot up my computer. Paul hasn't responded to my many emails begging him to believe me. I have a bad feeling about bringing these drugs to Boston. I must find another way; there's no guarantee Jose's way works. I know he's done this several times before, but I trust nothing he says. He's a criminal; I would be stupid to trust him.

My phone beeps, it's a text from Johnny.

I miss ya too babe. Where are ya?
In the Dominican

With who?

Myself

Bullshit, ya with that guy from the hotel?

What, how does he know about Ruben? I ignore his comment.

No, for real I'm by myself, call me…

I can't, Casey's over.

Do you have any connections at Logan?

Why?

I have some heavy luggage to get through customs

Huh?

The items in my luggage, they are HEAVY

Ava, you're crazy!!! I will never understand you

Good, so, you think you can help me

It's gonna cost ya

I just want a backup plan that's all

Okay, I'll call ya in the morning

It's my last day in the Dominican Republic. Johnny called from a secure line, late last night. I could tell by his voice he'd been drinking. It irritated him that I'd risk so much for such a small amount of cash, and he implied I should have asked him for the money. He cursed, bitched, talked down at me, but it was worth the earful. I got what I wanted. According to him, I won't have any issue at the airport. The luggage will be taken off the plane and delivered to Johnny. I'm putting all my trust in him. It makes me sick to my stomach to trust another person; a man.

After throwing a fit and yelling at me, he told me he was in love with me. He admitted he thinks about me all day. According to him he's called off the wedding and moved in with his parents. He wants to be with me and only me. He asks me if I love him and I say yes. I love him, but maybe not the same way he loves me. I don't want to be in a relationship, but I like the idea of having someone to lean on, and I know he'll do anything for me.

A migraine has entered my head, probably from all the stress. I fight through the headache and get dressed to head down to the bar. My favorite bartender is working. I have nicknamed him Nice Guy, because he's nice, but it's a front to get big tips. It rains most of the day, so I sit at the bar drinking and smoking cigarettes for at least five hours. My drinking fun ends when my luggage arrives. It is a strange hand off. The taxi driver doesn't look at me when he hands over my luggage. The bellman brings it to my room, and that is where I stay for the rest of the night. I'm so drunk I just sit on my bed staring at the luggage and thinking about opening it and doubting my choices in life.

I wake up extra early for time to calm my nerves. I smoke an entire pack of cigarettes while getting ready. I purposely dress like the average wealthy American woman: a white linen, collared button up with khaki capris and loafers. I complete the look with a small scarf tied around my neck and a petite silver bracelet and watch. I clip my hair into a French bun. I look like I'm going to watch my husband play golf. This look adds ten years to my age.

The bellman knocks on the door, I take one last glance at my neat hair in the mirror before opening the door.

AVA

CHAPTER 18

MI CASA

I refuse to sit in the window seat on the plane. Most people fight to sit near the window, but me, I prefer to sit in the aisle seat. I wouldn't consider myself claustrophobic, but I get anxious sitting near the window because if there is an emergency, I would need to depend on two strangers to get out of my way. It's the same when I'm in a new building; I want to know where all the exits are located. If I don't, the worry could give me a panic attack. When I'm in a stressful situation, I have an urge to urinate almost every hour or more.

Today's a stressful day because I'm losing my drug mule virginity. I don't know how this will turn out. I'm almost depending on Johnny to get my luggage past customs in Boston. Jose is expecting a quick transaction at an East Boston Hotel. He has strict rules and times in place. I'm to report any delays to him or any mishaps. He seems more stressed than me. I can only imagine the amount of product in these bags. I try to clear my mind by watching a free in-flight movie. I have a choice of a romantic comedy, a comic book hero or an animation. *Just fucking arrest me now and put me out of my misery.* I need a few drinks to get through this flight. I settle on vodka and tonic.

The pilot wakes me with his announcement we are preparing for landing. I spill the last drink I ordered all over my handbag and pants. There is no time for a bathroom trip, but I sneak past the flight attendant and hear her asking me to take a seat. I pretend I don't hear her. It's that or I piss my pants.

When I am exiting the bathroom, I find the flight attendant in my face with a scowling look.

"Miss, you must go to your seat".

I pretend I can't hear her by pointing at my ear. I'm screwing with her, pretending I can't hear her, and it is making her angrier.

I move slowly to my seat to annoy her more.

As soon as the plane lands I turn on my phone.

I text Johnny.

I'm in NYC

I have a three-hour layover, plenty of time to get through customs and grab a bite to eat.

I try not to sweat from the stress and fear of getting caught.

Before I go through customs, I need to pick up my checked bags, trying not to look obvious by looking around too to see if there's any undercover police. At Gate 5, I wait for my bags. The buzzer sounds, and the baggage carousel moves. I tied red ribbon around the luggage handle, so I can spot my luggage quickly. Everyone crowds around the carousel anxiously to grab their luggage, making it difficult for me to see mine. I think I see my luggage, but several times I'm wrong.

There're only a few people remaining, and this is when my panic sets in. I head to the restroom, lock myself in the disabled stall and start pacing back and forth. I've lost my shit. I switch from scared and calm, like someone has changed my emotion channels – next station, tears. If I go through customs, they'll arrest me. Johnny hasn't returned any of my texts. I call him, no answer. My mind is racing; maybe Johnny set me up, maybe he got caught, maybe the luggage is missing, or worse, the luggage is with customs and they're waiting for me – or maybe Jose set me up, maybe Alterman's message about my father was a warning. I'm entering a full-blown panic attack, the bathroom stall is shrinking, my breathing is short with my anxiety adding layers of bricks on my chest and my heart is pounding through my ears. I'm sure others can hear my heart pounding in my chest.

I remember I have valium; a muscle relaxer should calm me enough to get through customs. I haven't eaten anything today, so I take a half a pill. I force myself to get out of the stall. I wash my face and focus on slowing my breathing, counting from one to four on every inhale and exhale. The valium kicks in, the restroom walls are back to their original position. My internal earthquake is over. At this moment, for whatever reason, I mourn for my mother like she died yesterday. She was everything to me and she loved me like her own. She never wanted to tell me the truth about adopting me, but it hurt to keep such a secret from me. I thought the pain would go away when I moved on to college, a new boyfriend, job, but all these milestones just made it more painful. I don't feel I did enough to find her real killer. I thought a good job and getting to marry my first love was all going to blanket me with happy sparkle dust. But nothing could give me back the only person who truly loved me and no one could replace her. If I must risk it all to find her real killer, I will die trying, because it was not Lewis.

I stand up straight, push back my shoulders and leave the restroom. I take one last glance at the carousel; no luggage. I head straight through customs with no issues. If the luggage is never found, then so be it. I'll take care of Jose and find money another way. Now, I need to get some food in my stomach. I duck into the first restaurant I see and sit at the bar. Immediately, my phone rings – it's Johnny. I jump off the bar stool.

I don't let him make a sound before I speak. "Where's the fucking luggage?"

"No hi, how ah ya, just where's tha fuckin luggage. Ya know you can be an ungrateful little cunt," he says in a half-sarcastic tone.

"I had a fucking panic attack in the bathroom, you motherfucker."

"Chill tha fuck out, it was taken from the plane and one of my guys is driving it to Boston. At the last minute they told me Boston wasn't gonna to happen," he explains.

It's a relief to know it's not lost. But until it's in Jose's hands and the money is in my safe, I'm not satisfied.

"You okay?"

"No, I'm never going to see the money from Jose."

"You worry too much; it's annoying. Ya think I'm not gonna get you that money, ya don't know me."

"You're a dickhead, but I love you," the words melt off my lips. I bite my bottom lip to take back the words. I feel vulnerable, the secret is out, Johnny's my weakness.

There's a pause before he speaks. "I know."

"You knew?"

"We have chemistry, it's as if you're my soulmate. There's somethin' 'bout ya. I've held back, ya know."

I find his words to be all lies; I don't believe him. He was always nice to me but what he doesn't know is that the girls at work would share their sexual encounters with Johnny; the copy room, conference room and staircase to the garage, a new sex-capade every week. He's fucked every intern, new hire and there are even rumors of him fucking our boss, Susan. I know Johnny, he's forever a womanizer and the quintessential irresistible charming man. The women were using him just as much as he was using them. Some women use their pussy to get to the top, and men take advantage – why not?

I can't get off the phone fast enough; this love talk is making me uncomfortable. Johnny and I agree on a meeting point. I order two entrees because I can't decide; typical.

The plane ride is under an hour to Boston, so the flight attendant hands out bottled water, no snacks. I rush off the plane to exit the terminal to meet Johnny. The moment I turn off airplane mode my phone rings.

"The luggage was supposed to be here already," says Jose, getting to the point.

"There was a slight hiccup in plans. I'm off the plane and heading straight to you with the luggage.

"AVA, AVA, AVA... Someone lost their life tonight cause of your hiccup," he screams. "You did not follow the plan, you DIDN'T. FOLLOW. THE ... PLAN. I told ya to communicate with me and follow the plan."

"Jose, listen, I got paranoid, and had the luggage picked up in New York. It will be here in maybe the next couple hours.

"Bitch, I don't have a couple hours. I don't believe you... You will pay for this. Bring my luggage to the restaurant."

The phone goes dead.

I laugh to myself because I know Jose is all talk. He tries to act like a gangster, but he's fake. If he knew the Irish Mob was holding his drugs, he would shit his pants.

The doors open, and I'm hit with the agonizing chilled-to-the-bone cold winter. I'm underdressed for this temperature. Lucky, Johnny is here to greet me. He must see how frozen I look because he takes his heavy suede coat and throws it over my shoulders then pulls me into his arms, pressing me against his chest. The beeping from an impatient taxi breaks up our embrace. I worry Johnny will pull the taxi driver out of the car and beat the shit out of him. Maybe he decides it's not worth the risk, since the trunk has my drug-filled luggage.

Johnny opens the back door of the cab, which I find odd. Then I realize he hired a driver. It's out of character, but I'm too excited to have Johnny's attention.

We get comfortable in each other's arms in the back seat. With the warmth of the heat, my high declining and Johnny wrapped around my shoulders I just want to sleep but I know I have plenty of explaining to do.

"If you're wondering why I need the money, I can't say."

He pulls his hand away from me and stares straight ahead.

I find him attractive when he's angry with me. I predict his next mood will be forgiving.

Without looking in my direction he says, "You cannot bring drugs ta Boston without my approval, people get killed fah that shit all tha time. Ya lucky it was diverted to New York."

He reaches for me, but stops his hand inches from my neck, as if he was going to choke me. I look into his eyes, but the Johnny I know isn't inside.

I close my eyes, "Please Johnny, don't hurt me."

I peek out from one eye. His fists are still clenched but are back resting on the seat beside him.

"We will go see Jose together, you'll get ya money, trust that."

I keep trying to call Jose, but there's no answer.

Finally, Jose calls. "Where are ya?"

"We are here."

"WE?"

Johnny grabs my phone and hangs up on Jose.

Jose's restaurant is empty, no customers as usual, but there are several men outside smoking cigarettes. Johnny reaches under the seat and conceals several guns in his coat, boots and the back-ass pocket of his pants.

"Where's my gun, and what is going down here?"

Johnny dismisses my question.

The driver opens the car door, then heads to the trunk to grab Jose's drugs. The driver is built like a professional wrestler. He must stand at least 7-foot-tall, with wide shoulders. He's sporting thick black sideburns, slicked black greasy hair and a nose that's been broken before. He's one ugly son of a bitch. He's dressed in black from head to toe, a long trench coat, and a designer silk scarf that doesn't match his angry demeanor. The dragging sound from the suitcase wheels missing the pavement every few steps lets me know he is following closely behind. The men outside stare us down but nod us past them into the restaurant. Jose is sitting in the far back of the restaurant with a shirtless young girl who doesn't even look of age sitting on his lap. There are lines of cocaine on the table, ready to snort; a trigger for me.

Jose pushes the young girl off his lap, and she disappears to the back of the kitchen.

"You didn't have to bring friends, we are *familia*," he smiles wide. He points to a bag on the floor, getting the attention of his guy to pick up the bag and hand it to me. Johnny intercepts and grabs the bag; the driver rolls the luggage to Jose.

Johnny grabs my arm tight and walks towards the exit.

"Bad etiquette," he shakes his head. "You can't leave without me opening the suitcase to check my goods."

Johnny stops and turns around to look at Jose.

Just as Jose unzips the suitcase, I hear a loud bang. Something in the suitcase pops and the room fills with thick pink smoke. Johnny shoves a mask over my nose and mouth and presses down while dragging me out of the restaurant. I hear gun fire and see flashes of light reflecting in the glass window. The driver is not a wrestler or a driver, he's a hitman. Johnny pushes me onto the floor near the door.

"Stay down; don't move until I come back." He pulls out two guns from his back and steps outside. I close my eyes and hold the mask over my face. I hear more gunfire coming from outside. I'm scared Johnny is dead. I open my eyes, but my mask is covered with pink residue.

"GET UP!" yells Johnny. He grabs my arm, pulling me out

the front door.

I rip off the mask to get air as soon as we are outside. Johnny pushes me onto the back seat and jumps in the driver's seat. Hits the gas and drives to the front of the restaurant. My clothes are covered in a pink powder substance; the smell is unbearable; my lungs and eyes are burning. The passenger door flies open and the driver—still don't know his name—hops in the passenger seat. I'm so shocked I can't speak; my ears are ringing from the loud gunfire. *Am I dreaming? Did this just happen? Why the fuck did Johnny do this? There is no way we will get away with this; more blood on my hands. This is all my fault, damn, what am I thinking trusting Johnny?*

I rummage through my purse for makeup wipes. I find the pack and start rubbing the pink powder from my eyes. The burning subsides and I begin to pull myself together and sit up. I want to smoke a joint, but I'm afraid the mysterious pink powder is flammable or that I'll inhale dangerous chemicals. We pull up to a motel. Johnny tells me to grab my bag of belongings and the bag of money. The driver doesn't look my way and doesn't speak a word to even Johnny. It seems the plan was well in place before I stepped foot off the plane. I have so many questions I know Johnny will answer in his own time. I've learned to be patient when Johnny has that stressed look in his eye. I can easily set him off.

Johnny already has the key to the room. It's outdated, from the paneling on the wall to the bedspread. I don't even want to sit on the bed, so I pull out the desk chair that's missing a wheel.

"We don't have a lot of time," he says as he turns the shower on and takes his shirt off. "Shower and get this stuff off your skin." He motions me to the bathroom.

I drop my jacket on the floor and strip walking to the bathroom. Johnny tries to be polite by staring into my eyes but can't help looking over my naked body.

We shower with blue dishwashing soap, washing our skin like animals caught in an oil spill. Johnny steps out of the shower to grab towels for both of us.

He dries himself off and wraps the towel around his waist. He's erect, and I can't help but feel turned on. It's difficult to control myself around him. He takes it upon himself to dry me off, even dries in between my legs, spending more time than necessary. I can't help but let him take control. I'm always vulnerable in his presence. I take it upon myself to make the first move, pulling his hips towards me, pushing his erection against me. He grabs my face with both his hands, sticks his tongue down my throat and kisses me roughly. He moves his hands down to my back to grab my ass, pulling me out of the bathroom and onto the bed. I no longer care that the bedspread is ugly and the bed old. I will explode if he's not inside me right now. We skip the condom, not uncommon with us. He turns me over on my stomach, grabs my pussy from underneath and sticks his thumb inside before sticking his hard dick inside. Then takes it out slow and pushes himself back in. He repeats this, teasing me. He knows what I like. He massages my ass, leaving his dick inside then taking it out and laying his dick on top of my ass, rubbing it like he wants to stick it in my ass. I've never done that before, so I hope he doesn't try it. Thankfully, he turns me over, and we fuck missionary style while he licks my breasts. I widen my legs when I feel I may come, and I push up off the heels of my feet until I climax. It's all over in ten minutes. We're both satisfied, but tired. Naked, I search through my purse for a joint and a light. This is much needed for both of us. I sit on top of his limp penis and blow smoke in his face. My worries temporarily melt away as my high kicks in and my eyes close.

"Wake up, Ava, get up." Johnny is standing over me.

"I'm up."

He throws my bag at me.

"Get dressed, fast."

I dress and watch him run around gathering all the clothes we wore during the shootout, the towels, soap, mask, and anything that has the pink powder, and throw it in a trash bag.

"Why did you kill Jose?"

"Why do ya even care?"

"Cause, I don't think it was necessary."

"Trust me, it was."

"He would've given me the money."

"ENOUGH ALREADY, SHUT IT, OKAY! You must trust my judgement. You know nothin' about nothin'. You know nothin' about this world."

"I know, but I'm scared. Don't you worry about retaliation? I mean how do you sleep at night after murdering people?"

"I sleep fine, now get your shit and enough questions. You got ya cash, so stop bitchin'."

I do as he says, but I feel sick to my stomach. Jose was a friend to me when he was dating my roommate Samantha. He was a small-time crook. It's wrong, and now I have one more thing that will keep me awake at night.

We take a taxi to my house. Johnny insists on staying with

me, but I want to be alone, I'm too upset.

"At least let me check your house to make sure it's safe," says Johnny.

I let him search the closets, under the beds, and look around the back yard. He's not satisfied, so he walks around locking all the windows.

"A black car will be parked outside, that's my guy. Don't answer the door no mattah what."

"Yeah, okay."

"I'm not kidding, Ava. I promise we will talk tomorrow; you will get the answers you're looking for."

He kisses my forehead before he is leaving.

He's a liar; I'll never know, and if I ask, he will just start an argument.

It feels good to be home. I grab a wine glass, a bottle of pinot grigio and head straight to my room. I take a seat on the floor, leaning my back against my bed. I stare at the bag full of cash, while finishing off the first glass of wine before I open the duffel bag to count the money. $85,000 exact, just as Jose promised. He kept his promise and I didn't.

I lay on the floor and cry myself to sleep.

AVA

CHAPTER 19

PLAN B

It's already noon when I make my way to Mr. Alterman's office to discuss my father's visit. I don't know that much about my father, besides what I read on the internet, and I can assume he isn't looking for his long-lost daughter. My mother didn't talk much about him, but after her murder I uncovered a box of letters and pictures that answered some of my questions, but not all about their relationship. As innocent as my mother pretended to be, I could see she was living a fake life. When I was young, I would pull the grass from the yard to make sure it was real. We moved into a big house, seemed like the money came out of thin air. I know my mother and Lewis couldn't afford the home. At first, they both pretended to be renting the house from a family friend. The lie manifested into another lie until suddenly, the home is theirs and we never moved. I sold the house for obvious reasons; I couldn't live under the same roof where my mother was brutally murdered. Her murder replaced all the good childhood memories.

Alterman's receptionist is shocked to see me, like she's seen a ghost. What the hell does she know that I don't? She normally greets me with eye contact, and now her hands are shaking dialing his extension. Mr. Alterman approaches in the hall, motioning me to his office. I can smell the booze as soon as I walk in his office.

"Whiskey?"

"Yeah, sure."

Funny, I don't remember him having liquor in his office on my last visit. He slides a glass of whiskey in front of me. I never turn down a drink. We sit in awkward silence, sipping our whiskey, staring at each other. His eyes are glassy, his face unshaven and his hair—what's left of it—is disheveled. He looks angry and disappointed in me, for what, I don't know. I take the last sip and sit the glass on his desk. The alcohol burns my chest going down, but it's soothing. I get comfortable by leaning back in the brown leather chair, waiting for him to speak.

"Your father broke into my house and threatened my life if I didn't tell him everything, I know about you," he says in an angry tone. I go to speak, and he stands up quick. For a second, I think he's going to throw his glass at me.

"Don't speak until I say all I want to say to you. I gave you the option to be honest with me, and you lied – everything out of your mouth is a GODDAMN LIE! You know who your father is, and you still let me walk blindly into the devil's den. I can't leave my office without being tailed," he says pacing his office.

Without asking, he refills my glass and leans in to whisper,

"You're a criminal and a fraud." His words are shocking to me

"Mr. Alterman, I came here for your help and you're now accusing me of knowing who my father is. If I knew about him, why would I come here to ask for your help? Do you think I would associate myself with a group of criminals on purpose? I'm the victim here, I'm the one trying to avoid death or jail."

I'm now yelling, my anger has taken over. I could just smash this old man's face. Who does he think he is accusing me of such absurd lies? I walk to his liquor station and pour another glass of whiskey. I'm so angry that I shut down, I can no longer speak. I just sit and stare at him.

"Can we just discuss what he said to you, and I can leave. I don't want any trouble for you. Tell me how to get in contact with my father and I'll make sure he leaves you alone." I surrender, exhausted, with no fight left in me.

Mr. Alterman pulls out a yellow envelope with my name written on it in all caps. He throws it at me; a sign he wants me to leave.

"All he did is ask questions, and I answered them, and he demanded I give you this envelope." Looks like I can't trust Mr. Alterman. He sided with my father and is working for my father now, whether willingly or not.

Before I walk out of his office, I turn to him. "Thank you, for everything," I say, searching for his eyes, but he avoids eye contact. He leans back in his chair and stares into his empty glass. I find it difficult to believe he wants our business relationship to end. I always go with my gut instinct, and I feel I haven't seen the last of Mr. Alterman. It's weird he didn't ask for the money I owe him – that's unusual behavior because he always reminds me how much I owe.

I try to shake off the stressful meeting with Mr. Alterman by focusing on my list of things to accomplish by the end of today. I call Paul on the train. He doesn't answer; I guess it's to be expected after the incident with Mac. I leave him a message letting him know I'm coming over to give him the money I owe him. Maybe this can get us back on good terms.

It's a long, cold walk to Paul's from the train station. I am underdressed for this weather, no hat or gloves. Walking in the cold makes a ten-minute walk feel like a thirty-minute walk. Paul's windows are blacked out with black garbage bags. Every time I visit him, he seems more paranoid than my last visit.

"Paul, it's Ava, open the door," I yell while buzzing his apartment.

I do this for five minutes before giving up and going home. I'm afraid I lost my only friend.

AVA

CHAPTER 20

LIGHTS ON

From the looks of it, my roommate is home because all the lights are on at my apartment. I go to put the key in the door, but the door glides open. It's as if someone broke in. Strangely enough, I'm not scared. The old Ava wouldn't have dared walk through the door; she would've run and called the police.

I push the door wide open to find two men sitting at my kitchen table drinking my whiskey. It bothered me that they are so comfortable in my home, at my kitchen table, drinking my whiskey. These men are visually intimidating, but it doesn't faze me. I take a step back, just in case I see sense and need to make a run for it. I take another step, as if to not make a sudden noise, like these men are bears and will attack me at the sound of my foot snapping a branch. I get one foot on the stoop, when I feel a hand on my back pushing me all the way through the door. I turn to see who's behind me and find my Indian friend.

I'm relieved because I have his money, but frightened that I'm late with his payment. Hopefully, he will take the money and leave with his friends. He pushes my shoulder down until I'm seated at the kitchen table, sitting across from the drinking bears.

In walks an overweight, red bearded, middle-aged man and I recognize it's my father. He's much older and fatter than the mugshots on the internet. Regret hits me for not reading the envelope that Mr. Alterman gave me.

"Ava, hi," he says, walking over with his arms open wide for a hug.

I freeze. I'm frightened of this man. He's the only person on earth I fear, even more so than the Mob itself. There is no Mob without him. The files Paul dug up on my father were shocking and the unsolved murders the FBI had tried to build a case with were difficult to read because of the tortuous details of how the victims died. I couldn't finish reading most.

My legs shake, barely able to hold up my body enough to stand, and I hug fear itself. His beard is rough on my face and his embrace is tight enough to suffocate me. He smells like a wood stove and same aroma I smelled when I was at the Indian's home. He must have been in New Hampshire with the Indian. Our hug is awkward for us and the two bears and Indian. Perhaps, they've never seen my father hug anyone or maybe they're waiting for him to kill me.

When the hug is over, he grabs me by my biceps and stares at me.

"Bloody hell, ya look just like ya mothah," he says in a loud voice.

"Wow, you think." I turn my head to hide that I'm blushing at his comment.

The bears laugh after my father bursts out in a deep chuckle. The Indian's expression doesn't change.

"I need to be alone with my daughtah; wait for me in the cah," he orders the bears and Indian.

One bear grabs what is left of my whiskey, the bastard. No one else seems to notice, but it bugs me.

I follow my father to the table and sit. He doesn't take a seat. He's leaning against the front of my stove – to his right is my wood block stand with sharp steak knives. Either he's a rather smart man or it's just a coincidence.

"Ya can stop your acting and bullshit. I know ya not innocent, and the deal ya made with the Mob at Atlantic Financial. A rather clever deal, almost threatening. And now ya unwilling to take the heat of the case. Susan can't go to jail, she's too important to the Mob. I'm here to tell ya to take the deal the Mob has given. Ya may not even get time, just probation or if you get time maybe a year at the most."

I stand leaning my hands on the table and stare down my father.

"Where have you been my entire life? And to show up accusing me of working with the Mob and lying about it!" I scream. "I'm not you. I went to college and got a real job, like normal people."

"Ya ungrateful child! Do ya know what I went through to keep you…"

He doesn't finish his sentence but instead makes a fist with both hands and turns his back to me. His angry expression reflects through the kitchen window. He's looking through me.

"I came here to help you, ya my daughtah, but it looks like ya refusing my help. I think what I'm offering is a loving gesture. I'm warning you of danger, something I would never do for anyone working against my employer. If ya were not my daughter, ya would've been dead before ya put yah key in the lock."

It shocks me that he is so calm, but with a look of anger. I am the one out of control and yelling. I'm not angry that he is calling me a liar and doesn't believe me, but he won't even acknowledge the father-daughter relationship. He hasn't apologized for leaving me as a child and didn't even ask how I was doing. He is more concerned with himself and his work.

"I will promise ya this, they will kill ya, if ya give them a reason, without hesitation," he explains. I go to speak, but he stops me.

"I AM NOT KILLING MY DAUGHTAH!" he yells. "I am beggin' ya to take the deal, please Ava…"

In this moment, he has shown weakness. It's shocking, for a man so hardened and heartless. He's right, I will have to play their game, take the heat. I don't have a choice at this point. I am tired. I don't want to argue with my father.

"Tell them I will take the blame for Susan, you have my word," I exhale.

"Don't lie, Ava."

He gives me a big bear hug.

"Daddy, you have my word," I say sarcastically.

"That's my girl. Let's catch up in the mornin', we can go have breakfast. How does that sound?"

"Yes, I would love that," I say with bright eyes. "Um, I owe the Indian money, can you call him back into the house?"

"I already took care of him, ya all set. He owed me a favor

and we're even now. Get some sleep, see ya in the mornin'."

He kisses me on the forehead before leaving.

I take a few deep breaths after he leaves. It's surreal. I have waited for this moment all my life. To meet my father. I pictured it under different circumstances, but still my dream came true. I'm just hoping that he will answer some questions that have been on my mind since I was a little girl.

I'm frightened to stay home alone. I go upstairs and, without turning off the lights peek out my bedroom window. It is the only room that faces the street. Just as I suspected, there are two cars parked outside my house. I can't leave but doesn't mean I can't invite someone over.

I call Johnny.

AVA

CHAPTER 21

DADDY DAUGHTER DANCE

My father and the three bears pick me up at 9:30 a.m. The last time there were only two men who reminded me of bears and now it looks like we have a third. These men are so big in width and height; intimidating in looks alone. Scary men; I see why my dad keeps them around. My father takes me to a diner in Charlestown. It's so empty, I joke that he paid for a private diner. The bears sit at the long bar and my father and I grab a booth in the middle of the restaurant. There are long pauses of silence and no eye contact.

"This was the last place I took ya before I left Boston. Funny story, we were both almost murdered right over there in that parkin' lot. The lot was largah back then before they started buildin' all these condominiums," he says in excitement.

"Well, let's hope history doesn't repeat itself."

We both chuckle.

"Ya have a clevah sense of humor, like your old dad."

The waitress interrupts, topping up our coffee.

"What can I get ya?" she rasps.

My dad motions me to order first.

"I'll have blueberry pancakes, bacon, sausage, scrambled eggs."

"How many eggs?"

"Two."

"White or wheat?"

"White."

The waitress thinks I'm done and turns to my father.

"Home fries and extra syrup on the side, oh and whip cream, on the side," I add.

The waitress looks annoyed by my order.

My father looks shocked by the amount of food I am ordering. I drank so much, and am so hungry, plus I love eating breakfast leftovers.

"I'll have two eggs over easy, bacon and white toast."

"Is that all? Anythin' else?" says the waitress with an attitude.

"No that's all," I say politely because I don't want my food tampered with.

"Are ya sure ya don't need to ordah more food?" he jokes with me. "Rough night last night?"

"You could say that." I smirk. "And the fact that I eat more when I'm stressed."

"And who's to blame for that, Ava," he stresses my name.

"I didn't agree to have breakfast with you to discuss the trial." I blow on the coffee before sipping. "I want to know why you left me," I say, the tears building.

"I didn't want ya and your mom to get hurt because of me. After almost getting ya killed that day, I decided ya and your mother were best without me in your life. I made sure ya both had everything ya needed financially – and protection from harm. That's when I decided to go North."

I didn't let him know I already knew the story. I was just fascinated to hear him tell it. It was sort of like a fairy tale. In that moment, he was vulnerable, and no longer looked like a killer, but a concerned father.

"My mother told me a similar story, but made you sound like a bigger asshole," I smile.

"I loved that woman, and still do. I talk to her every night before I go to sleep. She was the only woman I ever loved, besides ya of course. I prayed for both of ya each night. You didn't know, but your mother sent me photos of ya a few times each year."

Now, I'm smelling bullshit. He is overdoing it. I don't believe him, but I'll let him have his moment.

He is interrupted by the arrival of our food. I have so many plates there isn't much room left on the table. We eat in silence, savoring each bite. I finish before him, even though he has less food to eat. My stomach is bigger than my eyes. I motion the waitress over to box up my food and refill our coffee.

Somebody approaches our table.

"Ava, how are you? Funny bumping into you."

At first, I don't recognize the face but quickly realize it's the FBI agent who interviewed me about the investigation, Connor McClean.

Before I can speak, he turns to look at my father.

"I knew you looked familiar," he says. Realizes who my father is.

"Connor, it's been a long time, buddy," he stands up and gives him a big hug and a pat on the back. "Sit, have some coffee." He waves to the waitress for more coffee.

Connor squeezes in the booth besides me, since my father takes up most of his booth.

"You failed to mention Jimmy Coonan is your father," he smiles.

"She was probably nervous under the circumstances," my father explains.

"Had I known, I wouldn't have asked you to come to the station; we could have made other arrangements. I hope you'll accept my apology."

"It really was nothing, not a problem. You were just doing your job."

My father's power is evident in Connor's face. It's obvious that Connor is worried. I knew he was a dirty cop when I met him. Even the suit and police station atmosphere weren't enough to cover up a crooked cop like him.

"Enough about the mix up, how's ya mothah, she still cooking every Sunday?"

"Yes, you should come over this Sunday or whenever you get a chance. My mother would love to see you, but you better come with an empty stomach. She still doesn't take to kindly to anyone who refuses to eat."

"I appreciate the invite, tell ya mothah to make a room for me at the table for supper this Sunday."

"I'm gonna to take my coffee to the bar and if you have a

minute after finishing breakfast with Ava, I would like to run something by you," he says, getting out of the booth.

My father agrees.

He stares at me for some time hesitating to speak.

"What?" I ask.

"Are you with Johnny?"

"Well, sort of, we just sometimes…"

"Stop, I don't need the details. Did he tell ya he's engaged, and his fiancé is pregnant? They just announced it yesterday."

The time has stopped, my ears are ringing, my dad's lips are moving, but I hear no sound. She's pregnant? She's pregnant… I don't believe it, or at least I don't want to believe it. My chest is tight, I feel the urge to throw up.

"Ava, are you okay? I thought you knew."

"I… Yeah, of course I knew, I just didn't know it was officially announced," I lie. "We broke it off, after he told me the news."

"Ya just told me ya were with Johnny. Messin' with someone like Johnny never ends good, I'm sorry ya had to learn ya lesson, but he isn't the most honest person, I mean, most criminals aren't."

"Dad, it's really no big deal. We were just having fun." The lies pile up.

"I hate to end our breakfast, but I have a lot of errands to run." Another lie.

"You just called me Dad, wow, how cool. If yah up to it, this Friday my friends are throwin' me a homecoming party. Ya will be there, won't ya?" he asks.

"Of course, I wouldn't miss it. Just call me with the details."

We awkwardly hug, and he calls one of the bears over to

take me home.

I hold back the tears until I get home.

I can't believe she's pregnant. Our relationship is over, this changes everything. He will never leave her, it will always be her over me, like it hasn't been in the past.

These last couple days have been stressful and lonely. Suicide enters my mind. It would be so easy. All my problems would be gone.

I need to get Johnny out of my mind, so I take a shower, get dressed and sneak out the back door to head for the bar down the street. I dress casual, but sexy. A long beige sweater dress with high black over the knee suede boots. I throw my hair up out of my face and put in some simple hoop earrings. I may as well go out since I'm not going to get any sleep. I walk to the closest bar to my house. It's a local hipster bar full of MIT and Harvard students, not my scene. You can tell this place is a bar because there are large floor to ceiling windows that open in the warmer months. There's bright lighting, stainless steel elements; it's over decorated with industrial fixtures. Many faces are familiar, but I don't know the names that go with the faces. Paul used to frequent the bar, until he started to develop paranoia, anxiety and whatever other social issues he's diagnosed himself with.

I get to the bar in under ten minutes. There's hardly anyone at the bar and a few pool tables vacant, which is usually never the case. I head to the middle section of the bar and take a seat. I order a double shot of whiskey and a beer from the only bartender. He is in his mid-forties at least. His arms are covered with tattoos, hair slicked back, his beard and mustache neatly trimmed. He has worked at this bar since I can remember. He is extremely untalkative for a bar tender, but friendly enough so you don't think he's rude.

I sit with my drink pretending to watch the hockey game. Every TV mounted on the wall is tuned into the hockey. They should have Jeopardy playing on the TV's, it would be more fitting for tonight's crowd. I finish my drink quickly so I can leave to find another bar or maybe just go back home. I wave to the bartender to close my tab, but a young man interrupts.

"This seat taken?" says the young man.

"No." I reposition my body so I'm now staring at him.

My interest is peaked, looking back at this young man. His amazing blue eyes shine though his thick oversized glasses. My immediate guess is that he's a college student.

He orders two beers and gets comfortable next to me.

"It's no coincidence that I'm sitting next to you," he says in a quiet voice. "Paul sent me to look for you."

He hands me a piece of paper. All that is on there is an email address.

"Did he say anything else to you?

"No, he just wanted me to give you this."

He grabs his beer and leaves the bar.

I'm so confused. *Why would Paul send someone? I was just at his house.*

I pay my tab this time and leave the bar to head to Paul's house.

I buzz his apartment over and over, but he never answers. I sit on his front apartment steps for a minute to think. I hear a cat meow from the bushes. It's Paul's cat – now I'm scared that something has happened to Paul. Without Paul, I'm shut out from the dark web completely. He's my only source and my payout from the Atlantic job would be lost. Then there's Mr. Alterman who's turned his back on me. A loneliness suddenly creeps up on me, like fog in the morning. I feel my back against the wall. I have no one on my side I can trust; everyone has left me. Paul's cat finds its way onto my lap. I decide to take the cat to my house until I can find him. I hate cats, but it's the only thing I have left of my friend Paul. I just hope he's okay.

I'm so exhausted that I forget about the envelope Mr. Alterman has given me. I hope it has the answers I am looking for.

I open the envelope and find a handwritten letter from Mr. Alterman and a bunch of legal documents from a lawyer's name I don't recognize.

Ava,

I have already told you how disappointed I am in you, so I won't waste it in this letter. I did some digging after your father's visit. The Mob's lawyers are pinning it all on you and this can get you up to ten years in prison, and that's the good news. I don't know what you have possibly done to piss them off, but I can assure you they do not have your best interests in mind. Their lawyers are showing you one deal, but they have made deals with the FBI to get Susan off with no charges. I have enclosed advice I sought from a lawyer who is a friend of mine; you can trust him. When you are ready for his help, just call him. He will be

expecting your call. I have already paid him upfront for your consultation. However, if you request his services for court, you will need to pay for his services.
I will be in touch only after I find it safe, please don't reach out to me.

Mr. Alterman

After I'm done reading the lawyer's letter, I flush it down the toilet. I send myself an email including the lawyer's phone number and first name. I might need this in the future with the trial less than a month away.

JOHNNY

CHAPTER 22

WITH CHILD

Casey jumps on my lap with a white stick in her hand, pushing it in my face. Her smile is bright, wide and excited. It makes me smile back, without knowing what I'm smiling about. I just love to see her happy; it brings all her beauty to the surface. I'm with my normal morning erection and her jumping up and down on my lap makes me want her.

"What is this?" I say, grabbing it from her hands. I sit up with her still on my lap and lean one shoulder into the bed, staring at a pregnancy test. There's two lines. I don't know how to read a pregnancy test, but by the look on her face, she must be pregnant. I'm disappointed but hide it from her. I grab her face and give her a long kiss. I know how long she has wanted to be pregnant and she's getting her way.

I don't want children. A child doesn't fit into my lifestyle. It gives my enemies a way to hurt me and something to use against me. I think of Ava; it will devastate her. This could end our relationship and fuck up my position with the Mob. It's a possibility she could lose this child. She has had two miscarriages in the past. Then I think, *I should have left Casey when I had the chance. When she found out about my affair with Ava.* Ava is the affair that has lasted the longest. I even admitted to Casey that I was in love with Ava one night after drinking.

"Are you happy, baby?"

"Come on, course I am, what kind of question is that?"

"I can't wait to announce the pregnancy." She jumps on top of me.

"Don't you think we should wait until you're further along? Also, shouldn't you confirm with a doctor?"

"Yeeeeaaah, you're right," she sighs, heading for the shower.

I light a cigarette and lay back down with one hand behind my head. I just stare at the ceiling, thinking about the future. I can't picture me as a father. It's doesn't feel right. I have a bad feeling. I can't shake it.

Casey breaks my train of thought walking out of the bathroom naked, drying her hair with the towel.

"You can't see her anymore, now I'm pregnant I won't put up with the cheating, it's me or Ava," she says.

"Whatever." I get up and walk to the bathroom.

"I mean it Johnny; you better end it." She follows me into the bathroom.

"It's not that simple, my job…"

"Fuck you and that fucking job."

"Fuck my job, fuck my job, how the fuck do you think we pay the bills?" I scream. "You don't understand my lifestyle;

it won't change, I have told you this a thousand times. My job comes first. This conversation is over."

"You're a dirtbag." She walks out of the bathroom and slams the door.

All we do is fight. She envisions a different life but doesn't understand it's not possible. She lives in a world she's created in her mind and now she's pregnant. I don't know how to tell Ava. I need to tell her before she finds out from someone else.

AVA

CHAPTER 23

DEEP WATER

Still hungover from last night, I return to the same bar where I bumped into Paul's mysterious nerdy friend. I'm hoping to see him again. I'm lost on what my next move should be. It's as if I've lost my sight; I'm blind without Paul's assistance. I take shot after shot, chasing them down with beer. I keep replaying Paul's last conversation with me. I want to call Johnny but decide to text him instead.

Congrats on the baby
I am SOOO happy for you
When's the wedding?
Asshole
Fuck you
Dickhead

I stop myself from texting more. It's pointless and not making me feel better. I feel the urge to throw up; I hurry to the restroom.

I push the first stall open and drop to my knees and throw up uncontrollably. It's coming out of my nose and mouth. The smell and look of it is making it hard for me to stop. Before I can get up on my knees, I hear the stall door open and look up to find a man with a black bag – it's over my head before I can react. My hands get zip tied behind my back. I feel a foot kick me in the side of my head and another one, this one hits my nose. I'm scared, even more so than the last time I was in the trunk of a car. I'm in a public place. I try to scream, but the music in the bar is louder than I am. It's no use.

The man drags me by my arms, my shoulders burning with pain. I feel the cold air hit my face, and it gets lighter. I must be outside. I hear a car peel up and I'm pushed into the back seat. The smell of vomit under the bag is making me nauseous. The bag over my head is wet from blood gushing from either my nose or head. I pass out.

I wake up cold and to the smell of ocean water. For a moment, I forget I'm kidnapped. We are moving, but not in a vehicle. I'm in a boat… I'm in a boat. They're going to dump me in the ocean. Panic sets in; I need to get my hands free.

"HELLO? HELLO?" No one answers me. "Why are you doing this? I think you have the wrong person. Do you know who my father is? He's Jimmy 'The Coroner' Coonan."

All I can hear are the waves hitting the boat.

"Ooh, we're so scared little girl. Don't worry – your body will never surface, people will think you just ran off," one of the kidnappers says.

I hear a second voice ask, "Who's Jimmy 'The Coroner' Coonan?"

The other responds, "I don't know".

"WHY … why are you doing this?" I beg, the tears rolling down my face.

"It's the boss's orders."

"I can pay you double their offer, whatever you want. And, I'll, I'll disappear, leave the country. You can collect both pay outs. Please, I'm begging you."

They're silent. I don't want to die, at least not at the hands of someone else. If I find no way out, I need to get them to kill me before they throw me in the water if my hands are still tied – but if I can get my hands loose, I can swim back to Boston or to one of the surrounding Boston Harbor Islands.

"Please, I can't swim." A lie.

"The bosses ordered you to be drowned," the second kidnapper chimes in. His accent is distinct.

I start twisting my wrists and rubbing them against the wall of the boat. The zip ties cut into my skin. My guess is it's been about ten minutes since the boat left the harbor. That means we can't be doing more than 40 mph. I'm trying to do the math in my head; we're maybe seven miles from the shore, but that depends if we are heading south. I can't be sure of how far I am from land.

I hear the kidnappers talking to each other about tying weights to my legs. I feel one of them grab my leg and suddenly he's dragging me. I kick at him, flaring my legs so they can't tie anything to them. He manages to tie a rope around one of my legs. I feel the second kidnapper grab my shoulders. I'm praying to God, asking for forgiveness. I don't want to die, not now. I don't want to be murdered, by people I don't know and for reasons unknown. My legs are cramping and getting tired, but I can't stop kicking at them or I'm dead.

"Bitch, stop moving; let's just shoot her."

"No, that's not the plan, we have to do it exactly the way the boss requested."

"Oh, you are a fucking pussy, the boss, the boss. Who cares?"

"Listen, fucker, it's the boss's way or no way. If her body washes up full of bullet holes, you think the boss will be happy?"

They are too busy arguing and it's my opportunity to jump to my feet. I can't see anything, but I'm standing. I don't know which way to run. The boat is rocking back and forth. I feel one of the kidnappers grab my shoulders. I kick him and swing my head into his forehead. We are now wrestling, and I'm over-powered. I step backwards and my thigh hits the side of the boat and I fall backwards into the water.

Hitting the water feels like hitting an ice rink. The water is horribly cold, and my body goes into shock. I shake the bag off my head. I kick my legs to try to get my head above the water to get air. Only my lips get above the water for a quick inhale. I swallow salt water with the little air. I'm choking underwater and slowly sinking. I keep trying to pull my wrists apart twist to loosen the zip ties. The water lubricates around the ties and I get one hand loose, leaving the zip tie around the other wrist. I quickly swim up for air, gasping and choking on the saltwater I swallowed. The kidnappers' flashlights skim the water while they argue back and forth.

"Where the fuck is, she, we have to make sure she's dead."

"You're a fucking idiot, we should've killed her then dumped her in the water."

I swim underwater towards the opposite side of the boat, away from where the kidnappers are as quietly as I can. Something rubs against my foot and I yelp, it freaks me out. My kidnappers spot me and start shooting in the water. My teeth begin to chatter. I try clenching my teeth together to stop it, but it's no use. My muscles are cramping, and my body is becoming tired and shaking uncontrollably. If I don't get out of the water, I will die from hypothermia. Even if I was closer to the shore, I wouldn't survive the swim. I feel the vibration from their boat engine start. They are leaving me to die. I panic, feeling around the outside of the boat, looking for a rope or something to hang onto, but there's nothing. I see a bright light shine over the top of the boat; it's another boat. I must get the attention of the people on that boat. It's my only change to survive. If I'm lucky they're not with my kidnappers.

"HELP, HELP me, they're trying to kill me."

I wave my hands in the air. The boat spotlight is on me, it's blinding.

I hear more gunshots, and duck under the water.

"This is the coastguards, put your weapons down."

The kidnappers' boat's engine takes off. Something hits the water in front of me. It's a flotation device with a rope on the other end. I grab it and feel it pull me closer to the boat. I'm praying this is really the coastguard. They pull me on the boat, and immediately wrap me in blankets. The coastguard puts his arms around me trying to warm up my body.

"Are you injured?

"Just cc…o…l..d."

The other coastguard brings a warm cup of tea and helps me sip it. I'm too tired, I just fall asleep.

I wake in an ambulance with an oxygen mask over my face and an IV in my arm. I lift my head and look out the ambulance doors and see a news reporter. My head feels heavy and quickly falls back onto the stretcher. I fall back into a deep sleep.

I hear machines beeping around me, but I don't open my eyes, I can't – that's how exhausted I feel. There're heavy warm blankets stacked on my chest. I hear a familiar voice in the distance beyond the beeping hospital machines. It's the FBI agent, Connor. He's speaking with the doctor. The doctor recommends he come back tomorrow morning because I need rest. I fall in and out of sleep.

It must be morning; the sun is peeking through the window. The burning sensation in my chest has my full attention. Each inhale feels like knives slicing and dicing the inside of my lungs. The sun is shining so brightly that I can see the white particles in the air. The oxygen under my nose feels cool and refreshing. I lift my hands, my wrists are wrapped in white gauze, blood stains seeping through. I turn my head to the door and see the day, date and time written on the small white markerboard. It doesn't feel like I've been here two days. In this time, I've had the craziest dreams that feel real. There were Indians chanting around my bed throwing red powder on my face and I swear I can still smell the incense from my dream. Drums were beating slow, then faster and more intense. My father was there amongst the Indians wearing a strange robe and headpiece. The Indian sliced my father's arm and positioned it so the blood would drip into a bowl. The Indian added sticks and sand to the bowl, like a witch making a potion. They forced me to drink the mixture from the bowl. I felt like I was choking and couldn't breathe. I looked at the ceiling to find hundreds of red birds flying around gracefully. They looked like Cardinals. The window opened and the birds flew out leaving my room empty and quiet. Everything in the room transformed into pure white. My mother was sat in the chair. She looked up from her book and smiled.

"Honey, you're awake." She grabbed my face and kissed my forehead.

"Mom, are you okay?"

"Of course I am, honey."

"I thought you were dead."

"I am."

"What are you doing here?"

"Your father asked me to visit you and make sure you are okay. Ava, listen to your father, he really loves you."

Then the drums came back, and the room was dark. Suddenly my mother was stabbed in the back by someone I didn't recognize, her blood spraying all over me. She screamed my name, and I woke.

I feel so comforted that my mother visited me. I haven't dreamed of her in so many years. Strange how she mentioned my father. She always spoke so badly of him, warning me to stay away from him. What she didn't know is her continuing to tell me to stay away from him aroused my curiosity in finding him.

I hear a knock on the door and I immediately close my eyes. I'm not in the mood to talk about my second near-death experience of the year. I want to cry just thinking about my fear while in the ocean. I can't talk about it because I will burst into tears. The door opens, and I hear unfamiliar voices. It's just the nurse and doctor. I turn my head and slowly open my eyes.

"Ava, I am Dr. Sleeper,"

The nurse is already wrapping the blood pressure cuff around my arm.

"When can I leave?" I ask.

"Well, as soon as you are feeling better, I suppose," he explains, looking at my chart. "However, I'm concerned about your blood pressure levels. They are high for someone your age and pregnant. I recommend a low dose of lisinopril and follow up with your primary care doctor in a months' time. Also, check your blood pressure at home daily. It is possible, that this traumatic event has temporarily driven up your blood pressure. High blood pressure is dangerous for your pregnancy."

"PREGNANT!" I say, grabbing my stomach.

"I'm sorry Ava, I thought you were aware. Don't worry, after the blood work came back, we immediately did an ultrasound to make sure everything was okay. It all looks fine, from what we can see."

He examines me and when he finishes up his notes, he says they will prepare me for discharge. The nurse grabs my belongings from the drawers and places them on the bed. She takes out my IV, suggests I take a shower and tells me lunch will be delivered soon.

Am I carrying Mac's baby? I should've taken a morning after pill; it completely slipped my mind that night. Although, it could be Johnny's since we hardly use protection. I don't know if I could be a mother and adoption is not an option. I'll likely get an abortion, but right now I have other pressing issues that concern me.

I'm feeling lonely sitting in this cold hospital room. The old Ava would have had a hospital room full of guests, flowers, balloons and someone to hold her hand when she woke. I wonder if anyone even knows I'm here. My cellphone is gone, I've no connection to others outside of this hospital room. I don't even have a ride home. I sit on the toilet and feel bad for myself before finally taking a shower. In the shower I look over my body's many bruises and rip off the gauze that wraps around my wrist. My cuts hurt under the shower water.

I just can't keep it together anymore and let myself cry. I sit on the shower floor and grab my knees rocking myself back and forth. I 'm giving up again, I'm tired of being chased. I just want to lose already. I think about admitting myself to a psychiatric hospital. Maybe that would keep me safe until the trial. I don't need to communicate with the outside world anymore. Paul's upset with me and has disappeared, Mr. Alterman wants nothing to do with me and Johnny's started a family. I don't trust my father or his followers. Even the FBI is on the Mob's side.

I can't narrow down who would want me killed. Atlantic was run by the Italians and the Irish were working with them, even though they won't admit it. Why else would the Italians allow the Irish to launder money through Atlantic? Then there's obviously the Mob, my father, and perhaps Jose's goons are after revenge for his death. I can't forget the two men who kidnapped me, but we know they were working with Atlantic. I can't put my finger on the accent of the men that tried to drown me. It wasn't a Boston accent. Similar to a New York, New Jersey or even

Connecticut. Instead of trying to find the men who almost killed me, I should be focusing on the trial and how to stay alive for the next three weeks. I need to get home and get to my computer; it's the safest way to try to get in touch with Paul. I will email him at the address the mysterious guy in the bar gave me.

I feel an urgency to get dressed and leave the hospital before the nurse returns, or the cops. I'm sure they want to question me about my ordeal and investigate what's happened. I dress quickly and peek out the door and down the hall. All the nurses sitting at the nurse's station are busy typing away on their computer, on the phone or talking with their patients. I decide to skip the elevator, I don't want to bump into anyone that may be looking for me. I take the stairs down to the garage and walk out the emergency vehicle entrance. The closest subway is just a few blocks away. I speed walk to there, realizing I have no wallet with me. I sneak behind a paying customer going through the turnstile. I left my wallet in the bar bathroom the night I was taken. It's probably in police custody along with my phone.

I sneak around the back of my house and crawl through an unlocked window, noticing immediately my house has been broken into. I run to my room and find it a mess. My safe's been turned over but was probably too heavy for them to take with them to open later. I lie on the floor and try the combination a few times before it opens. I grab all its contents. I find my computer under the floorboards where I hid it last. I head to the back door but stop and investigate my roommate's bedroom; the door is ajar. Something tells me not to enter the room. I feel something brush against the back of my leg. It's just the cat, but it almost gives me a heart attack. I notice blood on the cat's face and that's when I decide to look in my roommate's room. She's laying on the bed bloodied. There's a knife sticking out of her chest. I grab my mouth to stop myself from screaming and run out the back door. I almost forget to open the door, hitting my shoulder against the wall.

I run with my backpack through the back streets of Cambridge until I get to a subway station. There, I take the redline to the Amtrak station at South Station and buy the next two business class train tickets to New York City. It's the most frequent destination from Boston. The trains operate every hour. I buy two seats for myself, because I don't want anyone sitting next to me. I order fast food to bring to eat on the train later. I buy all the local newspapers to see if my attempted drowning story is in the news or anything about the upcoming trial and grab a prepaid phone from the pharmacy.

I finally settle in my seat on the train, putting my belongings on the seat next to me. I have four and a half hours to figure out my next move before my train stops in New York City. My first email is to Paul. I'm hoping he gets back to me. The next email is to the lawyer Mr. Alterman set me up with. I email Mr. Alterman even though he may not want to talk to me. I feel that not all is lost with our relationship. Then I text Johnny from my new phone.

I write, *it's me Ava, please don't give anyone this number and don't let anyone know I have reached out to you. Call me when you get this text.*

JIMMY

CHAPTER 24

REVENGE

Waiting for my meal to arrive, Silver interrupts me. My men know better than to interrupt me during supper. It's my favorite time of the day to eat; it's when I eat the most. It better be an emergency, or he will get a punch in his noggin. The look on his face says that someone must be dead.

"It's Ava, she's in the hospital," Silver says, handing me his cellphone.

"Jimmy, it's Connor. Ava's in the hospital, the doctors says she will be okay," he explains.

"What the fuck happened?" I say. I clench my teeth and feel my heart pound out of my chest. My temper flares. I can't hold in the anger; I slam my fist on top of the table.

"The coastguards found her nearly drowned in Boston Harbor. We don't know how she got there but assume someone was trying to kill her. I haven't spoken to her; the doctor has her sedated."

I've heard enough, I hang up the phone. I can't visit her at the hospital, the police and news reporters will have the place surrounded.

"Silver," I scream, "Get the boss on the phone. We need the news station to be paid to never run the story."

"Too late, boss." He points to the TV above the bar.

"FUCK, Let's go."

I call the Indian and demand he meet me at my house. I tell him to bring the white man. We need all my people looking for the cocksuckers that tried to kill my daughter. I need to find, torture and kill everyone involved. I'm heading straight to see Claire. That bitch better have all the right answers. They targeted my daughter, and I am sure this must be about the trial. I thought I made myself clear, when I said she's cooperating.

"Silver, drive." I throw him the keys.

He's driving fast and erratically, even running red lights.

"Are you trying to get us killed, asshole!" I yell.

"No boss, sorry boss," he stutters.

Silver is a nervous, skinny Irish boy. His looks are deceiving, but he's a featherweight retired boxer. He knows mixed martial arts and has a third-degree black belt. He wrestled in high school but was kicked out of school for fighting too much. Silver is my driver and I guess you could say sidekick. He won't hesitate to kill you and prefers to do it with his hands. He always carries a gun, but you will seldom see him pull it out. He's one ugly motherfucker. His nickname comes from his silver front tooth, not gold but silver. Most of his teeth are fake from all his fighting years and his nose is bent to the side. I don't think he even knows how many times his nose has been broken.

"Do you know Johnny Cormick's phone number?" I ask.

"Here's my phone boss, I think his number is saved in there under Cormick."

Johnny motherfucking Cormick. This bastard better answer his phone. It rings several times and goes to voicemail.

JOHNNY

CHAPTER 25

MR. COONAN

My phone won't stop vibrating. I'm getting calls from all sorts of numbers and even text messages. I'm trying to ignore my phone, but I know something has gone terribly wrong. Casey is laying on the doctor's table getting her first ultrasound. I'm kind of excited, but at the same time my mind is elsewhere. It's with Ava. I haven't spoken to her in over a week. I know she's alive, because the Mob would be the first to announce her death. They would be pissed since their plan is to use her to take the heat off Susan. The trial is almost here, and I need to make it right with Ava. Casey interrupts my worries.

"Look, Johnny, can you believe this, that's our baby, our baby," she says excitedly.

I squint at a black and white static TV monitor. I have no idea what the hell I'm looking at, but I can hear the heartbeat. To me the sound is more impressive than the blob on the screen.

"Ya, honey, it's great," I say trying to match her enthusiasm.

"Hey Doc, can I get one of those machines to listen to the baby at home?" I ask.

"Oh, yes, I think you can get them at a department store or large pharmacy," the doctor says, not looking at me.

I don't like that the doctor didn't look my way, I'm offended and want to punch him in the back of the head. I don't want this dickhead delivering my baby. My mood shifts to anger so quick I don't feel it coming. I stand up and look out the window. Finally, the doctor wraps up with Casey.

"Hey Doc, can I have a word with you. PRIVATELY?"

From the corner of my eye, I see Casey's head turn in my direction. She knows me too well; she can sense I'm annoyed.

"Sure, follow me to my office. Casey, make an appointment to see me in six weeks," he says, motioning me to follow him out the door.

We get to his office. He offers me a seat.

"This won't take long. Ya know my family, my history, so I suggest ya give me the same respect ya give my family members," I say, leaning in front of his desk, not breaking my glance.

"I don't..."

"Save it Doc, next time I ask you a question, and you don't answer me while making eye contact, I'm going to assume you don't care about your own family," I say, picking up his family photo off his desk.

"Johnny, I meant... I meant no disrespect, really," he stutters.

"Well, fuck, it must be a misunderstanding," I smile.

I pull out $10,000 cash and smack it down on his desk.

"I want my fiancé to get the best treatment and care; that should cover a few visits." I leave the office before he can refuse the money or speak.

"What was that about?" Casey whispers to me in the elevator.

"Nothing, I just had to pay him, and it was cash so thought it would be strange to slap the receptionist with a stack of bills. Plus, the receptionist looks like a junky whore."

Casey slaps my arm in disgust, but also laughs because she knows it's true.

I drop her off at her mother's, they have a shopping day planned and I must get to work. I listen to my voicemails – there are so many I don't know who to call back first. Shockingly they all must do with Ava. I can't believe someone tried to kill her; my blood is boiling. I must get to the hospital.

The hospital tells me she left without being discharged, so I look through my text messages to see if she has sent me a message. Yes, she has, I almost missed it because it's from an unknown phone number. Probably a burner phone. Something scared her because she left without checking out.

I call her on the number she texted me, but it goes straight to a voicemail that is not yet set up.

I get to my car to find an older man leaning against it. At first, I don't recognize him.

It's Jimmy "The Coroner" Coonan. I haven't seen him since I graduated high school. I remember not having a party to celebrate my graduation because we were at Mattie's funeral. Mattie was Jimmy's right-hand man.

When you bump into Jimmy, it's no coincidence, he's out to make a hit and you better hope it isn't you. When Jimmy isn't out making a hit, he is at the bar drinking like the fucking lush he is. I know he has never left the Mob, because no one does, but he did disappear from Boston for a long time.

"Jimmy, I haven't seen you since Mattie's funeral," I say, shaking his hand.

His hand crushes mine, and he smiles, holding my hand longer than necessary. I bet he wishes it was my neck.

"That long, huh? Well ya still as ugly as I remembah ya. How's ya fathah?" He lights a cigarette and gets comfortable leaning against the front bumper of my car.

"He's good, business is good."

I'm waiting for him to tell me the real reason why he is here.

"Have ya seen my daughtah, Ava?" he searches my face for answers.

A lump forms in my throat. Did he say daughter? I must be mistaken.

"Ya, daughter?"

"Ya, Ava, well, have ya seen her, boy?"

"I… I … didn't know she was your daughter. No, no, of course I haven't seen her. As soon as I heard what happened, I came straight here."

"Ya seem shocked that she's my daughtah. Why, what did she say about me?"

"Ava never mentioned that you … were her father."

I'm frightened of this man. Had I known, I would have never gotten involved romantically.

"Let's keep this between us, but ya need to go look for her now and bring her back here," he barks the orders. "I never got to ask her what happened, and the police want a statement. They're getting impatient and startin' to sniff around and ya know the more they sniff around the more it will cost us."

"Do we have any information about who tried to kill Ava?"

"I have some ideas of my own, but no solid names. I went to Boston Harbor to shake down some boat owners. It smells like the Italians, real meatball and sauce kind of shit."

"What the fuck is it with your problem with the Italians, ya stuck in the fuckin' past. Ya know my mother's Italian. Don't start this war again, the city doesn't need it, we have enough problems with outsiders trying to establish business in the city. The Italians are not a problem."

"Touchy topic for ya huh, don't forget who ya work with; the Irish. Ya know ya fathah wouldn't have it any other way. I don't know what ya and that Susan got ya self into, but ya made a damn mess for ya self trustin' Ava," explains Jimmy while shaking his head as if to say *I told you so.*

"Did I miss something? Are ya sayin she knew about what we were doing before the FBI raid?" I ask confused.

"Ava really has ya believin' she is innocent; damn my girl is good. Johnny, she was the brains behind this entire launderin'. She was you and Susan's puppet master."

"What? I know for a fact she had nothing to do with this, she's lying to you, Jimmy."

Jimmy grabs me by the collar of my shirt pushing his nose into mine so our eyes of level

"What are ya tryin' to say? I don't have time to talk with ya all day, I need to find my daughtah before someone else does. Call me as soon as ya hear from her, I know she's goin' to call ya. Ya know she's pretty upset about ya baby on the way."

He pushes his fist into my neck still holding the neck of my shirt crumbled in his hand. His force almost knocks me to the ground.

Before I can react, he's in his car, backing out of the parking lot. I wondered how Ava found out about the pregnancy. She was pissed, sending angry text messages a few days ago and wouldn't return any of my calls or messages. I guess she found out then.

Jimmy has never liked me or my family, I think it's because of my Italian heritage. He would never want a mutt like me dating his daughter. He still believes in the old way: Irish marry Irish, Italian marry Italian and so on. I can't believe that bitch Ava lied to me. She never mentioned her father. The Mob must know Jimmy is her father, but did they know when she was hired at Atlantic? I don't recall him having children. I'll have to discuss this with my father.

I try calling Ava again from the number she texted from. Still no answer. I light another cigarette and lean against my car thinking about where Ava could have gone. I'm so lost in thought I smoke the cigarette to the filter, burning my inner lips. The same thought keeps playing over and over in my mind. All Casey's dreams are coming true now that she is finally pregnant, but my nightmares have just begun. If Ava is truly Jimmy's daughter, the blame will shift from Ava to Susan and me. There is no way the Mob would prosecute the daughter of Jimmy Coonan. The Coonans are deep rooted in Mob history, no Coonan has gone to jail longer than a few months. I need to find Ava, now.

AVA

CHAPTER 26

DIRTY SOUTH

I don't waste time in NYC. I board a bus to New Orleans to meet up with Ruben; not the best time to visit, but I need his resources. An expense-free, safe place to lie low until the trial. Ruben thinks I'm taking a flight. I don't want him to know I'm saving the money he gave me for a plane ticket to cover my lawyer's fees. I don't feel comfortable telling Ruben about my problems because I really like him. It might scare him off if he knows everything.

The plan is to stop and get luggage, new clothes, rent a motel room, just to shower and clean up before meeting him. He insisted on picking me up at the airport or sending a car, but I convince him it's easier for me to just catch a cab. He's getting a hotel room for us, rather than have me at his home, so I assume he's married. It doesn't bother me and anyway I'd rather stay at a hotel, I'll feel more comfortable.

The bus ride is long and uncomfortable. I'm feeling nauseous and throwing up everything I eat. I either need to pin the blame on Susan or Johnny, and of course not before getting the Mob's approval. That's the tricky part, getting the Mob on my side. While I'm still upset with Johnny, I don't want him to go to jail, and it's not because he's having a baby. It's because I selfishly want him to myself. If Casey thinks this baby is going to stop me from continuing our relationship, she's dead wrong. If anything, the baby, stress and responsibility will only push Johnny further into my arms. Johnny has told me on several occasions he doesn't want a family with her, but maybe he would want one with me.

Without Paul, I don't know if I can pull off my plan. If Paul will ever talk to me again. I'll have him hack Atlantic and alter their accounting books – this will be leverage against the Mob. Not only will this prevent me from going to jail, but it will also prove to them they can't fuck with any Coonan and get away with it. My family has built a reputation for themselves, and I won't be the one to tear it down. This is no longer only about saving myself from serving jail time but keeping my family name creditable. With all the research and information Paul has sent me regarding my family, it's no wonder my mother insisted I keep her last name. If the Mob knew about me, then the Mob's enemies would know about me. This puts a permanent target on my back. Seems funny that all these years I lived such a simple life, until my mother's murder. I wouldn't say I've been in any real trouble. However, if my mother was still around, she could dig up some troubling stories from my childhood.

When I'm with my father, I feel like no one will try to or can hurt me. If the FBI agent Connor knew I was a Coonan that day in the interview, he wouldn't have had me come in. I enjoy the way Connor treated me when he found out who I was. It's as though I can have whatever I want. There is a mandated level of respect for my father. Once everyone knows who I am, everything will change. Even so, I know I can't testify against Claire and can never mention the Mob's association. Paul will have his work cut out for him because he needs to hack the Mob's lawyers and the FBI, but before that can happen, I need Mr. Alterman's lawyer to trust my plan. If I get truly desperate, I can admit to the Mob that I have been skimming off the top of Atlantic Financials' profits and the Italians, but will they believe that money I stole wasn't from their personal funds? They may not like the fact that I was going into business for myself. Only Paul has proof and he would never expose me. Deep in my gut I feel Paul will come back into my life. If he doesn't get in touch with me soon, I'll have no choice but to find another hacker. I worry that the Italians discovered our skimming scheme and made him disappear.

From the first day of my internship, my plan was to steal from Atlantic by copying the hard drives of executives, lawyers, and Susan and Johnny's computers. It was easy for them to trust me and hand over access to the shared drive. I was free labor, and they loved handing over work they couldn't be bothered doing. I was a good intern, always completing jobs in a timely manner and taking the initiative to ask for new projects, all while Paul sat at home on his computer remotely downloading confidential financial information. I'd play dumb and ask stupid questions, so everyone would think I didn't know what I was doing. That allowed them to trust me alone in their offices and even let me use their computers. Paul would put viruses on my computer, and I would log into someone's computer in the office to transfer the files. The only connection I didn't know of was that Johnny and Susan were working for the Mob. There was no way I could have known.

We'd later discover the Mafia owns Atlantic Financial –Paul uncovered that when he did a search and backtracked every executive's family tree and linked the Mafia to just about everyone working at Atlantic. I gave too much credit to Susan and Johnny when it came to the money laundering. I couldn't figure out how and where all the money was flowing into the company. When Johnny finally told me, several light bulbs began lighting up, like a string of Christmas tree lights.

I'm still worried the Mob will think I was stealing their direct funds from them. Paul wasn't the slightest fazed when we first found out it was the Mafia we were skimming funds from not Atlantic. He's sometimes too confident for his own good, but that's Paul. He gets off on uncovering secrets and being in dangerous situations. Like the time he discovered my father was a hitman for the Mob. It didn't stop there because Paul dug up files to uncover the lengthy history of the Coonan name. Rumor has it that my grandfather, Mr. Coonan, began his Mob career here in Massachusetts and expanded business throughout New England, New York, Philadelphia, Chicago and Canada. There is so much more history of the Coonans that cannot be found in any newspaper or FBI file. Only stories told between mobsters who care to carry on the legacy. Not many rats can blab to the cops before being a murder victim. Even if they get the chance, they wouldn't give up all they know to the FBI.

The bus ride feels like it is taking forever. I sit next to the back exit in case I need to make a quick getaway. I check my email account every ten minutes looking for a response from Paul. Then I spot thirty emails in my drafts folder. I click on the draft folder and read the first email addressed to me, from Sherry, my alias. *I didn't write the email, so who the hell did?* I click on the next draft email and the next, the emails are all identical. The email reads:

Dear Ava,

I'm still incredibly upset with your behavior that night. You put me in harm's way and could've destroyed all we worked for. At first, I was conflicted with the information about Thomas, but I know I'll never know the truth about what happened to Thomas because even if you did kill him, you would never admit to it. I've had a lot of time to think about us and with that in mind, I've decided to give you your share from the Atlantic scheme. However, after that transaction I don't want anything to do with you.

Burn in hell,
Sherry

I look through all the emails and delete the draft folder and then empty the trash folder. It's Paul; I'm so excited to hear from him. He's brilliant, and I'm relieved that at least he sent a response to my many emails, but also frightened that he has agreed to still give me my share. Paul is smarter than me, so I must be cautious. I have plenty of reasons for concern. He knows too much and could easily hand me to the FBI, and I would be lucky if I ever got out of jail. If I've learned anything from Paul, it's you can never be too paranoid.

I respond to Paul by the same method, with a draft email.

Dear Sherry,

I'll gladly burn in hell if you'll join me. Johnny took care of the situation, no one will ever know. I know you don't believe me, but I didn't kill Thomas. I wish I could prove it somehow. Thank you for keeping your end of the deal. I'm only accepting it because I'm in a lot of trouble. Someone tried to drown me in Boston Harbor and my roommate has been murdered. It gets worse, the doctors told me I'm pregnant. It's likely to be his. You know who I'm speaking of.

I miss you dearly and hope you are safe and okay.

Love always,
Ava

It hits me right then. I have no home to return to after seeing my roommate's lifeless body in my house. The second death in that house is enough for me. Luckily, the doctors are witnesses that I was in the hospital at the time of her murder. By the look of her body and the smell, she was dead for at least three days before I got there.

I decide to power down my computer to save the battery and take a nap to recharge my own battery. I'll check the draft emails again later. If it is deleted, I know Paul has read the email. Before I doze into a heavy sleep, I start to wonder how much

Paul is watching what I search on my computer. Paul is my friend; no matter how angry he is, he could never do anything to harm me. Could he?

JOHNNY

CHAPTER 27

SNAKES AND RATS

My knuckles are white from gripping the steering wheel too tight on the drive to my parents. I will pull all my resources to find Ava. She knows I love her, but she keeps pushing me away. We have our problems, but I thought our love would fix them. I must always prove my love and she is constantly testing my loyalty. I lie to her about Casey, but that's just because I don't want to hurt her. I'm in love with both Casey and Ava. It's a shitty situation, but I can't choose. Casey is loyal and a part of my family, and now she's pregnant, how could I ever leave her side? And Ava, she is the bad girl that every man fantasizes about. She doesn't care what others think, with her criminal mind – and the sex is something I could never turn down. She's wild in bed and pleasures me more than Casey. In an ideal world, I want to keep a relationship with both women. Not under the same roof kind of shit. They would kill each other. This fantasy life in my head is all great, but I know it will end with me possibly losing both women. I'm not a one-woman man. Casey is wrong if she thinks I will change because of a baby. Women who think like this are delusional.

It's difficult to keep tabs on Ava. In the beginning, she was easy to track; either she's getting smarter or she has help. With the news that Casey is pregnant, Ava has more reason to turn on me and blow the heat in my direction. If this happens, I'll get my father to put pressure on the Mob to keep me out of jail. With my child's birth approaching, jail is not the place I want to be. My parents raised me with some values, and I won't neglect my own. I may not be a good boyfriend or even a good future husband, but I'll be a good father. I'm not a deadbeat dad like Ava's father, Jimmy.

When I tell my father Ava is Jimmy's daughter, his look of intrigue changes to worry, and this frightens me. I rarely see this side of my father; usually he's wearing his poker face. My father doesn't like to show emotion, he claims this leaves him vulnerable. I guess in his line of work, dealing with criminals and phony politicians have made him expressionless. I value his opinion when it comes to the Mob because he's been part of that world since he first learned to walk.

"You better find Ava. That's your one job, don't keep screwing up," my father says in his typical disappointed tone.

"Don't ya think I know that. How am I gonna find her?"

"I'll dig into the new-found information about Jimmy being Ava's father. What's the last number she called you from?" says my father with a pen in his hand waiting for the number.

"Here." I give him Ava's last known phone number.

If anyone can find her, he can. He was the one who's been tracking her cellphone all along. She's been smashing phones and gluing the backs thinking that would work. She thinks she has it all figured out, but she can be a naïve bitch. Even though it's become increasingly challenging to keep track of her whereabouts, for the most part, I've known where she's been this entire time, until now. I even know about her eventful weekend at the casino with Ruben. I wasn't angry because I knew she was just trying to distract herself and get over me, but it didn't work. She was back in my arms as soon as she returned to Boston.

My father is writing something down. "Here's a list of places to check and who to contact when we get there. Don't skip any of these locations."

I call my boys to send them on a scavenger hunt. They'll check the airport, bus, train station and rental car locations. I doubt she's in Boston, Jimmy would have found her by now.

"You have to go tell her in person the news about Jimmy being Ava's father."

"What, why? That fucking bitch is crazy. She scares the shit out of me."

"I won't repeat myself. GO!"

My father never raises his voice. This is frightening and I better listen to his orders.

I drive to Dorchester, one of the more dangerous parts of Boston, to inform Claire what has come about. It is my job to keep tabs on Ava and I've failed again.

I find out Claire is having dinner in the North End. It's not dinner for eating, but a meeting to collect debts and make business transactions. I arrive at the restaurant and am told by the twins, Claire's doormen, that I'll have to wait. I smoke a cigarette, pacing the sidewalk, glancing up at the twins every so often looking for them to let me inside. The twins are tall, muscular, redheaded with large crooked noses. They used to play hockey in college hoping to go to play for the NHL, but were too clumsy on the ice, but great at fighting when time came to take off the gloves on the ice.

I'm let into the restaurant and led into the back-kitchen area. I walk in to find a makeshift torture chamber, plastic draped around the kitchen, covering the floor and countertops. There are human limbs on the kitchen counters, pools of blood puddling on the floor. Claire is standing behind a bloodied empty chair wearing a full body white disposable painter's jumpsuit and goggles. What's in her hands startles me. It's a small child's head with no body attached. I throw up in my mouth and force myself to swallow. I've never seen nothing like it; I mean, sure I've seen plenty of dead bodies, but never a child. Whose child is this and what could this person have done to deserve such pain brought into their lives? I can't peel my eyes off the bloodied teddy bear. I can't help but think about Casey and our unborn child. What am I walking in on?

Claire places the child's head on the kitchen counter and strolls towards me while peeling off the bloodied gloves and goggles.

"The Italians should never cross us and will pay what they owe us, or we will continue to murder their bastard children," she spits. She places the head in a box. "Deliver it to their father Piezo," she barks the orders into midair. "Throw the mother's body in the harbor along with the child's limbs. NOW," she screeches.

She cocks her head sideways, "Johnny, honey what are you doing here?" She touches my face.

I jerk away from her hands.

"I...." I freeze; the words won't come out.

"Let's get out of this room and sit and have a drink to talk." She guides me to the front of the restaurant.

I sit in the closest booth to the kitchen. She peels off her blood-stained disposable jumpsuit, rubber gloves and goggles, dropping them in a pile on the floor. Her face has splatters of blood, everywhere but where her googles covered her eyes and face. She sits with a smile.

Two pints of beer are slid in front of us.

I get straight to the point. "Ava is Jimmy's daughter?"

She doesn't answer me right away.

"NO!"

"Well, yes, yes she is"

There is silence, she's deep in thought staring into the beer glass.

"How old is Ava?"

"I'm not sure, twenty-five or twenty-six?"

"You worried you'll take the heat instead of Ava? Oh, Johnny, you're so silly. My loyalty lies with you over Ava any day. You look tired, go home and get some rest."

"But..."

Claire raises her hand signaling me to stop. She grabs my face and pulls me closer.

"You have nothing to worry about, just bring Ava here at once."

"Okay."

She waves me to leave.

"Johnny," Claire yells as I walk out. "Forgive me, I forgot to congratulate you and Casey on the new baby. Send Casey my best."

I turn around, wave and force a fake smile. She isn't fooling anyone with her congratulations. She couldn't care less about anyone around her. The old Claire use to care about family, friends and all the Irish in our neighborhoods. I don't recognize this Claire, murdering a child. This isn't the traditional Irish way. Rumors are circulating that she's making decisions without other members of the Mob. There're secret members of the Mob, that invest with the Mob for return profit and protection. There're comparable to a shareholder of a corporation, without the public's knowledge. The secret members' investments go to paying off the police, FBI and judges to keep us out of jail. They are the reason we have the most elite weapons, putting us ahead of other organized crime gangs. We even have access to chemicals that can erase traces of DNA, dissolve the oil left from fingerprints, gunpowder residue and blood splatter. It's near impossible for detectives to link anything back to us. Just like the pink powder I used to get rid of our DNA when we killed Jose. It isn't a cheap substance, so I had to steal it from the Mob.

We pay an enormous bill to hack phones, computers, and security systems and rig casino machines. With advances in technology and science the Mob knows they need more income to keep up with the ever-changing environment, if they want to maintain control of Boston. The Italians would tell you different, they would say they control Boston. It's like a boxer at a news conference; they always say they are the champs and will beat their opponent even though, deep down they doubt themselves.

A champ will never admit their weaknesses. Like Claire; I know she has weaknesses, but no one has yet found them. This would compromise her as a leader. Perhaps, that is why over time her extreme behavior keeps her relevant and helps her conceal her weaknesses.

I go to my parents to rest because Casey won't let me sleep. She's been jumping down my throat with things to do before the baby is born and a wedding to-do list. Her mood is up and down; my mother takes Casey's side no matter what and says it's just the hormones. It's annoying – my mother has always made me feel I couldn't do no wrong. She doesn't get along with Casey but has made more of an effort since she found out she's pregnant. My father could give a shit. He never gets excited about much of what's going on in my life. He has put all his energy as a father into Stan. As soon as I filled him in on what was going on, he called Stan to get him to help. It's insulting to know my father thinks of me as a shithead who can't do anything right or on my own. I know he blames my mother for the way I am. As I child, I always heard him saying, "Don't baby him, let him cry, it won't hurt. You aren't helping him; you are enabling him."

I think my mother wanted me to steer straight and get out of the family business of crime. She just wants a normal life, I can tell, the way she pretends all the time. Her friends, family and neighbors know better. She isn't fooling anyone. She tries to stay humble and not buy things that give off the impression my parents have money. It's hard when my father buys lavish cars and throws elaborate parties. He's no longer a politician but keeps up with who's running for office no matter if its City

Council or Mayor. He attends every white tie charity event and helps raise money for hospitals and other various charities. On the outside, he looks like a law-abiding citizen, but he is a crook. You will never get him to choose a side because he does business with everyone and anyone. It doesn't matter if you're Irish, Italian, black or Hispanic. Business is just business, that is what he always says.

Many people don't like that my father works with many associations or different races or religion. Some believe their god is the only god or that their religious ways are better, and their culture was the first to arrive. The Irish hate the fact that history books say the North End used to be Irish, until the Italians ran them out. The Irish claim that the Italians were dirty and didn't want to live side by side with them. At a young age, I learned the racist terms to describe Italians: ginzos, guidos and greasers. The Italians had their own terms for the Irish too: paddies, micks and snouts. Since my mother is Italian and my father Irish, I used to be called mick greaser. It stuck with me for some time, until I fought every kid that ever gave me trouble at the playground or in school. My mother was constantly at the school apologizing for my behavior, until I got smart and waited until after school to kick their asses off school property. I learned at an early age my fist earns respect.

My mother slaps my chest with one of her slippers.

"Johnny, go wash up, dinner will be ready in fifteen minutes," she says putting her slipper back on.

I check the clock, it's 6:30 p.m. I've slept for over three hours. I go to the bathroom to splash water on my face then go into my old bedroom to grab an extra gun and cash. Casey doesn't know I hide money at my parents. She spends money faster than I earn it. Plus, I know it's safe here. No one would ever come after my parents. They would be stupid because they wouldn't even make it onto the street before they were stopped.

I get to the table as my mother is putting out hot baked bread. Stan is sitting in his usual spot. He eats dinner every night with my parents, except on the weekends and that's because they always eat out.

"Stan the man, what's going on?" I ask, walking behind him grabbing his arms.

"Nothing much, I hear ya blessing this world with ya ugly children now," he chuckles.

"Ya wish ya were as pretty as me."

My mother hushes us and tells everyone to sit.

"Johnny, say grace," she insists.

I rest my elbows on the table and push my face into my locked hands.

"Father, we have gathered to share a meal in ya honor. Thank ya for putting us together as family and thank ya for this food. Bless it to our bodies, Lord. We thank ya for all the gifts you've given to those around this table. Help each member of our family use these gifts to ya glory. Guide our mealtime conversations and steer our hearts to ya purpose for our lives. In Jesus' Name, Amen."

"Johnny, you need to have dinner with us more often. I hope to see our new grandchild and Casey sitting at this table with us. Casey knows she is welcome over here anytime," my mother says.

My father adjusts the waist of his pants. Just the mention of

Casey makes my father uncomfortable. He doesn't like Casey. That's the reason she doesn't visit my parents' house. He's told her several times to her face she's classless. He feels she talks too much and that there are things one should keep to oneself. When he heard I was having a child, he was less than enthused.

"Yes, Mom, I'll let Casey know she's welcome here for dinner anytime."

The rest of the dinner conversation revolves around what is in the local news. My mother always blabs about the neighborhood gossip; did you know so and so is getting married, divorced, pregnant, a gambler, drug addict, is dead. I don't know half the people she talks about. My father on the other hand is all about baseball and politics.

My phone beeps. My mother looks at me in disgust. There are two things my mother won't tolerate: swearing, and phones during dinner time. I can't help but read the text. Ava's location is revealed: New Orleans. Looks like I better get to her before her father. I don't trust his intentions for Ava. He may be her father, but he's still a violent killer.

MR. ALTERMAN

CHAPTER 28

SHRED

Who would have known that someone could fool me in my old age? Ava's lies spilled from her mouth the first moment we met. A part of me wants to know why she lied, and another part doesn't care. My first impression of Ava was that she was an innocent, timid twenty-something-year-old scared of being framed by Atlantic Financial. She did an excellent job making me feel bad for her. I guess she thought no one would believe her because her father is a hitman for the Irish. She's right, but I still would have helped her for my entertainment and the opportunity to get close to the Mob, so I can finally try to give them what they deserve. I gave up years ago because I was being dragged in circles. Now I know the daughter of the Mob's hitman, the anger and pain has resurfaced. The last thing on my bucket list is to take down the Mob, starting from the top, and Ava is the in. I've been waiting for to accomplish this last attempt.

Jimmy doesn't believe I have cut ties with Ava. He knows I'm a retired Boston cop and as he says, cops are scum and can't be trusted. Evil seeps from his pores; I can smell the death on him. It scares me, but I lie anyway. I didn't really cut ties with Ava, that was all acting. If Ava's father was listening, I wasn't about to give them any helpful information. At the time I only had a feeling my office is bugged, but I discovered the proof during my office move.

Against my better judgement, I set Ava up with my good friend, Waylon Wilson, a Criminal Defense Lawyer, the best of the best. I feel bad for her; as mad as I am, I don't want to see her spend time in jail on behalf of the Mob.

I'm shredding paper, dismantling my office and ripping out the hard drives to my computers to keep my information away from Jimmy. I've dealt with the Italian Mafia in the past and I know the extent they'll go to to get information. I will break the Boston office lease and move my business to Texas, until things blow over and the dust kicked up settles back to the ground.

As an ex Boston cop, my experience is the Italians and Irish are both dangerous and intelligent – they have created standing relationships with the police, judges and political figures in office. Our city is powerless against them. Over the years, I've seen the crime spread to other states in New England in the towns bordering Canada. The small towns are the first to be consumed by gangs, then they work their way to the inner cities. There're no books in the library to prepare law enforcement for their devilish ways and how they move into New England. Throughout my many years working for the Boston Police Department as a cop, then as a detective, there's been little I haven't seen.

Though it wasn't my choice to retire from the police early, being a private investigator was the next best career choice. I've always had a general interest in criminals and the way their minds work. It didn't take long to discover there's no solution to eliminating crime; it's a cat and mouse game. I've walked the line that divides the honest cops and corrupt cops but could never quite bring myself to cross over like my fellow corrupt officers – but I admit I turned a blind eye to their cooperation with criminals. Having a clear conscience was more valuable than the extra cash. I have a big heart – the characteristic that made me good at my job but also terrible. I feel sorry for some criminals because that is all they've ever known. It isn't easy changing. I don't always agree with the laws in place but with a lack of energy or resources to make any effort to change laws is daunting. Sure, I've let several criminals fly under the radar. Minor criminals were never worth my time – we left those for the rookie cops. Rookies are eager to fight any crime, no matter how big or small. I miss being a cop, but it was best to exit just before the infamous accusations when the FBI was caught working with the Irish. At the time, I didn't know what was about to go down, but in hindsight, I was thankful the Captain gave me the heads up. We both knew that we would never speak again after my early retirement, it just wasn't safe for some of us to stay on as detectives when the FBI was under investigation. Fingers were even being pointed at the innocent. Everyone was under surveillance for several years, even after the trials. The Captain has since passed and as far as I know he carried his secrets with him to his grave. His funeral was the largest I've ever attended.

Officers, fire fighters, veterans and active military came from all over the state to say goodbye to the Captain. At the time, I was frightened to attend for fear of my life but did so anyways. It was good seeing some of my old colleagues, but others I tried to hide from. Moving South after retirement was necessary, and a great excuse to lose contact with everyone from my past. I've been back in Boston for almost five years and now I'm sitting here packing things up again. Running from my problems has always worked for me in the past but running today at my old age just doesn't sit right with me.

I'm also feeling terrible about the way I spoke to and treated Ava the day she was in my office. I had been drinking all day and stewing in anger for days. It was only a matter of time before I exploded on her. I want to at least have one more conversation before I decide to cut her out of my life forever. I just hope she takes my advice and hires Wilson as her defense attorney.

AVA

CHAPTER 29

SECOND LINE

My skin is crawling from that long, dirty, miserable bus ride from New York to New Orleans. I take the longest shower of my life. I throw away the clothes I wore on the bus because I sat in them for the entire duration of the trip. I take a long bath, shaving between my legs, underarms and legs. I then head directly to the hotel spa to get my hair styled, makeup applied, and nails manicured. There are times when it takes some pampering to feel beautiful.

After hours at the spa, I look damn good, the best I've looked since the first year I was with Mac. My body fat has melted off since being unemployed, but I'm now noticing a little bloating. Still, I'm skinnier than in my high school years. It does help that I only eat once per day. Not the healthiest diet plan, but it's working for me.

I must look my best for Ruben because he isn't exactly your

average looking man. His skin is flawless; he always looks like he's just spent the day at a spa. The short time we've spent together I've only ever seen him wearing suits. He smells of designer cologne all the time. He's the most charming and gorgeous man I've ever laid eyes on. In comparison, if Johnny stood next to Ruben, Johnny would look homeless. Ruben makes me step up my game and want to look my very best. Now, if this was Johnny I was going to see, he would be lucky if I even brushed my teeth. It's not that Johnny doesn't dress nice, smell good or anything like that. He's a jeans and t-shirt, full beard type of guy for the most part – since he no longer works at Atlantic, he's let himself go. Also, the comfort I feel with Johnny is different because he is so laidback, completely the opposite of Ruben. Ruben is more serious than fun, but he can be entertaining to be around, especially when he binges on coke.

I take one last glance in the mirror after tipping the many ladies that worked on getting me looking my best. My town car is waiting outside to bring me to the Roosevelt Hotel, where hopefully I will be greeted immediately by Ruben. I'm a very impatient person, so he better be waiting for me. I'm wearing a black floral halter dress that falls just above my knee. My cropped jean jacket hangs softly over my shoulders, perfectly complementing my leather wedge sandals. I purposely bought expensive designer luggage with a matching purse to impress Ruben. I plan to return the luggage before returning to Boston because I cannot afford such an outlandish purchase with the lawyer fees I owe.

It is humid outside, so the driver has the air conditioning blasting, but my body still finds a way to sweat; my legs are sticking to the seat. My anxiety and nervousness at seeing Ruben again is taking my mind away from the mess I left in Boston. The confined interior in the car makes me feel the urge to get out. It must be the post-traumatic stress from the two kidnapping attempts. I'm counting my breaths and trying to focus on the beautiful scenery and architecture the City of New Orleans has to offer.

We pull up to the grand, historic hotel, the kind where the bellhops wear white gloves and a full uniform, hat included. I don't wait for the driver to open my door, rushing him with the tip and running past the bellman. I go to the hotel desk to check in, but Ruben is already standing in the lobby with a bright smile. He's wearing a purple suit like those I've seen men wear on Easter Sunday matched with a white and purple plaid shirt with a two-button suit jacket with no tie. His hands sit comfortably in his pockets, his shoes are light brown leather cap-toe oxfords. The outline of his biceps is visible through his blazer. His hair is closely shaven to his head and his face is clean shaven; even his eyebrows are perfectly groomed. He doesn't wait for me to walk to him. We meet in the middle of the lobby, like a scene from a love story.

He hugs me tight and grabs my face softly to kiss me. I can taste the cocaine in his mouth. I'm turned on from feeling his erection against my leg.

"You look so darn beautiful. You've lost a lot of weight since the last time I saw you."

He grabs my arms and steps back, looking my body up and down.

"Thank you, you don't look so bad yourself," I say jokingly.

He continues to stare at me, making me feel uncomfortable. I'm not used to so much attention from a man. Mac was never like this, even in the beginning of our relationship.

"I ordered lunch to be sent up to our room. I figured you would want to relax after your flight."

"Sounds perfect."

He directs the bellman to bring my bags to the room. I hesitate to leave my bags with the bellman – they contain my computer and the only cash I have left. Before I can say anything, he grabs my hand to lead me to the elevator. He hugs me from behind and kisses my neck until the elevator opens into the penthouse suite.

The wall outside the elevator reads *Presidential Suite*. It is the largest hotel suite I've ever seen. The windows span the wall from the floor to ceiling. White shiny marble covers the floors, a matching color on the walls. The furnishings are high-end modern, but work well with the traditional moldings, fireplaces and detailed woodwork. There are paintings and sculptures throughout the many rooms. There are a ridiculous number of decorative pillows on every chair, couch and bed. The hotel room is the entire size of one side of the hotel floor, with the private elevator sitting in the middle as if it is a centerpiece for the room. There are three bedrooms and a study, with a tiny balcony in every room. The main room has a large terrace that wraps around two sides with a jacuzzi, lounge chairs and an outdoor dining table. There's no reason to leave the suite; you have everything you need right here. The view from the terrace takes your breath away – there are rows of buildings, the smell of seafood cooking makes my stomach growl, and in the far distance I see the dark water of the Mississippi river. All I can think is, *What a beautiful city, full of life and culture*. I could see myself visiting here more often but would never picture myself living anywhere outside New England.

There is a table spread of fruit, vegetables, cocktail shrimp and a dessert table nearby. I am suddenly starving, so I pick at the fruit.

"Grab a plate and come sit with me."

His bossy ways and dominance are attractive. I obey my master and sit beside him with a plate of fruit. He's removed his jacket and shoes. Both of his arms are resting on the top of the sofa and his feet are comfortably resting on the matching ottoman.

He gently grabs the plate of fruit from me and starts feeding me, one piece of fruit at a time. In between bites, he rubs his free hand on the back of my head, moving his fingers in a circular motion through my hair, turning me on. I'm no longer interested in the plate of fruit. I stand in front of him, grab the fruit and gently place it on the ottoman. I place my hands on the tops of his legs, grabbing a handful of his thighs while leaning in for a kiss. I bring myself to my knees kneeling in front of him. I unbutton and unzip his pants, pulling his penis from the hole of his boxes. He is fully erect. I'm not in the mood for sex, but I feel this will help get me get my way when the time comes to ask for favors. I place my cold lips over just the tip and begin dragging my tongue in a circular motion and occasionally pressing my tongue in the pee hole. I grab him with both my hands and start moving my head up and down, keeping my mouth around his penis. He grabs my hair and pulls gently. I can feel his excitement rise with his moaning and moving his hips. He is now pushing harder on my head to move my head in a faster motion. I can feel his penis pulsing as if he is about to explode. Then he stops my head moving, holding it so I can't take it out of my mouth. I feel it pulsing as the warm stickiness fills my throat. I gag but hold back the urge to throw up. I've never gagged with Johnny in my mouth because he's not as thick as Ruben, but they're similar in size. When he finally let's go of my head, I get up in a hurry, rushing to the bathroom and spitting into the sink and rinsing my mouth. I look up at myself in the mirror and Ruben is behind me.

"Just making sure you don't plan to keep any of that to harvest babies." He's smiling.

"I don't want kids, trust me I'm not the motherly type."

My thoughts scream out in my head: *Egotistic pigfucker. If he only knew I'm thinking of aborting the baby growing inside me.*

While he's cleaning up in the bathroom, I check my phone. Johnny has responded to my text. He wants to know where I am. I write back, *I'm safe don't worry* and put my phone away.

Ruben orders dinner without asking me what I want. I find that unattractive, but I'm not a picky eater, so I brush it off. We eat jambalaya, crawfish and steak on the outside terrace. The night would've been perfect were I not thinking of all the shit I need to handle back in Boston. I'm uncomfortable with the amount of cash, my house is a crime scene, Johnny is having a baby, my father is working with the Mob against me and all trying to build a defense without pissing off the Irish. I'm afraid to ask Ruben for cash to pay my lawyer. I'm hoping he just offers cash up like the first time we met. I know I don't have enough to pay for my lawyers, and Alterman made it clear he would not be paying.

At least I'm in the company of a rich, sexy man. Life isn't so bad now, if I keep my mind positive and try to remove my anxiety and negative inner monologue. I know I can depend on Paul and having one person is sometimes all you need. For now, I choose to live in the moment, fuck the trial and the Mob.

After dinner, Ruben says he must grab something from the concierge. He seems to be nervous and sneaking out for some reason. He likely needs to call his wife. I'm nuts, I make up these things in my head. I don't know for sure that he has a wife. I just have a feeling that he's hiding something.

I'm lying on my back smoking a cigarette when I hear the elevator ding and the doors open. I hear a heavy thud hit the floor. I lean over and put my cigarette out in the ashtray.

"Ruben, do you need help with anything?"

I get on my knees and lean over the back of the couch for a better view of the elevator. I hear mumbles and a gurgling noise. I see Ruben's leg sticking out from near the elevator. I immediately see two masked men turn the corner, charging towards me. I run to the bedroom and slam the door closed. There's nowhere for me to go. I reach for the phone, when the door is pushed open.

"Ava, it's me Johnny, put the damn phone down," one of the men says, ripping off his mask.

I'm relieved, but embarrassed that Johnny has found me with another man. I don't ask him why he's here because I already know he's here to take me back to Boston.

"Is this guy ya boyfriend?"

"He … he is someone I like."

"What the fuck does that mean?"

"Please don't hurt him, let's just go."

"How cute, Ava has a boyfriend. I'm sure Daddy will be happy to hear, considerin' I doubt he's Irish by the looks of him." He is pacing the floor looking down at his every step.

"If you hurt him, I will... I will hurt Casey."

He stops pacing and turns his head, looking at me.

"You're ah slut and a liar. Get ya shit and let's go before I shoot that bastard in the head."

I hurry around the hotel room gathering my things. I notice Ruben's wallet and take the cash and the bag of coke next to the lamp. I walk over to Ruben who has a gun to his head and his face to the ground. I say nothing, hoping this will prevent any further aggression from Johnny and his guys. Ruben starts to get up on one knee before the elevator doors close.

Johnny is holding my arm so tightly and pinching the back of my arm. I'm embarrassed and angry. On this trip, I have accomplished nothing, just made matters worse.

We pile into the SUV in the hotel garage.

Johnny's his usual angry, quiet self for the next hour. It's going to be a long drive back to Boston.

I take the coke out of my pocket, a mirror from my purse and a hundred-dollar bill I stole from Ruben. Maybe the coke will help me miscarry. Johnny looks at me in shock, but he's intrigued by the coke lines I draw up on the compact mirror. I snort a line and offer the mirror and a bill to Johnny without saying a word. He accepts. He hands it to the passenger who snorts two lines, his large nose sucking up both lines at once. The driver and the passenger look like twins, tall, skinny redheads with large noses that look like they have been broken once or twice before. The coke quickly changes the mood in the car. Johnny is chatting with his criminal twins, no one is really talking to me, but I don't give a shit. I'm happy because my high has kicked in, but still contemplating the injuries I could sustain from jumping out of this moving vehicle. I'm tired of running from problems I brought on myself.

After four hours of driving, we pull into a hotel parking lot. We all get out of the car and go into the motel and to our separate rooms. The rooms are directly across the hall from one another.

Johnny hasn't spoken to me directly, but now that we are alone in the hotel room, he will eventually break. Whenever I get Johnny alone, he's most vulnerable. He likes to act hard, cold when he his Mob buddies are around, but when we're alone, he's weak for me, I can have anything I want. His anger with me always subsides. He resets his mind, forgetting all my wrongdoing, and we start all over like we just met.

"I'm scared Johnny, scared of being killed. This wasn't the first time I was kidnapped and almost murdered. I saved myself from being thrown in the harbor with concrete chained to my feet." I can feel myself rushing my conversation. "In New Hampshire, I was thrown in the trunk of a car and duck taped to a chair in a motel. Johnny, someone wants me dead, and they won't stop until I'm gone."

I fall to my knees.

"Who wants me dead, please just tell me!" I yell.

Johnny sits on the bed, runs his hands through his hair over and over.

"Get off the floor."

"Do you blame me for running away?"

Johnny finally speaks. "Ya father is an important member of the Mob, one step from bein' in Claire's position; this is information ya shouldn't have kept from me. Ya father has never liked me and probably wishes he could break my legs."

"Johnny, I didn't know he was my father until I hired a private investigator."

"Ya hired a private investigator? Ya going to get us both killed. I've gravely underestimated ya and ya have underestimated your worth."

"It doesn't matter that Jimmy is my father because he still wants me to be a witness in the trial."

Johnny looks at me as if he doesn't believe what I'm saying. Maybe he's right, I may have overlooked that. He's acting strange and seems more anxious than usual.

"If the Irish wanted ya dead, it would have happened already. You are underestimatin' them. If I had to guess, Atlantic is behind the New Hampshire incident – and Jose's crew at the Harbor, whoever they are, they're either inexperienced or ya are just one lucky bitch."

Johnny walks behind me and hugs me and kisses my neck. He whispers in my ear, "I'm glad yah okay, but shocked at your choice in boyfriends. He hardly looks Irish; yah father will wish ya stayed with me."

Johnny knows he cannot be too mad, maybe jealous, but not mad. He has his pregnant girlfriend.

He spins me around so I'm facing him. He kisses me hard, holding my face in his hands. While we are embraced in a kiss, someone knocks on the door.

Johnny grabs his gun and tells me to get in the bathroom. He peeks through the door.

"What do you want?" Johnny yells through the door.

"I want to make sure Ava's okay; I don't want any trouble with you or your men."

I know that voice anywhere.

"Johnny it's Ruben, just let him in, so he can see I am okay."

Johnny hesitates, but opens the door.

Ruben doesn't enter until I ask him to.

"I need to have a word alone with Ava," demands Ruben.

"Fuck you, just have your words here with me in the room."

"How can I really know she is okay with you standing here?"

Ruben gets in Johnny's face and they stare at each other for an uncomfortable time. I'm holding Johnny's right arm, not that I could stop him from breaking Ruben's face or worse, shooting him dead.

"I should've killed ya when I had the chance. I'll give ya two lovebirds some alone time."

Johnny goes into the hallway and knocks on the twin's door.

"Ava, you haven't been forthcoming with me, but I'm not here to judge the skeletons in your closet, I'm just as guilty keeping things from you."

I try to speak, but it's clear he's not done talking.

"I had my men follow you because I wanted to make sure you're okay."

Ruben leans down and pushes the loose hair behind my ear.

"I'm okay, I promise, I don't have enough time to explain everything, but I ran from Boston to avoid some trouble from my past."

"And this is your boyfriend?"

"He is not my…"

"It's okay, you don't have to explain. How can I help you out of your trouble?"

This is my opportunity to ask him for money.

"I need to pay a lawyer, then I should be free from any jail time."

"Give me your lawyer's information and I will personally make sure he's paid."

I rummage through my purse for the cryptic note from Mr. Alterman. I write the information on the hotel room's note paper.

Ruben puts the note in his pocket and locks the hotel door quietly so as not to alert Johnny. He drops his pants and sits in the chair. Then pulls my pants and underwear down around my ankles, so one pant leg is out. He grabs me by the ass and pushes me to down on his condom-less erection. I ride him slowly, teasing him, allowing the tip of him to almost come out of me before pushing back down on top. He comes before I can get the chance, but it's exciting to ride him with Johnny outside the door. We clean up in the bathroom and smoke a cigarette before Ruben leaves. He assures me that he will reach out to my lawyer today and pay all the fees up front. This is the major difference between Johnny and Ruben.

Johnny returns to the room in a shitty mood. I'm too tired to pay him any attention. I lay on the bed, staring at the popcorn ceiling, smoking a joint.

I awake to one strip of sunlight shining through the opening of dingy floral vertical blinds. I put my arms behind my head and turn over to see Johnny laying on his stomach. His hair is getting long, it's covering his entire face. His biceps have grown since the last time we were together. I want to wake him for morning sex, but don't feel sexy. If I can catch a shower before he wakes, he won't bother trying to have sex.

I sit on the toilet smoking a joint while the shower water warms up. Johnny really doesn't care where he sleeps. He always picks motels over hotels. It's really a turn off. He chooses the biggest shitholes.

My mind has convinced me last night was a dream and Ruben never showed up like a Prince and offered to take care of my lawyer's fees. I almost want to ask Johnny if it is real. It's probably all the drugs I've been doing. I text Mr. Alterman asking him to reach out to the lawyer to ask if he received the payment. Without Ruben paying for the lawyer and Mr. Alterman doing me this favor, I'll be fucked. Mr. Alterman is not doing all this for nothing, and I need to know what's in it for him. That's at the bottom of my list of things to do. I also need to deal with my roommate's murder. Let's hope Ruben makes the payment in time for me to contact my lawyer before I get back to Boston. My lawyer will instruct me on how I should proceed.

MR. ALTERMAN

CHAPTER 30

RANCH

Wilson's ranch sits on over 100 acres of Texas farmland just outside of Waco, TX. His driveway alone is at least a mile long and today my drive feels longer; maybe it's because of my excitement to see my old friend. The tires kick up dust making it near impossible to see more than a foot in front of me. The driveway is barely wide enough for one car at a time and forget about trying to pull over if a car is coming in the opposite direction. The fences run on both sides leaving no room. If another car is driving in the opposite direction, one of the vehicles would need to reverse backwards. It's happened to me on several of my visits.

Waylon is not your typical criminal attorney; he gets down and dirty and only chooses to represent cases that he finds interesting. People will pay him just for advice. He's practically retired but makes time for friends even if they come to him for business. I met Waylon in college when he was studying to be an attorney and I was studying criminal justice. I wanted to be a detective. He practiced in Boston for many years before going country on me and moving to Texas. He was tired of the corrupt judges, and I can't blame him; Boston is a politically corrupt city. He lost his passion for being a lawyer. His practicing license almost got taken away from him permanently when he beat the shit out of one of the judges in a parking garage. Waylon was tired of this judge scheming the system. He was putting away the innocent, so gang members could be free to walk. I admit I too was tired of seeing these sorts of things, but I didn't have the balls to stand up to them like Waylon. After this incident he decided it was time for him to move on, but we always stayed in touch. He lent me his ear when I wanted to complain about my boss and other detectives. We are both old men now, overweight, gray haired and balding.

I pull up to his modest one-story white farmhouse with a full wrap-around porch. Waylon and his wife Carol are sitting in their matching rocking chairs with the dogs lying lazily at their feet. Never far from his side is his rifle and his wife's shotgun. Carol is a true Texan, very familiar and comfortable with guns, but her love is the double-barrel shotgun. She likes that one shot is all you need.

My friend is looking old, but his wife doesn't look a day older. Waylon takes credit for his wife's ageless beauty. He jokes with her that he bottles up all the stress, so she can live carefree. Carol always responds with "My love for animals and nature keep me looking young, not this old man".

Waylon has since trimmed his salt and pepper beard. He's

wearing a cowboy hat, leather boots to match, and a white t-shirt with suspenders and jeans. He dresses the same each time I see him, until of course he has his day in court, then he cleans up real nice.

Waylon assures me over the phone that Ava paid him handsomely for his time, more than what was due upfront. The cash was wired over by a man named Ruben with no last name.

I decided to take the trip not only to see my friend but to help him with Ava's case. I want him to know who he can and cannot piss off in Boston.

Ava continues to play the victim, but I know she must be getting her hands dirty because why else would someone attempt to kill her twice and how much bad luck can one person even have? At first the news stations were all over the story about her abduction, "The Girl Found in the Harbor", but just like that, not 24 hours later, no more news on it. Waylon and I know the media can easily be paid off by someone – it's an all too familiar tactic. The rumors from a few of my informants say the Italians put a hit out on Ava and the Irish cleaned up the media mess. The other rumor is the Irish put out the hit and are trying to cover it up by spreading rumors it was the Italians. A lot of missing bodies have been washing upon the shores of South Boston beaches and along the Charles River banks, all of which happen to be of Irish descent. Now either we are back to the era of the Irish killing the Irish or the Italians are back to fighting over control.

"I thought I smelled bagels and lox. Get over here and give your friend a hug, your old Jewish bastard."

"Woo Eh, you smell like pig balls and cow shit," I reply.

"Can you boys cut that out, be nice to one another," Carol chimes in.

Waylon lifts me up, gives me a tight bear hug. He's put on a lot of weight since the last time I saw him but looks happy.

I hug Carol gently. She's a petite, frail woman with long black hair with silver strands peeking through. She always has a lit cigarette in her hand and another one sitting in the ashtray ready to light up.

"Good to see you, Alterman. Would you like some iced tea, just brewed?" she asks.

"Yes, and spice it up for me." By spice I mean alcohol, but she already knows how I like my iced tea.

I take Carol's seat next to Waylon. The view from their porch is endless fields full of neat farmed rows of crops and randomly placed farm equipment. There's a horse barn to the far right of the land. Waylon isn't big on farm animals, but he can't say no to Carol. In fact, every time I visit, Carol walks me around the land to show me all her animals, and there's most always a new animal to show off.

Carol brings me a glass of tea and sets the pitcher nearby. The glass is filled to the rim with ice. It's so cold and refreshing in this dry Texas heat, I drink the entire glass in one gulp. I pour another glass for myself, offer to fill Waylon's glass. She goes back in the house; law talk isn't of any interest to her.

"I know you didn't fly to Texas for my wife's famous tea. Let's get to talking about Ms. Madden's case. There's a lot of holes in the story you must explain. Like, why in the hell are you helping this young lady?" Waylon looks concerned.

"Simple; Ava is connected with someone who inadvertently

ruined my police career and so many of my friends."

"And, who is this person?"

"Jesus, Waylon, let me finish. When I was young, I dreamed of being a cop, catching the bad guys and being a hero. I went from fighting crime, to solving murders, to being forced to retire from a job I loved and losing my friends. Admittedly, I was scared for my life, a damn coward. When everything went to shit in Boston, I did what I was told, kept my mouth shut, never spoke to my colleagues again, and left Boston. I'm not the man I set out to be. I'm a lonely old man with a severe booze problem. I don't have much more time; I mean, I'm not sick, but I feel that if I must live this hell, I created any longer, I'll want to kill myself. I'm just not willing to leave this earth without taking down the very people that destroyed my happiness."

My elbows are leaning on my knees, my head slouched between my legs. I'm doing that thing where I feel sorry for myself.

Waylon gets out of his chair and stands in front of me silently. I look up at him expecting to see his familiar disappointed frown, but his face is hidden behind the shadow from his cowboy hat.

"Blaming others about your troubles is a symptom of narcissism. My father always reminded me that if a fool listens to your problems and feels bad for you, that fool is no friend. And I don't feel bad for you. Get your ass out of that chair and bring yourself inside. We have a trial to prepare, but first we need to eat lunch."

I grab the empty pitcher of iced tea and my glass and follow him into the house. Carol refills the pitcher. I take a seat on the couch and look in the reflection of the television, admiring the way Waylon helps Carol set the dining table. I'm staring at the reflection of true love. That could have been me, but I'm too much of a coward. The only woman that every loved me ran from me the first chance she got, and when I returned it was too late, she had moved on. I was selfish to think she would have waited for me.

"Boy, the food is getting cold, stop your daydreaming and come get a plate."

Mashed potatoes, corn on the cob, greens, steak tips, biscuits, and more of Carol's iced tea. I can see how Waylon has put on so much weight.

"Carol, this looks and smells amazing, thank you for cooking."

"It's never trouble for a good friend. I don't cook for many, so you count this as a blessing."

"This may be the best meal I've had in sometime."

While we eat, Carol tells us stories of her animals on the farm. I don't chime in much because I'm too busy shoveling the food in my mouth. My train of thought is interrupted when my phone beeps. It's a text from Ava. Johnny found her and is taking her back to Boston. She asks if she should try to run.

"Waylon, it's Ava, she was found, and they're returning her to Boston. She wants to know if she should go with them."

"Yes, she should return. Tell her to go right to the police station to turn herself in. They will want a statement about her roommate's murder. Tell her to answer questions, until she feels the questions become accusatory, which they will, we both know that. She then should lawyer up. We should be in Boston in a few weeks before the trial."

I text her Waylon's advice. She agrees to the plan.

After lunch, we lounge in Waylon's oversized office, and drink whiskey straight up and smoke cigars.

Waylon has already started working out the details of the trial by filling out two large white boards with all the key players in the trial, and others that don't seem to fit in. I explain in detail who everyone is, and their role.

"Ava disclosed that she was stealing money directly from Atlantic accounts, and without allegedly tapping into any of the Irish funds. She has proof this was transpiring right under Susan and Johnny's management. She hopes this information will influence the Mob's lawyers to settle for a plea deal for Susan and not try to push her to take the blame," I explain.

"I'm not following."

"It's my understanding her angle is to prove Susan's mistakes were the direct cause of the FBI investigating Atlantic laundering money, that she didn't even notice Ava was skimming from Atlantic's funds. Her hopes are the Irish will see her potential and make a deal with them instead of going to jail."

"As her Attorney, I don't see a better way? After reading through the documents sent over by the Law Office of Dillon and Associates, they are trying to make it look like they are helping Ava. They want her to stand trial and admit to some wrongdoing to accounting errors to lessen Susan's jail time or get her off completely. Ava can't admit to the FBI that she knew about the laundering, because that will guarantee her jail time. For all we know the Mob has evidence that Ava knowingly accepted laundered cash in accounts."

"Waylon, is there a way to get more information from them, like hack the lawyers? I mean Ava knows someone that can do that, if she hasn't done it already."

"We need to focus on the facts of the case. It's fun to talk about the what if's, but we are not at that point and furthermore, hacked information wouldn't stand up as evidence in court because, as you know, it's illegal. The FBI obviously have enough for a conviction against Susan, since she is still sitting in jail. We need to get inside information on the FBI. I assume the Mob's lawyers are hiding that information. It really is up to Ava to figure out what plan she wants to go with, and I will build a case around that. Right now, this looks like a big pile of shit that no shovel in my barn can tackle."

"You're right, this is Ava's decision."

"In the end, maybe we will fuck those Boston mobsters after all, and if we can pull this off, we old men still got some tricks left."

"Watch your mouth, Waylon," Carol yells from the other room.

Waylon pours two more glasses of whiskey and we click our glasses together. This motion seals the deal. Waylon has that old look in his eyes, like when he was an attorney in Boston. He's just as excited as me to take on Boston's criminal world one final time.

JIMMY

CHAPTER 31

RACE

"I found Ava with some black guy in a New Orleans hotel," Johnny says.

"Ouch, someone is jealous. Who cares that tha guys black? Aren't ya a little too young to be racist? I mean I know you are half Italian and ya all have a history of hatred towards the blacks, but damn."

"Fuck you, Jimmy, if anyone's racist it's you, pig."

"Me? Oh Johnny, ya have me all wrong. I'm a church goin' man now, God's people love all his creations."

"You're such an asshole and ya daughter's a slut."

"Well, I can't argue with you on that, if she is anything like her mothah."

"That's nice, ya know Ava's mother's dead, don't ya?"

"Her adoptive mothah is dead, her real mothah is alive, and she's a whore.

"Anyway, I called to let ya know I'm bringing Ava home. Is her house still a crime scene?"

"No, the Indian and White Man cleaned it up, changed out the furniture, painted the walls. The police still want to question Ava; they have no suspect. The detectives have been to the house several times. Ava told me ya robbed and murdered her roommate's ex-boyfriend. I think his name is Jose. Ya don't think that has anything to do with her roommate's murder, do ya?"

"Ava didn't tell you shit. The Dominicans used Ava as a drug mule to traffic drugs from the Dominican Republic to Boston. Jose is the ex-boyfriend of Ava's roommate. Anyway, I interjected the drug drop in New York and went straight to pay those motherfuckers a visit, and you know the rest. It's part of my job to stop drugs coming into Boston that are not the Mob's dealings. I brought the drugs to the Mob and gave Ava the money Jose promised for drug muling. The Mob runs this city, and I can't willingly allow those transactions to come through."

"Boy, Ava has ya for a fool. Just make sure she gets back here safe."

"Relax old man, I ain't gonna harm her."

"Ya, bettah text me as soon as she's home."

"I will, and don't evah call me a racist. Not all Italians are, ya know."

"Ya, ya. Oh, and just so ya know, I was the one who told Ava Casey was pregnant. Ya welcome. And do me a favor, tell ya fuckin' fathah to return my calls."

Nothing but silence on the other line.

"You son of a…"

I hang up on Johnny, just to piss him off a little more. I

love fucking with him. I don't really care that he's with Ava, Christ, I don't want to hear about my daughter's relationships. She's obviously using him, and he's just too dumb to realize. I have more important things on my mind. Like the two fuckers that tried to drown my daughter. It wasn't difficult to find out who they were. I tracked the boat they used, thanks to Connor McClean. It was rented in Gloucester, about a 90-minute boat ride to the Boston Harbor. The kidnappers must be amateurs because my daughter is still alive. I know just about everyone who owns a boat docked in Boston, so I eliminated them fast. The type of rope that was found tied around Ava's ankles is used by local fisherman. Who rents a fucking fishing boat to kill someone? What a bunch of idiots. If it was me, I would have stolen the boat, and not a damn fishing boat. I can't eliminate the Mafia or the Irish, but I know whoever it was they outsourced the job on purpose and didn't want it to come back to them. This was the second attempted murder of my daughter. The men that kidnapped her in New Hampshire were also amateurs. I assume she's stolen a lot of money or has something she can use against them.

She's a smart girl, I know from seeing her report cards, SAT scores and college grades. Just because I wasn't physically in Ava's life, doesn't mean I didn't hear all about her progress and big events. My agreement with Mary was for her to mail me letters and photos of Ava to keep me updated. I thought about my daughter every day, and regret giving her to Mary to be raised, but I was selfish. I chose the Mob over my daughter. I had to, I'm a killer. I was afraid if I got too mad or frustrated, I could kill her. Now looking back, it's a stupid thought. To think I could kill my own daughter. It's my mind playing tricks. That's why I write stuff down to make sure it's real because my mind thinks of the craziest shit. Likely schizophrenia. I mean no doctor has ever diagnosed me, but I read a lot, and the symptoms check out.

When Mary began dating Lewis Lorcan, I wasn't onboard at first because I was scared, he would molest her. Stepfathers have a bad rap for this behavior. The truth was I was just jealous of Lewis. I wished I was Lewis.

I surveilled the home and saw Lewis outside in the backyard teaching her how to ride a tricycle. Mary admired them from the porch. Ava never looked so happy. I've never witnessed such a happy family moment, that I wanted to be a part of. Never in my life have I regretted anything, and in that very moment I felt regret. I wanted to do it all over. I wish I'd stayed in Ireland and raised Ava myself. I wanted to run into the backyard and take my daughter, but I knew Ava would miss out on a happy home, something I didn't know how to maintain. The regret helps me pick up another bottle, the sadness makes me pour another glass, and the pain drives me to another bar or liquor store. I lie to myself every morning when I wake up and say I will not drink today.

I gave Ava to Mary to keep her safe, so she could live a normal life and now it all seems for nothing. I'm afraid that after this trial, the Mob will want her dead anyway, no matter how good the trial goes. She knows too much about the Mob. They wouldn't kill her if they knew she was my daughter. Johnny, the Indian and the White Man know, and whoever Ava told. The more people who know the more danger both of us are in.

I may have enemies on every street in Boston. I've murdered

so many people, I've lost count. I used to keep count in the beginning but writing this information down anywhere is risky and if caught I wouldn't want to be categorized as a serial killer, so I refrained from keeping items from those I've murdered. That's how most of them get caught. I prefer to be labeled a hitman, and a damn good one. I dress up for every planned hit, some are unexpected, but when I have time to plan, I wear a suit. Others think it's strange, but I respect the victim. Let them have a nice-looking man kill them. Also, I find humor in the way most people trust me simply because I'm wearing a suit, and this includes the police.

I wear my trench coat to better conceal my rifle. I've hidden a knife in each boot, a double gun holster to carry my two handguns, plastic tie wraps and duct tape. I look back in the mirror. I look so goddamn handsome. After I handle business, I will get a nice lay from one lucky lady tonight. I just hope I don't get blood on my white undershirt. I grab my keys and head to the North Shore to pay a visit to my daughter's killers. Their day job is running a construction business, and apparently, they're working late tonight in the office. If they weren't at work, I'd go to their homes and kill them and their entire family.

I turn off my car headlights and drive slowly down the dirt road. The office lights are still on, and their vehicles are parked out front. I know everything about them, because I've wasted my days doing a full week of surveillance. There's another vehicle in the driveway, one I've never seen. This could bring some trouble, but mostly for the sorry son of a bitch who owns the car. I hang out in the car for a little while to see if any more people are coming or going into the building. I use my night vision goggles on the scope of my rifle to check the surrounding area. This scope is unique because it takes pictures and video. I take photos of the car and a closeup on the license plate of the unknown vehicle.

An hour later, a man walks out the front door. I take multiple photos of this guy. I don't know him, but I can easily find out this information another time. Nothing is going to stop me from killing these men tonight. I wait thirty minutes before I enter the back door, which is always left unlocked by their lazy staff. Up the two flights of stairs, through a second unlocked door. It's eerie to get into the building that easily; I get a bad feeling but brush it off.

The hall leading to their office is dark and only lit by the light coming out of the main office where they should be working.

"Knock, knock," I say.

The men don't stand, just look up at me, as if they were expecting me. My immediate instinct is someone else is in the building, so I exit the room and duck into a nearby room and wait. The room is so dark, someone else could be in the room and I wouldn't know. I'm too old for these games. It was much easier to kill people in the old days. I'm sure that their friend in the car didn't really leave and instead hid out; probably drove his car down the street and came back on foot.

"You better get the fuck out of here before you end up dead, old man," a voice yells from the other room.

I keep quiet. If I respond they'll know what room I'm in.

I could probably kill them by shooting through this office wall, but they don't deserve a quick death. I hear the floor creak; that must be the surprise they were planning. I'm holding both handguns. What they don't know is I can stand in this room all night; this isn't my first time. I've got a talent for keeping still and quiet. I've spent many nights standing in closets waiting for my victims to get home.

The sound of footsteps gets closer, and they are so close I can hear their fast, heavy breathing. A sign this person is nervous, and inexperienced. He's likely a larger fella by the sound of his heavy footsteps. I hear him stop in the doorway before opening the door. I switch the light on in the room. Before they can unload their gun into me, one of my guns is pressed between the eyes of this unlucky soul. With my other hand I smack his gun out of his hand, likely breaking his wrist from the blunt force.

"You unlucky son of a bitch. Do you know who I am?" I yell so the others can hear me clearly.

"No," the man gulps.

"You motherfuckers listen. I'm Jimmy 'The Coroner' Coonan. Mob's one and only psychotic hitman, and you are?"

"I... Stan," he stutters.

"I, Stan, that's a strange name. I think you mean Stan. Stan, you just tried to kill me, so that means...?"

I wait for Stan's answer.

"I'm dead," Stan replies.

"Well, that depends if you tell me the truth."

Holding Stan by the back of his neck I walk him into the room with the other men. I push Stan into the doorway of the room. Gun fire erupts, Stan is shot several times and takes off down the hallway limping. I let him get away for now, because I know he'll probably pass out from the look of his wounds.

I let them continue to fire their guns, and when I hear nothing

I peek into the room. One is attempting to reload his gun. I shoot the inside of his wrist, and his gun falls to the ground. The other man is nervously holding a gun pointed at me. He would've shot already if it was loaded.

"Drop your weapon and walk towards me," I say to both men.

They hesitate but do as I say.

"Get on your knees."

"Jimmy, please, you remember me," one of them says, holding his wounded hand.

"I don't know you, boy."

"It's Bobby, I used to work at Mr. Cormick's restaurant in the North End. Every Friday you came to the restaurant to get a pastrami sandwich with extra mustard."

"Mr. Cormick's restaurant had the best pastrami sandwich in Boston, and you always made it just perfect. I'm sorry boy, I don't recognize you as a grown man. Who's your friend?"

"That's Larry, my cousin."

I pull up a chair behind them since they are facing the door. I can't put my back to an open door just in case Stan decides to save his friends. With the gun still pointed at them, I use my free hand to grab a cigarette. I take a few drags staring at the back of their heads. Contemplate blowing their heads off at that moment. I confirm they are my daughters' kidnappers.

"Who paid you to hit Ava Madden?"

Nothing but silence from them both. I can hear their hearts beat faster and can see their breathing pace increase.

I shoot Larry's left ear off. He screams then drops on the ground, grabbing the hole where his ear used to be.

"Sean Cormick, he ... put a hit on Ava for $100,000. He said she stole money from him." Larry hides his head in his arms.

Stole money from Johnny's father? This doesn't make sense.

"How did Ava steal money?"

"I think … um, something about a company she worked for."

I've heard enough.

"Get up and start walking."

"Oh, my god he's going to kill us Bobby." Larry is sobbing like a child.

"Jimmy, please let us go, we will kill Mr. Cormick for you. It's his fault, plus Ava is safe, she didn't die."

"Shut your bastard mouths," I yell.

We walk through the warehouse following Stan's blood drops outside next to his car. Looks like he's passed out from the blood loss.

I kick him in his side.

"Get up, Stan – we're bringing you to the hospital."

He wakes up, scared and slowly rises to his feet.

"Walk with them."

I bring them to the back of the warehouse where I left the cement truck running before I entered the building. It should be ready to pour any minute.

"Turn around and line up," I instruct them.

I tie their hands behind them, attaching the rope to all three men. I wrap duct tape around their mouths, all around their heads. This will keep them from calling for help, not that they are remotely close to any residential homes, just businesses that will probably not reopen until Tuesday morning – most businesses are closed the day after St. Patrick's Day.

"Get in the bed of the truck."

I see the fear build in their eyes; they know they're going to die.

"Sit."

They sit with their backs to the bed of the truck. I take a rope and tie them to the truck, so they can't move.

I tie a rope across their chests and lean them against the wall bed of the truck, closest to the back window.

"You're probably wondering why I'm here, how I found you, and what will happen next? Ava Madden, who you kidnapped, tied up, and tried to drown in Boston Harbor is my daughtah. Of course, I don't expect you to know that because it's been a secret. I guess the old saying, 'What you don't know won't hurt you' is a lie."

Danny and Larry are crying, but Stan just glares angrily into my eyes, like he's prepared to die.

"I'm going to hop in this truck and pour cement to cover the bottom half of your torsos. Do you boys know how long it takes to set?"

I pause as if expecting them to answer with their mouths bound with duct tape.

I raise my hand. "I know: it takes 24 hours give or take, so I suggest you boys put your heads together and try to get loose and out of this truck. You're all probably curious why I don't fill it up to the top. Well, I want you to panic just as my daughter did when she was drowning, her hands bound behind her back, struggling to swim to safety in the dark cold harbor, unsure what direction to swim.

"Larry, STOP your sobbing and listen with that one ear. Have either of you heard of Tycho Brahe, a scientist from the 16th century? He was a strange man who had a silver or gold nose, I can't remember which or how he lost his nose, anyway, doesn't matter. It's how he died that is fascinating. His bladder burst from not relieving himself. Such a strange way to die for an intelligent person. The story goes along the lines of this. He was attending a banquet and didn't leave to relieve himself, got home and couldn't piss, and sometime later he died when his bladder exploded. That can happen to you if this cement sets and you don't urinate or pass a bowel movement. A bladder takes just ten hours to fill, that's on average 1,500 ml of urine. Not to mention your bowels; shit can back up in your system and the shit can literally come out of your mouth."

I laugh in their faces.

"Now that you have all the information you need, let's get this party started, shall we?"

I climb in the truck, and hit the lever to begin the pour, hopping back out of the truck to make sure it fills just past their waists. When the pour reaches the right height, I shut off the truck.

"Well boys, it's been a pleasure meeting you all, and I hope God chooses to give you the strength to get out of your harrowing situation and saves your souls. Well, go on, try to get loose, don't wait on my behalf."

I walk away listening to them swoosh their legs around in the cement. They will soon tire themselves out because there is no possible way, they will be untying a double fisherman's knot, unless they cut it, but that won't happen. Also, I know there is only a two percent chance their bladders will burst, because Tycho Brache likely died from infection, not his bladder erupting. Larry and Stan will probably bleed to death from their gunshot wounds. Danny could survive, but likely won't because once the cement hardens it will cut off circulation below his torso, killing him. I can't wait to hear about the outcome in the newspapers. Before I leave, I take all their video footage, computers, and the small safe in the office. I check myself in the bathroom mirror, not a spot of blood on my suit. This calls for a night out at the bar, and some lucky whore will have her opportunity to take me home tonight.

PAUL

CHAPTER 32

ADIOS

It was effortless picking up my life and leaving Boston without a trace. My hacking capabilities have outclassed any FBI specialist, software developers who work for the most prestigious technology establishments, politicians, or any hackers I've met on the dark web. Anyone can be a hacker; all they need to learn is how to program a computer and be secretive. Not everyone can keep a secret. Inexperienced hackers brag about their riches online. They become overly confident fast, and poof they vanish without a trace, never to be found in the dark web again. The majority of hackers are killed because they brag in chat rooms to others. Inexperienced attributors brag online which puts a price tag on their head. If other hackers can find you, and physically get access to your computer, they will drain your funds – and sometimes, even with all the money at stake, they hire a killer online faster than ordering a pizza. It's a simple ten minutes, and several murderers will offer their services. Especially criminals that know they're going to jail on different charges anyway; they may kill just to have money for commissary. It's a dangerous place to play when you are new to hacking. You can never be too sure who you are talking to online. I'm constantly quizzing my other hacking buddies just to make sure I'm chatting with the right person.

There are places you can walk into to hire services you can only find on the dark web. These people are called internet bookies. You tell them what you need, they request payment for your service plus a twenty percent service fee, cash only of course, and the bookie will put your order in on the dark web.

I still refer to myself as a hacker, or that I'm hacking, but once you graduate from tinkering around on the dark web and cross over into hacking for malicious reasons, you are no longer referred to as a hacker, but rather a cracker – or instead of hacking, you're cracking. What a strange word. It's quite possible I'm the best at what I do unless I'm put against a full team of hackers. That's really a disadvantage but still I'd like to think I could succeed. When other hackers find out how good you are, they want your help solving their own puzzles. The most common service request I receive is for assistance getting through the backdoor of a website. When you go through the front door, you are entering with a username and password, but the front door is a bore, and limited.

Recently, I've been getting multiple "chore" requests; what the dark web defines as a job offer. I have so much money that I choose only the high rolling chore requests. The money we skimmed from Atlantic is enough for both of us to live lavish lifestyles and stay off the grid for the rest of our lives. Ava and I are greedy; we both want ultimate power to control our surroundings, and we must have the money to make it happen.

I do feel homesick here in the Dominican Republic. There are only so many men I can sleep with to comfort my need to feel loved. It's Ava I miss. I'm in love with her. Even if she did kill Thomas, I feel I need her in my life. If Ava was a man, I would dive into a relationship with her or at least try. I believe we are soulmates. I would do anything she asked. She's the first person I came out to as gay. Her response? "I know, I love you, and I don't care." That night she cuddled me a little tighter and closer than ever before. She made me feel like being gay didn't matter. That's how much of a good friend she is. She's the only person I love and that loves me back. I hate that I left her to clean up the mess, but I don't blame her for killing him – he was an asshole and rapist. I feel bad leaving her behind in Boston with all those dangerous people following her, trying to kill her, and now her father's popped up. I express all the time how much I don't trust

Johnny or her father. I just hope I'm right when I think she's capable of handling herself.

I miss my cat and regret not taking her along. I got attached to the fluffy creature. I tried not to because I used my cat to test a new military tracking device. The military has been testing this new technology on their enemies for years and finally the device was beginning to make progress. I purchased several testers from a biohacker, a real mad scientist. This tracking device is practically invisible to the naked eye. It's as thin as a sticker, a quarter of the size of your pinky fingernail. It is programmable to connect to the home host DNA, but once it gets the taste of a new DNA it is programmed to disengage with is home host. When you want to track someone, you stick it on the palm of your hand or tips of your fingers, and when you shake their hand or touch them, the tiniest needle fiber attaches to their skin pulling away from their host. It absorbs under the skin of its new host, so it's no longer visible to the human eye. Once this bug is imbedded, it logs into the nearest Wi-Fi network and sends messages to the home host. And just like that you are tracking the individual's every move; although they're still working out the side effects, and they are at about seventy-five percent success rate for transfers to host. Recent military reports I found on the web show that the longest time the bug has lived on a host is for about a month. I tested this device on my cat, and a few times on myself. It feels like a static shock when it attaches itself, but not enough to be suspicious. I can still track my cat – she's either with her new adoptive family on Ava's street or she's just living outside.

I decide to forgive Ava and assist her with her trial and any monetary purchases, since I oversee her funds from the Atlantic job. I need to take care of myself first, or I'll be useless to Ava. Before the Mac incident, we both agreed on telling the Irish she was skimming from Atlantic, leaving me completely out of the picture. Even though she doesn't want to admit any wrongdoing altogether, they need to know the Irish accounts were not touched; maybe the Italians' funds, but that's not where she wants them to home in on. This was the only way to get their attention before the trial. They'll want more information about the how's: How did you do it, how much did you skim and how did we not catch you? We hope this will give her a get out of jail free card. However, if Ava isn't indicted on charges, the FBI will demand someone be charged in her place. Ava wants to put Johnny in her place, he's the only one that makes the most sense since he worked directly under Susan. We're predicting the Irish will be angry with Johnny because Ava was able to skim funds right under his nose. He wouldn't fight the decision because he cannot undermine Claire.

A man that has everything to lose is the most fearful. Johnny's fiancé is about to give birth to his first child, so I assume he will play nice to keep his new family safe. Ava claims she truly loves Johnny and I have witnessed her obsess over him but can't understand how she can throw him in jail when he is having a child. Sure, I understand she's just thinking of herself, but if you truly care for someone you wouldn't want them behind bars. I'm not judging, but maybe she's upset that Casey's pregnant.

Ava made a promise to me that I would remain anonymous, and I trust she will not break that promise because if she does, I'll have to rat on her about killing Mac. Her laptop recorded the entire event; I installed a live video feed on her laptop before I gave it to her. I have proof that she killed him, so if presented with this data, she won't try me.

This FBI investigation into Atlantic has screwed up our opportunity to take the biggest paycheck home in hacking history. Atlantic has so much money that I bet they wouldn't even have noticed a billion dollars missing. There is nothing better than getting someone inside a company to assist with hacking. Plugging into their office computers is like playing yourself at a card game. The guarantee to win is right there, no doubts.

Not to mention the bonus you take home from selling Atlantic's financial stock purchases and sales. Financial analysts get a hard-on learning inside information because it gives them the psychic ability to predict the market to know the right times to buy and sell stocks. Who doesn't want to be a fortune teller for a day?

I feel one can never be too careful when you're a criminal hacker. Any documents or emails I send to anyone I automatically delete. This is hacker 101, but sometimes in the dark web, hackers get lazy and comfortable. They think they're safe and the next thing you know, you never hear from them again. I assume they're dead because hacking is more addictive than heroin. If you have a successful hack, it's impossible to not return to the scene of the crime, just as a murderer likes to visit the murder site or keep a souvenir from the kill. Most people refer to the hacking world as the dark web, and it's fitting because a lot of dark shit happens.

Picture the internet as a body of water. On top of the water the boats that float are the search engines that everyday people use. If you go snorkeling, you're safely floating on top of the water looking down – those snorkeling are the more intelligent people that can use the web to find some leaked government or company information available to the public; stuff that takes some digging to find. Now, if you go diving in that same body of water, you are encroaching on new discoveries, things you've never seen; new fish are discovered. This is the part of the ocean the government controls, but just below the non-diveable depths of the internet are sharks, and you need special equipment to safely dive that deep down. It takes serious money to get that far down in the water of the dark web.

When I enter the dark web, I can be in there for a full day, and it can feel like just hours, like a gambler in a casino – it's as if oxygen keeps pumping into the room to keep the gambler playing tables. The dark web has so many windows that you can get lost, and not know how to get back to where you began without starting over. Sometimes I just need to x out of everything and shut down my computer because too many windows keep popping open, dragging you in deeper. I have developed several software prototypes to block the things I don't want to see on the dark web. The first popup blocker I developed was to block child porn. It utterly disgusts me, and in the beginning, like every rookie hacker, I thought I could take down all the porn sites and save the children and the world. It's like a cop, fighting never-ending crime, but never, never will there be enough cops to keep up with the corruption, just as there will never be enough hackers to take down all the child porn sites. As soon as you shut down a porn site, a new one pops up.

I can name several extremely powerful people in this world, who do not believe in God, but rather believe they are God themselves. These people are dangerous, fear nothing, and do as they want, pleasuring themselves with fantasies sane people would never even consider. Imagine being able to buy any fantasy you want. If your fantasy is to kill someone, kidnap a child, turn the power off in a city, cause plane crashes, rob a bank, anything - all you need is the right amount of money.

The dark web has its own currency called HSAC: cash spelled backwards. The exchange rate means $1.00 HSAC currency equals just $0.10 in US dollars. HSAC has increasingly become run like a corporate banking system; their fees have increased twice in the last year. I've been working on setting up a similar banking system to HSAC, another place to safely store online funds, but I charge just $ 0.01 cent. I don't profit, I just need to charge something to make it a valid transaction. I started by only offering this to certain hacker friends, but then it spread to their friends and before I knew it, it spread like a wildfire. The more hackers that can trust me on the dark web, the more protection and power I accumulate. It's all about building trust.

I have never taken a job from another hacker friend; if I know they're working on a job, I avoid bidding on that job. Others don't play by the hacking rules, but I choose to show respect. Things went south when I moved my funds from HSAC to my new banking system. HSAC threatened my life and before I knew it, people were following me. The HSAC wants to monopolize banking on the dark web, but they can't, and I think I have made them realize it, along with my hacker friends. I didn't do it alone. Now that all my funds are safely stored and out of the hands of HSAC, I'm no longer concerned about losing my fortune, but it's never enough. You can't put all your eggs in one basket.

I've set up a charity for the school Ava visited, to help build a kitchen and cafeteria. The bank regulations are a joke in this country. This is my own little paradise. Endless nice-looking men, and easy hacking opportunities right here at the resort. Every vacationer is using the resort's free public Wi-Fi. I even bribe the concierge to give me the password to the non-public Wi-Fi. The first rule is to never use public Wi-Fi, particularly while doing banking business or purchases. These rich folks are so careless, especially while on vacation. I doubt any of them even look at their itemized bill at checkout. All week I have been adding my restaurant bills to other hotel guest's checkout bills. If the guest does complain, the hotel management will likely brush it off as the waiter's mistake.

I can't wait to share all my news with Ava, but I can't – it's not safe to talk over the phone. She can bring me trouble and I can bring her just as much trouble. All we can do now is communicate with each other through ridiculous draft emails. She has already agreed that if she is jail free after the trial she's coming to the Dominican. Once the trial ends it will take time for the many angry sides to settle. If she can just focus on something other than dick, she will be in a better place. I can't wait to brag to Ava how right I was about Johnny. He turned out to be just as I expected, a weak loser, and now she's chosen revenge over her love. She's playing dangerously with his life and her heart.

AVA

CHAPTER 33

BACK IN BLACK

Johnny pushes open the bathroom door, knocking my phone out of my hand. A text response from Mr. Alterman pops up on the screen as the phone hits the dirty linoleum. He picks up my phone and hands it over, thankfully not opening the text message. The fact that he doesn't pay it any attention is unlike Johnny. He enjoys getting jealous and arguing with me.

"Sorry, I didn't mean to startle ya," he says.

He motions me off the toilet. I don't leave the bathroom while he takes a piss. I look back at myself in the mirror. My makeup has blackened under my eyes and one fake eyelash has peeled away. I wash my face while Johnny relieves himself. He pushes his way in front of the sink to wash his hands and face. I lean against the wall with my arms crossed, watching and waiting for him to finish. He moves to the side to finish brushing his teeth. With his free hand he motions me that the sink is all mine. We stare at each other brushing our teeth.

"I still love you and want to be with you, Ruben was a mistake," I say, spitting out the remaining toothpaste.

He's silent, just looks back at me with angry eyes.

"I can't trust you," he replies in disgust.

"Trust, really, that's the deal breaker, trust – like you are so damn trustworthy."

"Casey was never a secret; ya knew I would never leave her, but ya slut your way around. I'm more shocked about who ya father is, and how it must have slipped your mind, or how about yah new job as a drug mule for the Dominicans and I'm sure there ah more surprises coming my way."

"Johnny, if anyone is a liar, it's you, you told me on several occasions you could leave Casey for me, and then I find out she's pregnant."

"She tricked me; ya know I don't want fuckin' kids."

"I will never have you to myself, so what's the point, what are we doing here?"

"We aren't doin' anythin', I'm done with ya."

"You fucking pussy. You scared the Mob will side with me over you because of Jimmy being my father? How does it feel, to not be in control?"

He grabs me by the throat with both hands and slams me against the closed bathroom door. This is Johnny's go-to: when he's mad, he hurts me.

"I will kill ya if ya try me."

His hands tighten around my neck. I stare into his eyes, but Johnny is not inside. Evil has possessed him. It's as if he's blacked out in a rage. I scratch at his hands to loosen them from my neck. I can't breathe, and I begin to see black and white dots, I feel my legs give out.

I whisper his name with the last of my breath, and my body goes numb. I try to speak again, but nothing comes out. He lets go of my neck allowing me to drop to the ground. He stands over me while I sit on the floor covering my head, waiting for another kick or punch.

I stare into his eyes – the evil shell of Johnny. It's as if some evil has taken over, and this happens more and more frequently lately. He blacks out during his fits of rage. It's not like Johnny to hurt me this much. His hands hit fast, and it's over, but today feels different. I stay in this position until my breathing is at a normal pace.

"Fuck, Johnny are you trying to kill me?"

I peek from behind my hands to see Johnny sitting on the toilet with his face in his hands crying.

"I love you, Ava, I love you, and ya don't even see it. You only see what ya want to see. It's a game to you. My life is in the hands of my boss and your father will make sure ya don't go to jail and will probably plant all the blame with me. He fuckin' hates me… I'm fucked. Please don't let them send me to jail."

I've never seen Johnny cry. I get to my feet and lean on the sink, looking my neck over in the mirror. The bruises are already forming. The bruises get bigger, his hits hurt more each time, but I love him. It's not his fault. I provoke him, I know how to push his buttons. I know just what to say at the right time to get him hitting me. And after his anger climaxes and he has a moment to reflect, I swoop in just in time to manipulate him into feeling this is normal, it's my fault and that I forgive him.

I kneel in front of Johnny and hug him close.

"Everything will be okay, please don't worry. My father only cares about the Mob, he doesn't care about me. I'll go to jail before I let them blame you. Susan should be the one to take all the heat."

"Claire will never let that happen. Her and Susan are close. Plus, there's been a long-standing rumor that either they're lovers, or Susan has somethin' over Claire."

"What do you think it is?"

"I don't know."

"Well, we need to find out to save both our asses."

"It's no use, it's too risky."

This is the part of Johnny I hate. He can be a coward and pessimistic when he's outside his comfort zone. It's the old cliché saying, he's a sheep in a wolf's world and the Mob is the wolf. He fears the Mob, his father and probably Casey. According to Johnny, the only reason he has a position in the Mob is because his father was owed favors. Nepotism exists even in the Mob.

I'm done talking to Johnny about Susan because it's a waste of time. Johnny would never agree to help me get more information, he's almost useless to me, if I didn't love him.

I pull Johnny from the bathroom and make him sit on the bed next to me. I light a joint and we hand it back and forth in silence until the joint is burning our fingertips. Johnny apologizes and kisses the bruises on my neck. We are interrupted by the knocks on the door.

"Johnny, we filled up the tank – we're ready to go, meet us downstairs," one of the twins yells through the door.

"Okay!"

I'm not looking forward to the twenty hours or so drive back to Boston. My coke supply has diminished into a small eight ball. I refuse to share it with others. I text Alterman to confirm Ruben has wired the $20,000 retainer to Waylon. Alterman's reply makes me feel relieved that he has paid. Waylon charges $700 per hour. The bill could reach half a million if he charges me the two weeks he will be in Boston.

Johnny doesn't know I've hired my own lawyer. He'll eventually find out from Claire and my father. I startup my computer to check for any sign from Paul. There's nothing. I draft an email to myself meant for Paul.

Sherry,
Can you call me, so we can discuss my needs?
Love Always,
Ava

This email shit is ridiculous. I need Paul to call me. I need my cut of the money and I need it now. Without Paul puppeteering the strings of my life, using the dark web, I wouldn't be this close to accomplishing my plans.

We drive all night and arrive in Boston the next day in the late afternoon. Johnny tries to drop me off at my house, but I refuse to get out of the car. Instead I convince him to drop me at the police station. I need to give my official statement for the night of my abduction and I'm sure there will be plenty of questions about my roommate's murder.

"You want me to come with ya?" he asks.

"Nah, go home and get some rest, I'll be fine."

"Okay, I'll call ya later tonight."

He hugs me tight and kisses me outside the vehicle. He grabs my luggage and walks me to the entrance of the police station.

Before we get to the entrance, I see out of the corner of my eye someone approaching us fast.

"Johnny, you fucking liar, you are still fucking her. Is this the work that has kept you from me and the baby? You have missed appointments. How can you sleep at night? I'm over here pregnant, planning a wedding…" Casey screams.

"Get the fuck in the car and I'll explain." Johnny is pissed.

"Ava is that you, you like fucking my Johnny? She grabs her belly as if it's a trophy she won.

"Yes, as a matter of fact, we just cleaned up after fucking in the backseat," I lie.

She lunges at me, pulling my hair. Johnny puts himself in the middle of us, blocking her from hitting me.

"Both of ya, shut the fuck up," he yells.

With so much commotion outside the police station, a crowd begins to form.

"What's going on out here?"

I hear a familiar voice behind me. I turn to see Connor glaring at us.

"Are you guys fucking animals or something? Take this shit somewhere else," he says.

Connor turns to Johnny. "You know better."

"Ava, come inside," Connor insists.

I follow him inside the police station, but not before looking back at Casey and Johnny. Casey is still flailing her arms as Johnny gently ushers her into her vehicle.

Connor doesn't speak until the doors of the elevator are closed.

"Your father is very concerned for your safety."

"How so?"

"There's a rumor that you have sought counsel."

"That's not a rumor, it's true."

He hits the emergency button in the elevator making it stop suddenly.

"Ava, are you suicidal? Your actions are putting everyone in your path in danger."

"I know, and I need your help. I don't want to go to jail."

"You have to take the plea."

"I'm not going to jail for anyone's actions but my own. If I can get my father on board, how much would it cost for you to help me?"

"Your father is the least of your worries. He is not in the position he used to be, not since he returned from Ireland. He disappeared shortly after to Maine. The streets are talking since his return to Boston. The trouble has followed you, his secret daughter, since his return, but that's not what I want to talk to you about. There's an undisclosed amount of money taken indirectly from the Mafia that connects Atlantic and the Mob. I haven't done this, but if I was to display all the photos of the persons involved, I would think that the strings may all tack to your photo. So, I can with great confidence be extremely helpful. Before I consider a deal, I need to know who you're working with."

I laugh hysterically. "You will never get that information"

"So, you're admitting this rumor is true."

"That depends if you would hypothetically accept my offer that would allow you to retire comfortably at an early age. I need to know how to beat this case."

"Are you bribing a Federal Agent?"

"Are you accepting my bribe?"

"I am."

I'm turned on by the deal I'm making with Connor. He's only maybe ten years older than me, but if he made a move, I would spend the night with him. The few times I've seen him he looked unkempt. Today his beard is trimmed neatly, matching his parted, slicked down hair. His clothes are casual, but more form fitting. He looks more like an FBI agent and less like a rundown drug addict.

"$250,000 and I can guarantee no jail time."

"And if I get even one day in jail, you get nothing," I reply.

I need his assistance with another matter, but I don't have all the details.

He's silent, but extends his hand, sealing the deal.

If Connor knew the real amount we stole, his number would have been different. I'm not convinced that he knows as much as he's saying.

"What happened to your neck?" he asks.

Without flinching I lie, "It's from the rope that was around my neck when the attackers tried to drown me."

I can tell he doesn't believe me.

"You have another problem," says Connor.

He leans against the elevator wall, folding his arms.

"Your ex-boyfriends' wife was at the station filling out a missing person report. Your name was mentioned as the last person to see him."

I swallow hard. I don't care that Connor sees me nervous.

"Really? He's my ex-boyfriend. It's not unusual for us to hang out from time to time."

I avoid eye contact. I feel acid coming up my throat. I've had so much heartburn lately.

"Save the bullshit for someone else. What happened to Mac?"

"How the hell should I know? I didn't know he was missing."

"It will cost you if this case shows up on your doorstep. You can save me a lot of trouble looking for a missing person that isn't really missing."

He's trying to break me, perhaps bribe me for more money.

"Honestly, I don't know where Mac could be."

He smiles with his eyes, but his frown shows he's not convinced.

We agree to meet up in a week to discuss our deal. Just like that there's no further mention of the attempted drowning, and I'm satisfied because I don't want to relive that event by telling my side of the story.

He brings me to the lead detective working the murder case on my roommate. The detective only has a few questions because they rule me out as a suspect due to the time of death. The nurses confirm I was in the hospital recovering. Even if they press me with more questions, I will lawyer up and end the questioning. I can only guess she was killed as revenge for Jose's murder and really the killer was trying to get to me.

I leave the police station, not wanting to go home, but I really have no choice. I walk home to give myself time to think about the deal I made with Connor. He could easily go to Claire or the Mafia and tell them everything, especially since he seems to possibly have proof or a solid informant. To accomplish what I set out to do the day my mother died, I need to take chances and be fearless or my plan will fail for sure. I get to the front door of my house. I take a deep breath and enter.

Finally, today is the day I get to meet Waylon. Mr. Alterman has arranged for the three of us to meet at a cigar bar in downtown Boston. It's attached to a hotel, where I assume Waylon is staying. Our meeting is to go over the plea-bargaining agreement before we meet with the Dillon brother lawyers. I get to the cigar bar, but the door is locked. I peek inside; it's dark, so I can't see very far inside. I knock on the door and immediately the door is answered by what looks to be the bartender.

"We are closed."

"Waylon and Mr. Alterman are expecting me."

"Oh, my apologies, of course, come in."

The sweet smell of cigar smoke filters through my nose. Dim lighting and dark wood throughout make it difficult to see too far ahead. I follow the bartender to the back of the bar where a dim green light fixture hangs above four oversized leather chairs with a round glass coffee table in the middle. Waylon and Mr. Alterman are sitting with cigars in one hand and what looks like a glass of whiskey in the other hand. They both stand as I approach.

"Ava, this is Waylon Wilson." Mr. Alterman makes the

introductions.

He grabs my hand, consuming it with his swollen fingers.

"It's a pleasure to meet you, young lady."

I like him immediately. I'm thankful Mr. Alterman is helping me.

I don't shake Mr. Alterman's hand; we only shook hands the first time we met.

I take a seat across from them both. Mr. Alterman pours me a glass of whiskey.

I drink it down in one sip.

"Woo, lady, slow down, we have a long meeting," Waylon laughs.

"I've had one hell of day," I reply.

"Seems like you're having one hell of a life."

"It's been adventurous at times," I laugh.

"Ava, we need to get on the same page before we go see the Dillon's. Let's begin with the motion filed by the defense, the Dillon's. They are seeking to dismiss the charges against Susan O'Daire. The prosecutor requested a reciprocal disclosure, in other words requested the defendant to disclose the evidence. We need to know what exactly the Dillon's are going to disclose; that is the purpose of our meeting today. My hunch is that Susan may plead guilty only if it is foreseen that she would get house arrest or probation, and that means the Dillon's are looking for someone to pin it on. It would be the closest parties to Susan: first Johnny and then you. The Dillon's goal is to plea bargain before trial. However, I am here to make sure you are not a part of that plea bargaining. By law, it is not required that a federal court accept a plea agreement. If the court rejects the plea agreement, the defendant may withdraw the guilty pleas, and this would mean the case will proceed to trial," Waylon explains.

He takes a break from speaking to smoke and sip his whiskey.

"Your Irish friends certainly want to avoid trial at all cost," he continues. "So, my question to you is … do you want to stick to the original plan we discussed?"

"Yes," I reply, handing over two identical USB drives. The files on the USB drives prove my innocence of no involvement with the accounts they were laundering or approved access to Susan's financial spreadsheets, all thanks to Paul coming through for me at the last minute. I'm still wary that he hasn't really forgiven me, but all I have is his word. He brilliantly made sure it shows I had no access to their computer software or login and hides all the other guilty pleasures we were getting ourselves into at Atlantic. One copy is for the Dillon's and the other for the prosecutors if the Mob tries to throw me to the wolves.

The most important thing that's missing on this file is proof that I wasn't involved with skimming accounts owned by the Mob. This information will be used, if necessary, at tomorrow's meeting, but Waylon doesn't need this information. This is my leverage against the Mob.

"Bartender, get us another bottle and a cigar for my friend Ava." Waylon is feeling generous.

We drink, smoke and I listen to them reminisce about the good old days when Mr. Alterman was a cop and Waylon was battling criminal cases in Boston. Waylon doesn't seem to have a care in the world. His demeanor puts my mind at ease. Mr. Alterman wasn't kidding when he said he was the best man for the job.

It was a long night of drinking and I'm not looking forward to the meeting with the Dillon's. Waylon will meet me at their offices. I walk by my old employer's office building. There's a sign in the first-floor window advertising office space for rent.

The Dillon and Associate's office is located on the 42nd floor. I check in with the receptionist and she kindly offers me coffee or water. I decline and take a seat in the waiting room. The lights are so bright that I can hardly open my eyes. I decide to put my sunglasses on and tilt my head back while I wait for Waylon to arrive.

"Ava, wake up," Waylon says, shaking me.

I jump to my feet and follow him through the office.

In the far back of the office is an oversized corner conference room. There's a long dark table in the middle. And there they sit, the two sleazy brother lawyers, the Dillon's. I could smash both their faces into the table, but instead I take a seat next to Waylon.

"Terry Dillon, Brennan Dillion, I am here today with my client Ava Madden

to ensure she is not used as your scapegoat to get Susan O'Daire's charges nullified. I understand you have already submitted your plea agreement. My client will not take the blame for Susan's money laundering at Atlantic. Furthermore," Waylon slides one of the USB drives across the table to the Dillon's, "here is proof that my client is completely innocent of any wrongdoing. In fact, the files on the USB are evidence that will further damage your client's credibility. Ava has provided proof of Susan's transactions and where she made mistakes. If I am not misguided, the Mob might be interested in Susan's incompetence as an accountant, and truly she is the sole reason the Mob has had to deal with this entire muddle. And, if the Mob decides they want to continue to stick out their necks for Susan, that is their decision to make. I must advise, Johnny is just as guilty as Susan. We both know Ava is in no way affiliated with the Mob," Waylon takes a pause to inhale a deep breath. "We have photographic evidence that Johnny has been abusive towards Ava, and if our backs are against the wall, we will push 'abusive supervisor' who cheats on his pregnant wife. Poor Ava was forced to work in a dangerously controlling environment. Giving the prosecutors this new evidence will surely deny your plea and head to trial. A jury will eat up a pretty, smart, young, naive girl, who was just trying to survive another workday in hell at Atlantic." He slides colored photos of my bruised face and neck across the table.

Waylon pushes his chair back to give him room to cross one of his legs. He just stares at the Dillon's. They whisper back and forth before asking us to leave the room, so they can consult together in private.

We are ushered back to the waiting area.

"What do you think?" I ask anxiously.

"Does a hen lay eggs?"

"Yes?"

"Remain positive, until you aren't."

I put my sunglasses back on and sit in silence.

Less than thirty minutes goes by when the model-like receptionist tells us we can go back in.

I can feel my heart pounding up my neck into my ears. Waylon looks unbothered, and a real badass.

We take our seats in the same spots.

"We have consulted with our client. She wants you to know she's not pleased about you stealing funds but is impressed with your knowledge and would like to meet with you to come to an agreement," Terry informs us.

"No," Waylon replies. "We will not waste any more time with this nonsense—"

"Yes, tell her I will meet with her, without my lawyer present. I have more information that is confidential and would like to share it only with your client," I interrupt before Waylon can continue.

"Well, then, we are done here and will be in contact."

Waylon is hesitant to get out of his chair, but eventually does and follows me out.

We don't speak until we are in the elevator.

"You've just agreed to a meeting with the devil herself."

"I've met Claire before; she doesn't intimidate me. Plus, it sounds like if I don't, there will be no deal. I can take it from here, Waylon."

"It's your life, I trust you are making the right decision."

We part ways at Atlantic. Waylon will remain in Boston for the week because that's how long Ruben paid him to be in the city. I don't think we will need him any longer, since I have Connor working in the background. I won't pressure the Mob to accuse Johnny unless I'm pushed to breaking point. Of course, I love Johnny and would rather see Susan in jail, but it's my life over his any day.

JOHNNY

CHAPTER 34

BIRDS ARE SINGING

I lie with one arm behind my head and the other wrapped around Ava. I've been lying in bed watching her and listening to the birds chirping outside. The sound tells me that Spring is soon approaching. We were up all night talking about the future. I promised her the impossible more than once. I told her I'm done with Casey, will move back to my parents, and share custody of my soon to be son. This is the only way I can get Ava to even consider letting me in her house and doing what she does best, pleasuring me all night. She's better in bed than Casey. Especially now that Casey is putting on weight – her belly gets in the way.

My father reaches out to me this morning with concerns about Stan. He hasn't been in contact with anyone for a about a week. My father went to visit his boxing gym, and the guys at the gym claim he hasn't been in to workout in over a week.

It's not like Stan to miss even one day at the gym. Even on his resting day, he goes to the gym to hang out with his boxing buddies. I've never heard my father this stressed. He demands I come to the house immediately, but I'm in no rush to look for Stan. I'm sure he's fine.

I roll Ava over on her side, lift her leg and push myself inside of her. She hates fucking in the morning, but she never says no. I finish so quick I don't even think she has the chance to fully awaken. I smack her on her ass and tell her to come take a shower with me. She grunts but follows me into the shower. I enjoy taking showers with Ava now that she has lost weight. I love watching her wash her body, the soap suds dripping down and around her perky full breasts and pink nipples. Her breasts are unusually full and I notice she's putting on some weight around the waist. When she tilts her head back under the shower, she closes her eyes the same as when I'm pleasuring her. Sometimes I catch her biting her lip. I think she does it on purpose if she feels me watching her.

"My father needs my help around the house today," I lie. Will ya be around later tonight?"

"Yeah, I'll be here. My father's coming over soon. We have a lot of catching up to do."

I kiss her on the forehead before exiting the shower.

My father is already outside when I pull up to the house. He gets in my car just before I stop in the driveway. It's strange behavior.

"Johnny, I'm worried sick," he says.

The alcohol on his breath is fresh. He doesn't drink in the

morning.

"Dad, calm down, Stan's fine, we will find him."

"No, this is not like him at all. We talk every morning. Stan would never miss a call."

It's as if he's bragging about his and Stan's relationship. I think what he wants to say is, "My own flesh and blood son doesn't call me every day".

"You got his cellphone records?"

"I already have them. His cellphone's last ping location was in Falmouth, MA. It's a five-mile radius, so there's a lot of ground to cover."

"Okay, let's get going then."

I understand my father's concerns, especially since Stan's phone hasn't been used in a week. The last resort is getting the police involved and if we did, we would make an anonymous call to the police. Stan isn't exactly a model citizen. He has a lengthy arrest record. I just hope that we can find him alive.

We have about an hour's drive, so I decide this is a good time to discuss the trial.

"Have ya heard anythin' more about the trial?" I ask.

There's no response. I think he doesn't hear me, so I repeat myself.

"I hear you, Johnny, but do ya really think this is the time to discuss this? We have enough shit going on."

"Okay, well, when the hell is the best time then?"

"Jesus Christ Johnny, I don't know."

"Dad, you always put Stan before me, always, and it's bullshit, just pure bullshit."

"That's not true."

"Stan has always been your favorite, and ya know it."

"Johnny, you're just a spoiled, selfish, incompetent boy. I told your damn mother a long time ago not to give you everything you asked for, but no, she spoiled you anyway, rotten to the core."

"Don't blame your problems on Mom, you've been an asshole to me all by yourself."

I feel something hit the side of my face. To my shock, it's my father's fist. I yank the steering wheel and pull the car over in the breakdown lane and exit the vehicle. If I didn't exit the car right then and there I would have hit the old man, but I know I would have regretted it for the rest of my life. Instead I decide to start walking back to the city or keep walking until I'm too tired to be angry.

"Johnny, come back, let's talk. I didn't mean to hit you. I'm stressed, I love you, you are my only child. Stan will never replace you. Stan is like a son, but no one can take your place."

I keep walking, ignoring his words, instead focusing on the sound of cars passing by.

My phone is vibrating in my pocket. I stop walking to check who's calling. It's my mother.

"Hi Mom."

"Johnny, thank goodness you answered."

I can hear the stress in her voice.

"Mom, what's wrong?"

"Honey are you with your—"

She doesn't finish her sentence. She's sobbing uncontrollably. I immediately think something has happened to Casey or my unborn child.

"Your father, is he with you?"

"Yes, Mom, I'm with Dad, what's, what's wrong?"

"Stan … dead."

"Stan is dead?" As soon as the words spill from my lips my knees feel weak. Every happy memory of Stan floods my thoughts as if someone pressed fast forward in my mind. My chest tightens, and a lump forms in my throat.

"Johnny, Johnny, oh Johnny please be gentle breaking the news to your father. Please Johnny, please I can't, I can't tell him."

She's silent, but I can hear her sobbing and wiping her nose.

"How?"

"Johnny, how is not important right now. Bring your father home right now."

I know Stan was murdered by the panic in her voice. If it was natural causes or an accident my mother would explain in more detail. It's not a question of who would want Stan killed, it's a question of who did it. Working with my father's business dealings is not exactly a safe means of employment. While Stan is not affiliated with the Irish or Italians, he's dealing with them in some form of business relations, since my father works closely with both.

I walk back to my father who is sitting on the hood of the car, his legs blocking one of the headlights. His head is hanging low as if ashamed. I lean against the car next to him and light a cigarette.

"I'm sorry, Johnny."

"It's okay, Dad. I love you and I was out of line."

I take a deep drag of my cigarette before breaking my father's heart.

"Mom called. Stan is ... dead."

My father drops to his knees, screaming Stan's name. I kneel next to him to try to comfort him, but he shrugs me off. It's clear he doesn't want me to touch him. I climb in the driver's seat because I feel so uncomfortable seeing my father cry. I'm sure he appreciates me not sticking around. I wait patiently in the car chain smoking. My father will get in the car when he is ready. Several minutes pass before my father climbs to his feet. He's on his phone when he climbs in the car.

"Drive to Falmouth Hospital," my father demands.

I don't question him and just drive. I can only assume Stan's body is at the hospital. The drive is long and depressing. My father has stopped crying and returned to his everyday expression: anger. I'm not done crying for my brother, but hold back the tears, too embarrassed to cry. I will just stay quiet until we arrive at the hospital. I pull up to the front of the hospital, dropping my father off before looking for parking. My phone is ringing nonstop. It's my mother, but I don't answer. She knows my father will not rest until he knows who murdered Stan and why.

I head into the hospital and give Stan's name at the main reception desk. I'm directed to the hospital's morgue on the ground floor. As soon as the elevator doors open, I no longer feel like I'm in the same hospital I just entered. The cold air whips around my body. There are very few signs for direction and no one to greet you at the elevator. I roam the hallways, pushing through the first set of gray double swinging doors to another hall with more of the exact same doors. Finally, I come to a hallway where my father sits in the only chair. This must be where Stan's body is. My father is staring at the door that reads

MORGUE in large capital letters. He's either contemplating going in or has already identified Stan. I quietly stand next to my father, waiting for him to speak.

"I can't, Johnny."

"What, Dad?"

"I can't go in there because I know he's in there, but I can't go in. I don't want to see him this way."

I know he wants me to offer to go in. We are Stan's only family, so someone needs to identify him so we can lay him to rest.

"I will go in Dad, wait here."

"Thank you, son, you're a good boy."

I haven't heard him say this in a long time. I hold back my tears.

Without hesitation I push through the double doors. It's a quiet, large dark room. All I can hear is the creaky sound of the rusting swinging from the doors behind.

"Sir, are you here to identify Mr. Stanley Cormick?" asks the tall, pale bald man wearing white scrubs.

"Ya."

"I'm Bob, the hospital's mortician."

Bob walks to door number seven, unlocks the freezer door and pulls out what may be Stan. Strangely, he doesn't pull out the entire body.

"Come," says Bob.

I walk slowly to door seven because my legs and feet are heavy with sadness. There is only a blue sheet separating me from the dead body. Without warning the man pulls the sheet back exposing me to Stan's gray, pale face, eyes sewn shut and missing more than the lower half of his body. The smell and sight fill my throat with vomit. I hurry to the closest trash can and throw up. When I stand up, I don't expect Bob to be standing next to me offering me paper towels to clean up.

"Well, is it him?" asked Bob, somewhat impatiently.

"Ya, it is, but where the fuck is the rest of him?"

Bob ignores my questions. He walks over to a desk and grabs a clipboard. My patience is gone.

"Where is the rest of him?" I ask again.

Again, Bob doesn't answer or acknowledge me. I snap, grabbing him by the collar of his shirt, pulling him close to my face. He turns his head to avoid eye contact.

"I'm not gonna ask ya again. Where is the rest of his body?"

"I don't know... I... I don't know, he was brought here like this. The story is in the newspaper, over there," Bob points to the newspaper on the desk.

I loosen my grip on Bob and pull him with me to get the newspaper. Pushing him to sit in the chair I grab the newspaper. Stan's murder is front page news: THREE MEN FOUND DEAD AT CONSTRUCTION SITE. I read the first paragraph. Stan and two other men were found buried in cement up to their chests.

"Show me the other two bodies," I demand.

Bob doesn't ask questions. He nervously grabs the keys and opens freezer doors two and four. I rip the sheets off the bodies before Bob has the chance. I don't recognize either man, or their names.

I cover Stan's body carefully with the sheet and close the freezer door. I walk back to the hallway where my father is still sitting. I hand him the news article.

"Dad, who are the two men found with Stan? Come look at them, maybe we can figure out who did this to him."

My father gets to his feet slowly. For the first time in my life, my father looks every one of his sixty years.

When we return inside the morgue Bob is on the phone. I grab the phone from his hand and put it back on the hook.

"I was calling the detective on your case to see if he can meet with you guys," Bob explains.

I ignore Bob and bring my father to the men. My father immediately goes pale.

"Fucking stupid cocksucker, motherfuckers," he yells. He storms out of the morgue. I follow him, and we leave the hospital without even signing the paperwork.

"Who are they?" I ask.

"Don't worry about it, I will take care of it."

I fold the newspaper article and stuff it in my coat. Something about all of this is not making sense. When I get a chance, I'm going to look into how these men are connected to Stan and my father. Right now, I just want to mourn my brother in private, but my father has other plans. He instructs me to drive to Top Bar in South Boston to pay a visit to Claire.

"Why are we goin' to see Claire?" I ask.

"Its obvious Jimmy is involved with Stan's murder."

"I'm not following, Dad. Am I missin' somethin'?"

"Stan and those two men were killed by Jimmy."

"Jimmy? How do ya know?"

"The bodies were staged in a way only Jimmy would do," he responds, this time more loudly

I decide it's best not to pick at the subject any longer.

Top Bar is full of loud, obnoxious Mob members, bikers and local drunks and druggies. This is not exactly the bar to visit if you are looking to have a cold beer and watch the game. This place is full of spilled drinks, fights and half-naked waitresses most old enough to be my mother.

Claire is sitting in a booth with Connor McClean and Jimmy. They're drinking beer and laughing.

I pull my father aside, "You think this is a good idea, accusin' Jimmy of murderin' Stan?"

"Everyone fears Jimmy, not me, so ya, I think I will go ahead with my plan."

My father's not in his right mind right now. I feel like I need to do something before he ends up in more trouble than he can get himself out of, but I don't.

"Claire, can I speak to you in private?" my father asks.

The laughter stops, and everyone at the table gets serious.

"Of course, follow me." Claire pushes by Jimmy to get out of the booth.

Jimmy smiles sneakily at us but doesn't speak. If I find out he killed Stan, I'll kill him myself.

We follow Claire to the back of the bar, into a tiny office. Her usual watchmen are just outside the door.

"Sean, what is the urgency of this meeting?"

"I found out just hours ago that my son Stan was murdered."

My father hangs his head low as if to hide the tears. Hearing my father say it out loud makes it a reality. My brother is gone.

Claire stands up and hugs my father and then hugs me. It

seemed genuine enough.

She sits down, lighting a cigarette.

"It was not ordered by me, I can assure you," she replies, exhaling smoke.

"I know, but I also know who is responsible, and it's someone very close to you."

"I see, and why should I get involved with this person close to me and your matters?"

My father turns around as if to walk out of the office.

"Have I not done you enough favors, have I not given so much to you and your members?" he yells.

The door flings open; it's Claire's watchmen trying to squeeze their way into the office.

"Boys, I'm okay, please stay outside," she orders.

"Cormick, sit down and relax. You don't know the trouble we are facing. I can't pile anymore onto my plate, it's full and I still haven't even had dessert. I don't mean to disregard your pain, but I'm limited in my involvement and I can't get into the reasons with someone other than my members."

I very seldom hear anyone call my father "Cormick", only his older associates.

"My son's a member, doesn't he deserve your time and ear to just listen to what he is going through losing his brother?"

She motions him to continue.

"I think Stan's murder is somehow connected to Ava, and that's why Jimmy killed him and those two men."

Claire doesn't show a flicker of emotion.

"Ava is not who you think she is. I have information that proves Ava was skimming the Atlantic accounts under Susan's watch. How the FBI hasn't discovered this is astonishing. There's more; I haven't gotten to the part you will find most interesting. Ava is Jimmy's daughter."

It's disturbing to see my father look so excited to spill the news about Ava and Jimmy. It's as if he is expecting a gift after giving her this information.

My father continues, "I am not here to avenge Jimmy. I am here to save my only surviving son. I am begging you to not go back on your word you gave Johnny. You told him he wouldn't get any heat from the Atlantic job. Susan oversaw everything, and Johnny always did what Susan asked of him. Johnny has a baby on the way, and I just have a feeling Jimmy won't let his daughter serve time."

I'm touched that my father is here to see Claire for me and not Stan. Maybe this has scared him so much, he wants to make sure I am okay.

"Johnny, how old is Ava?"

I wasn't expecting that question.

"Um … maybe 23 or 24, I'm not sure, but her birthday is in January or February."

Claire turns away as if to hide her expression. "I never knew of Jimmy having a child and was curious what year this all happened. Cormick, I'm meeting with my lawyers in a few days. I will make sure the plan is still in place as we discussed. As for Jimmy possibly being Stan's killer, I will try to get more information."

"Please don't bother, I want to bury my boy and digging for answers will only bring more truth and pain. Leave it alone. But as for Ava, you might want to take a closer look at how much money she stole, you know, for the trial."

Claire hugs us both goodbye.

I'm shocked to hear Ava stole from Atlantic. Again, I have misjudged her character. It's as if I don't know the true Ava. She stole directly from the mouths of the Mafia, not the Mob. How didn't I know? My father seems to know more about Ava than I do. I got a bad feeling my father has some guilt about Stan's death.

JIMMY

CHAPTER 35

THE TALK

Johnny and his dirtbag father walk by the booth with their tails between their legs. Like father, like son, both cowards. They're lucky I didn't go to their house, fuck his mother and shoot them both in the head.

"I saw Ava today at the station," Connor says.

"And she didn't bother getting in touch with her father," I reply.

"We should leave to pay a visit," the Indian adds.

Claire squeezes into the booth across from me and next to Connor. I throw back the rest of my drink because the look on Claire's face tell me she wants to talk immediately. Fucking snitch, Johnny's father.

"What?" I ask before she speaks.

"You want to explain why you killed Stan and those men?"

"No, I do not," I pout.

"You work for me and you will hit who I say you hit; you can't just pick who you want."

"This was a personal matter."

"Personal, like, Ava being your daughter," she spits.

"And, so she's my daughter, what does that have to do with you, Claire?"

Claire never wanted Ava, and I chose to go against her orders to kill Ava as a baby. As soon as she found out her father and brothers' plane went down and she was next up to control the Irish, she had no interest in Ava. I hid my daughter from her for fear she would kill her and have me killed. I'm tired of hiding this secret and I'm ready to have the weight taken off my shoulders.

"Do you really want to have this discussion now, in front of the Indian and Connor?"

"I don't give a shit who hears me. You let me believe that my daughter was dead all these years. You could've told me the truth, even after I cried so many nights on your shoulder about my baby. I don't give a fuck who hears me. You have no heart," she says, now crying into her hands.

I have never seen Claire so upset and in front of others. The bar is reaching full silence and all eyes are on us.

"You told me to get rid of her and left me in Ireland," I yell back.

"I went back to find you hours later, and you were nowhere to be found; I changed my mind."

"You fucking liar, liar … you are a liar," I scream.

The Indian puts his arm on my shoulder to calm me and keep me from grabbing that bitch by her throat.

"I've spent years feeling guilt and you let me. Who raised our daughter?"

"Mary Madden, a girl that I went to high school with. She did a great job, until she was murdered by her boyfriend, Lewis Lorcan."

Claire stopped crying and looked for me to keep talking.

"I think I will give you all some privacy," Connor says awkwardly.

Claire lets Connor slip by her out of the booth.

The Indian takes the hint and follows Connor.

I'm left sitting across from a vulnerable Claire. The music is turned back up and people at the bar are back to being loud and obnoxious.

I grab Claire's hand and rub it.

"I'm sorry I kept this from you, but I was scared you would hurt her or me."

She doesn't speak or look at me.

"I love Ava and I want the best-case scenario for her. For the first three years of her life I was a part-time father, but one dangerous incident made me realize me being close to her made her my enemy's target. That's when I watched her from a distance and Mary sent me videos, photos, drawings from our daughter and letters telling me stories of her milestones. I have them all, I can show you. Lewis was a great stepfather, and when I felt like she was in good hands, I offered to assist our member in upstate Maine, during the drug smuggling expansion. The distance helped with the pain. Boston just kept reminding me that I was not a good father."

"When I met Ava, she reminded me of someone, and now it

makes complete sense."

"She does look a lot like you but has my beautiful eyes."

"Okay, you old bastard, I don't think so."

"I hope you can forgive me someday."

In translation, don't have me murdered. Especially since I'm the next up to control the Irish if she dies, but only because I'm the father of her child. The Irish changed the rule when shortly after I found out she was pregnant with Ava. Claire being the only remaining Spillane; The only chance she could keep the Spillane name going is through me and then Ava or whoever doesn't die first. There is a clause in the rule. If Claire were to get married, her husband would take my place. If I know Claire, she will get married just to spite me.

"Does Ava know I'm her mother?"

"Nope, I always planned I would leave it up to you, if you found out. I will keep my word."

"Why did you kill Stan?"

"Cormick hired those men who tried to kill Ava by drowning her in Boston Harbor. I didn't know Stan was his son, or I swear to you I would have let him live. Stan was never my target; he was just in the wrong place at the wrong time. Not to mention he tried to kill me. I see why Cormick left that detail out – because Johnny was with him. Johnny is deeply in love with Ava. That's not all; the first attempt to have her murdered was when Atlantic hired a hitman to kill her, but the Indian and the White Man saved her."

"How did she happen to come work for Atlantic?"

This I can't explain. I don't know.

"I'm not sure," I reply. I'm not lying. I really don't know.

"Doesn't make any sense to me," Claire says.

"So, what happens now? You can't possibly continue to push to get Susan out over putting your own daughter in jail."

Her response is too slow which means she's considering sticking with the plan.

"I'm not sure until I meet with my lawyers. Anyway, how do I know she's really my daughter?"

"We could always do a DNA test."

"And what will the members think of me, of all of this? I need more time to think about all this. For now, I'm going home to get some rest."

"I love you, Claire, and whatever decision you make, I will support it."

I lie right to her old, shriveled face. All her tears are an act. I never told her anything all those years because she's evil. I see this side in Ava and it frightens me that she could easily be just like her mother.

AVA

CHAPTER 36

TRIAL

Finally, the call comes I've been waiting for.

"Hello," I answer.

"Ava, it's Waylon."

"What's the news?" I ask impatiently.

"You got everything you asked for, no jail time. However, the Dillon's are demanding you meet with Claire today."

"Oh really. Did they say what for?"

"I reckon there's some unfinished business regarding the funds. They didn't say much, but my guess is something about the financial statements. I advise you go to the meet somewhere public, just to be safe. I wouldn't trust those potato eaters. Well, let me end this call before I must send you another bill you can't afford. I wish you the best, young lady."

"Thank you, Waylon. I really—"

He hangs up before I can express my gratitude.

Sure, it's good news I won't face any jail time, but even without the jail bars, I'll forever feel imprisoned with fear of being killed by the Mob. Something will need to be done about this.

I take a drive I haven't done in a while, to Walpole prison to visit Lewis. We have some serious unfinished business to discuss. I hated him for killing my mother, but the more I read into the trial, which Paul hacked a copy of, the more I still don't believe he killed her. Paul agrees with me and even wants to run new DNA tests. We could get him out of prison.

I get to the jail, parking my rental car as far from the entrance as possible to use the distance to walk off my anxiety. It's difficult to contain my emotions; I've lived with anxiety and depression since I was a child. My mother and Lewis were the only two who could console me during my nightly attacks.

I take off my jewelry, grab my ID, light a cigarette and head to the entrance. As soon as you walk through the doors, the life is sucked out of your body. The guards are sour faced, angry, matching the cold, gray concrete atmosphere. After signing in, they usher me into a room with tables and stools bolted to the cement where we wait for the guards to bring in the prisoners. In the waiting room are single mothers there with their children, the elderly and several pregnant women waiting to be single mothers.

The guards yell and the doors open. I stand up from being too nervous. Lewis has tattoos all over his neck and face. He looks like a white supremacist now he's shaved his head.

He smiles wide with a missing front tooth. That's new, since the last time I've seen him.

"Dad," I say, opening my arms wide.

"Ava, honey, oh my god, oh my god," he says pulling me in for a big hug.

We hug until the guard tells us to sit down.

I push back my tears. I'm flooded with guilt; I should've believed him and stood by him. He told me he didn't do it, and that the cops won't believe him, so he had to plead guilty to get a lesser sentence.

"Ava, I love ya honey, I'm happy to see ya, and oh my god, ya so beautiful, so beautiful just like ya mothah."

"Dad, I'm sorry for not believing you."

"That don't matter and don't let that nonsense fill our visit time. I want to know all about ya life."

"Well, I have had an interesting year."

"Well, go on, tell me."

"I found my biological father."

His face goes pale.

"Don't talk so loud," he says, reaching his hand to put it over my mouth, pulling his arm back quickly before the guards see him.

"Why?" I look around the room.

"They could be listenin'."

"Who?"

"Tha Irish."

"Dad, I know you didn't do this, and I think I can get you out of here."

"Ava, don't you dare even try it, don't dig up old bones, you don't know what dog buried them. Can you buy a coke from the vending machine?" He changes the subject quickly.

"Ok."

I go to the vending machine.

I slip the baggie of oxycodone underneath the can of coke. I know from my last visits what my father likes.

When I turn around to return to the table, my father is talking with a guard, but he returns to the table before I take a seat.

I set the coke down on top the drugs and slide it across the table.

"There is nothing like a cold can of coke." He pulls the can to him and the drugs fall in his lap and he puts them down his pants.

"I also came here for a favor. I have a friend that will be transferred to this prison soon."

"Who?"

"Johnny Cormick, he's my boyfriend."

I leave out the important details because my father would say no otherwise.

He doesn't need to know about the charges against me being dropped and that instead the FBI arrested Johnny based on new evidence. He pleaded guilty like he was instructed, and his sentencing is in the next few weeks. It was no surprise the Mob chose Susan over Johnny. Claire and Susan are close.

"What are his charges?

"Money laundering from a corporation."

My father laughs.

"Anything for my baby girl."

"Time's up people," the guards yell.

"I will replenish your commissary every month with the maximum amount allowed. I will be back to visit you soon."

"I love ya Ava, ya such a good girl."

We hug goodbye. I take the coke can my father was drinking as if to throw it away in the trash, but I hang onto it to test his DNA. Paul gave me a contact in Boston that will run my father's DNA. I want to see if it matches what the police found at my mother's murder scene. Paul informs me that the Mob has in the past altered DNA results to avoid their members going to prison. This makes me believe my father was framed. If I can prove his innocence, I can get him out of jail.

Next stop, a visit to Johnny's parents' house. I hear Casey has moved in with them since learning Johnny will do time. My father gives me Johnny's parents' address with a promise that I won't harm them. It is a strange thing for my father to say, I mean, it feels as though he knows I have killed before. There is no way he would know about me murdering Mac, unless Johnny ran off at the mouth. It worries me he has that leverage over me. If he wanted to rat on me, he could, but that behavior is highly frowned upon on the streets.

I won't kill Johnny's parents today, but I will threaten their lives, since Johnny's father Cormick put a hit out on me. Almost drowning in the harbor and finding out who's responsible makes you want to show up at a person's house. I still love Johnny but harming his family will mean losing him.

I turn off the headlights as I edge closer to the house on the hill. I find street parking a few blocks from the driveway.

I pull my sweatshirt hood over my head, tucking in my hair. I put on black gloves and check the gun to ensure the safety is on, I'm just here to threaten them, not kill them.

I stand at the back door. I call the house phone and hear

someone's footsteps walking to the ringing phone.

"Hello," a man's voice answers.

"Cormick, it's Ava, I'm at your back door. I just want to talk."

I hear him sigh.

The phone hangs up and the back door opens and out comes Cormick.

"Come in," he says.

I follow him through his kitchen past a woman sipping tea in her nightgown, her hair in curlers.

"Sean, who's this?" she asks as we walk past.

"Irene, stay put. Ava, sit."

"I'm not here to apologize that Johnny is going to jail instead of me. You know why, don't you Cormick?" I ask.

"Don't you dare say anything more, not around my wife."

"If you even ever think about trying that again, you will pay. I'll kill your wife, your future grandson and his whore of a mother."

I blackout daydreaming about blowing his head off.

He leans in. "Try my family, bitch and I will kill you first. Leave me and my family alone. I won't bother you if you leave us alone and that includes Johnny."

I hear the stairs creak and feel a presence behind me. We turn to see Casey looking very pregnant.

"You ruined my baby's life; he won't be raised with his daddy. I hope you rot in hell you fucking slut!" she screams.

Irene runs to be next to Casey's side and hushes her up the stairs.

"I think it's time you got the hell out of my house."

Cormick gets to his feet.

"Don't take my threats seriously and I'll be back, but this time you won't be warned. And me and Johnny are in love, he will forgive me, he can't resist. Just like you and all your prostitute whores you fuck out back of the church during service. You wonder where Johnny gets his need to be with multiple women…" I walk out before he can respond.

Johnny won't talk now and won't be any happier when he learns I threatened his family, but I know in time he'll see things clearer. I can't worry about that now. I have a few more task to complete before I leave for the Dominican Republic to join Paul. I need to meet with Koda. I just hope my plan works and he will agree.

INDIAN

CHAPTER 37

MY LAND

Ava burying her father alive is the final vision I receive from my most recent tribal ceremony. It's a sign she's becoming more powerful than him. It is cautioning that times are changing. The wind has twisted with summer approaching, but this wind is not because of the weather. It's the spirits; they are twisting, causing this wind. I only agreed to meet with Ava because she has news that will help me get back ownership of my people's land.

I grab an old wooden kitchen chair and drag it out to the small open porch to wait for Ava. I take out my favorite knife and begin carving a new tobacco pipe. The air is crisp. I see every breath I exhale. I don't mind the cold, I never did. New Englanders always complain about the long winters and that they're cold, but me I never say out loud I'm cold, even if that's the truth. A healthy mind can trick their body into thinking they're okay. A sick mind complains all the time about weather and everything bothering them.

She pulls up a few hours before the sun sets. She doesn't get out of her car. Possibly too cold for her.

"Koda, get in – I want to show you something," she yells out the car window.

I don't like surprises. I grab my rifle and knife and walk to the driver side window and tap on it.

"Where are we going?" I ask.

"It's a surprise, come, it's cold."

I go with my instincts. I sense no harm and unwillingly get in her car.

"How have you been?" she asks.

I don't respond. I hope she gets the hint I don't like small talk.

The drive is familiar, like every drive through the mountains. I have a feeling I know where we are heading.

We get to my ancestor's mountain, the Shawmut, which was absorbed by the white man and transformed into ski resorts that share the various mountain sides and valleys, as if to divide this mountain into many mountains.

We pull up to a popular scenic rest area that used to be filled with tiny food huts where my people sold their fruit and vegetables to locals and tourists visiting the White Mountain region. The view is spectacular, but not as I remember its beauty before it was over developed.

"Come, get out, look at this beautiful view," she says as if I've never seen this.

The moon is full, reflecting off the treetops along the mountain and reflecting exactly the river in the valley. Makes you see double.

"It was more beautiful before the ski lifts and electric poles.

There used to be more birds, owls, bald eagles and hawks," I respond.

"Koda, I got it all back, it's yours again. You can remove these ski resorts and restore the land. Here is the deed to all the land that makes up Mount Shawmut."

I read the deed in disbelief. It looks real from what I can see, but it's unimaginable.

"Here is a map of the current layout of the mountain and development. This top layer of the map is how we determined where Mount Shawmut begins and ends. The first land your indigenous people settled," she says with a wide smile.

"I don't need a map to know which land is my people's," I say, handing the map back.

"I didn't mean to insult you. I'm sorry," she says, looking at the ground, pushing snow into piles with her boots.

She's shivering cold. I motion her back into the car.

Ava turns the car heat on so strong it's burning my face. I slap the heat vents closed.

"Koda, my father told me of the many rituals you performed on him to keep him in good spirits. You know, I remember the rituals, drums pounding, and red dust tossed over my body while I was recovering in the hospital. At first, I thought they were dreams until my father explained your traditions. When I was a child, I remember the same red dust. My father told me the sandman sent the red sand to protect me. My father believes in your spirits and therefore I do."

"Thank you, but I cannot accept the land."

"This is when I ask for a favor."

"How did you pay for this land and what was the cost?"

"It's cost me everything," she half smiles. "I need you to keep an eye on a friend. He's a private investigator that may be in danger. I need you to keep him alive. Connor McClean is tracking him as well, but I think I made the mistake of trusting Connor. You need to keep him alive. I owe him for helping me with the trial."

"And if your friend is murdered, no mountain?"

"The land is yours no matter what. It was never our land to take from your people."

For a moment she has me trusting her word and then I remember who her parents are and know deep inside there are demons hiding in this girl. Some she may not be familiar with, but they will eventually introduce themselves to her and anyone in her way. Perhaps that is why her father continues to ask for more of my spiritual red sand.

"Koda, can I ask you something? Why do you allow people to refer to you as 'The Indian'? Aren't you offended?"

"The people that call me 'The Indian' are those who respect me, so why would I feel like they are disrespecting me? I am unlike other indigenous people. They are conservative Indians, everything can offend them, even the animals and spirits."

She's silent and I sense she's not done asking for favors.

"I have one more favor. I don't want an answer today or tomorrow. I just want you to think about it for some time before you give me your answer. Perhaps we can discuss it over some dinner."

I know what she wants before she even asks, but I'll let her ask me anyway.

"Take us home. The White Man has soup warming on the woodstove."

MR. ALTERMAN

CHAPTER 38

SUICIDE

It's an immaculate win for Ava. Only Waylon Wilson could have pulled this off. I know Ava is not happy about throwing all the dirt toward Johnny, but it was the only way she could keep herself out of jail. The Irish agreed with the conclusion, but on their terms. They were impressed with Ava's hacking scheme put in place with the help of her anonymous hacker friend, skimming the Italian's funds and laundering through Atlantic. Even though she's not all the brains behind it, she established the connections and made this all happen. It satisfies the FBI incriminating Johnny in Ava's place, and that's really all they care about, putting the blame on someone. Ava is not out of the woods yet, because the Italians aren't happy with the idea someone was stealing from them – even with the promise Ava will return the funds.

With the information that Ava offered regarding her case, I

reached out to the informants I pay to keep their ears close to the streets. I was told that Johnny's father, Cormick is looking to avenge his son Stan's killer. He accused Coonan, but the detective on the case found no proof that Ava's father killed Stan. It's obvious who did it, since it's rumored that Ava's attempted killers were hired directly by Cormick, not to mention the grotesque way the three men were killed. It has "The Coroner" written all over it.

Ava won't live to see her twenty-fifth birthday, especially after putting Johnny in jail.

I am waiting at the only breakfast diner on Massachusetts Avenue, better known as Meth Mile, because of all the methadone clinics. The food, service and even the coffee is terrible, but neither of us are here for the food or ambience.

I sit with my back to the wall facing the door. Being in law enforcement for so long, I never sit in a position where I can't see the entire room or nearest exit. In today's world, people just walk into public places shooting up everyone for religious reasons, terrorism, or for no reason at all. Ava told me I may not recognize her at first, but I don't know what that means.

I check the menu while waiting for her to show. I must order something, or it looks suspicious. I hear someone slide into the booth across from me. I peek from behind the menu. It's Ava, I think. Short black wig, and heavy makeup.

"Hello. I warned you, don't look at me so strangely," she says.

"Sorry, I just … never mind."

"Did you order? I'm starving. I only have an hour before I need to leave for the airport."

"Not yet." I wave the waitress over.

"Ready ta ordah?" the waitress asks as in an annoying tone.

I motion to Ava to order first.

"I'll get pancakes with extra butter on the side, bacon—well done—sausage, white toast darkened, with extra butter, hash browns, an English muffin with strawberry jam on the side and … um, can you heat the syrup? And for a drink, just coffee please? That's all."

"Two eggs over easy, whole wheat toast, oatmeal, and coffee," I order.

"Jesus, Ava, how do you stay skinny eating like that?"

"I eat all my calorie intake in one sitting. So far it's working for me."

"Let's get to the point of why we are here."

Ava pulls out a device that looks like a phone. "This is a GPS; this will guide you to your destination."

Ava is choosing her words carefully and I don't blame her. The device is tracking Mob boss Claire Spillane. She's been in control of the Mob since before I first joined the police force. She's ruined my life and the lives of my friends. Boston changed for worse the day she was promoted to Mob boss. When her father oversaw the Mob, there was less violence, especially against officers and innocent residents. The Mob stuck to killing only members from rival gangs. Many of my colleagues were killed because of the Mob or were forced to resign or relocate – or ended up drinking too much or getting into drugs. Under her rule, she murders for her own enjoyment. Her goal is to instill fear in others in order to maintain control.

When I knew Ava was linked to the Mob in such a unique way, I knew this could be my one opportunity to get to Claire. All those years as an officer trying to keep Boston safe, I admit I gave up, but now this opportunity. I can finally get rid of the most perilous leader of the Irish Boston has seen. I know crime will never be conquered, but I owe it to my friends and the families she destroyed. I love this city, and the people who live here. I've been around the world, and there is nothing that compares to Boston, nothing. The history, politics, culture, diversity, education, and beauty shall be restored.

"This device will not tell you who is around here, so please be careful. She's known to have many lookouts; people you wouldn't expect are on her side."

"I don't have any plans to live through this experience. I am old, I have nothing left to live for."

"What do you mean? You're just going to let them…"

She didn't finish her sentence. I've already set in my mind that I will die attempting to kill Claire. I don't have a backup plan; I don't have anyone to watch my back. I can't afford to pay for backup anyway. Plus, the more people who know, the more likely it is Claire will be warned I'm planning the hit.

"Ava, I have lived my life, I am okay to end it on my own terms."

Ava leans in and whispers, "They will torture you and everyone you know, they will want to know why, and they won't believe you because your motive is nonsense. So … this is goodbye?"

"Yes, I'm afraid so, kid."

The mood changes, and when our food arrives, we eat in

silence. There's nothing more to say.

"When?" Ava asks.

"You know I can't tell you."

"You don't trust me?"

"Don't take offense, I trust no one."

"Me either." We both chuckle.

"Don't you have a flight to catch?"

"Yes. But are you sure you don't want a different ending to your life story? I mean, I can help hide you, and even get you out after, but you need to give me more information."

"Ava, please, my mind is made up. Don't waste your energy. I believe people enter your life for a reason, and they also exit for a reason. This all feels right. It's my time to stop running, hiding and being scared."

A single tear rolls down her cheek. She looks down without making eye contact.

"Thank you."

"Thank you."

She stands, holding out her hand. We shake, and just like that she's gone.

I sit finishing my coffee and thinking about what I would do if I did survive. I'm making a mistake. I quickly push those thoughts out of my mind. Suddenly, my wrist stings. I look at my wrist but there is nothing there.

1 month later

Today is the day… I've been following Claire for a few weeks. The only day that she has a routine is Sunday. She goes to church at the same time, same location, same car and the same guys are with her. I won't kill her in the church because, after all, I'm Jewish, and I refuse to ruin a sacred place for the worshippers even if it's not my religious choice. I will catch her at her favorite restaurant where she goes after church. I've been going to the church and the restaurant for the last couple of weeks. She sits in the same booth, and I have been sitting in the same booth further down, but when you need to go to the bathroom, you walk right by her booth. I will get up to go to the bathroom, pull out the gun and shoot her in the side of her head. I have two shots, one for her head and one for mine. I have four seconds to reach into my pocket and shoot her in the head and two seconds to pull the gun and shoot myself before I am surrounded.

I don't go to church today because I want to get to the restaurant just before she arrives. The restaurant is unusually crowded today; there are a few new faces, but nothing out of the ordinary. I order my food as her vehicle pulls up. I try not to look in her direction. I have my newspaper in front of me, pretending to read the news. She sits down, and I take note of the clock. The waitress will be at her table in five minutes to take the drink order, then return three minutes later with coffee. She will place an order, which takes about two minutes, and the waitress will walk off.

It's time. I get up and begin my twenty-three second walk to her table. My hand is to my side, ready to reach in my pocket. I have practiced this over and over in my bathroom mirror. I know the level my arm needs to be and where on her head I need to shoot to kill her. I am ten seconds away when I see someone walk out of the bathroom; he is walking on the side I need to be to kill

Claire. He looks dead in my eyes. He is a Native American man, and I've never seen him before in my life. He needs to move to another aisle, or he will bump into me. I'm not budging; I am here to kill this bitch. I don't break eye contact with the Native American. We both arrive at Claire's booth at the same time, but before I can even reach into my pocket, he dives in front of me, pulls Claire's head back by her hair and slices her neck from ear to ear. I dive into the booth next to her and take cover. The bullets are flying in all directions. I look over and Claire is staring at me with her dead eyes, thick blood spreading across the table and dripping on the floor. I am angry, angry that I didn't kill her and angry that I am once again hiding under the table.

The room fills with smoke. I cover my mouth, trying not to inhale the substance. It smells all-too familiar. Perhaps I remember the smell from a homicide case in the past. Gangs have been using a substance like this to get rid of DNA left at the scene. Although this substance is stronger. My eyes are burning, I need to get out or this chemical is going to kill me. I crawl over what seem to be dead bodies. I hesitate to open the front door for fear of being captured and tortured. I didn't kill Claire, someone else killed Claire, but I will stick to my original plan. I pull out my gun, because suicide was always the plan.

AVA

CHAPTER 39

IN THE RED

All I can see is bright blue-sky peeking through the blowing palm leaves. My lounge chair is in a fully horizontal position. The sand fleas bite at my ankles every so often, reminding me I am disturbing their home. My upper body is shaded from the brutal sun, but as the sun shifts more of my legs are exposed to the sun. I throw a towel over my legs. All I can hear is the waves crashing and the resort getting ready for the day ahead. I know it has just turned 10:30 a.m. because the music at the beach bar is blasting reggae; *Three Little Birds* is playing in the background. I'm too familiar with the music rotation. Island life is just as repetitive as the days in the city; there's just a different scenery with a slower hustle. I'm craving my first drink of the day, a mimosa. It's my first drink every morning. All I need to do is wave in the bar's direction and the drink will be in my hands in minutes. Tipping well and for every service gets you special attention. I can't imagine the amount I tip in the evenings when I'm drunk. It's a routine habit for me now. The heat keeps you drinking all day and will dehydrate you while you get drunk. Paul suggests I drink a glass of water for every alcoholic beverage I have. I know I shouldn't be drinking while pregnant, but I'm guessing my subconscious knows I won't end up keeping the baby. I'm uncertain if Mac's the father or Johnny. I'm having difficulty going through with the abortion, but if I keep putting it off, I'll be too far along for doctors to even consider doing the procedure. I can't tell if it's my hormones or just depression I feel. This time the weather is not to blame. It's a mixture of homesickness and being upset with myself for putting Johnny in prison. I have cycled back to that old dirt road of deep depression before I lost my job.

I didn't foresee Johnny pleading guilty to keep Susan out of jail. I was certain they would charge Susan with all the proof provided. The DEA was just happy to charge someone and connect the crime. I wish Johnny would have trusted me enough to tell me his plan because I would have done all I could to push Susan in front of the prison bus. He doesn't deserve to be in jail, with his son's birth approaching. Fuck Casey, but his son is a different story. I love Johnny and will always care for him no matter how much he hates me, even if he never speaks to me again.

I've paid everyone I can at the prison in return for Johnny's safety. He hasn't made many friends. I know the Mob claims to protect him, but I don't trust their promises. I've written to him every week since he's been locked up. I'm living in hope for a collect call or a letter returned. He has not tried to reach me.

I have tried to call the jail to check if I am on the visitors list. Paul is working on setting up a meeting with Johnny, bypassing the visiting regulations.

I've begged Lewis to make sure he is not harmed in prison. I expressed my love for Johnny, so he will take my request seriously. He hates Johnny and his family. He won't tell me the reasons, but I imagine there is a laundry list of issues. Johnny isn't a likeable person. He appears an arrogant, ungrateful prick. He isn't nice to many people; I have firsthand experience of him treating me like I'm less than him. Still, he has this way of making everything better.

Paul and I are running low on cash. We have credit in the dark world of hacking but favors in the form of credit can only get you so far. I spent all I had from the Atlantic job on buying back Koda's mountain. I knew only Koda would be able to success-fully carry out Claire's murder. I never had faith Mr. Alterman could kill her, instead I used him as bait. If Alterman was stalking Claire, the Indian would stalk Mr. Alterman. The deal I made with Connor McClean was to follow Mr. Alterman and make sure he didn't do anything stupid – and protect him from being hurt. I knew Connor would discover what Mr. Alterman was up to and possibly warn the Mob. When I shook Mr. Alterman's hand that day at the diner, I transferred the tracking device Paul sent me. I gave this information to both Connor and The Indian. The Indian wouldn't get blamed for Claire's murder; instead Mr. Alterman would be blamed. I just hope he's dead before the Mob discovers Claire's lifeless body, or I fear he will suffer a torturous death.

The non-profit Paul set up has proved successful for cleaning dirty money, but between the profits and funding the non-profit, money trickles in like a leaky faucet. We are spending more than we are taking in, leaving our balance negative, in other words, no profit. The accounting books have more percentages in red than I would like to see. We cannot afford to go back to the States. It's cheaper to stay living in the Dominican for now, until we figure out our next plan. Not to mention, I have spent a good amount of cash trying to win back Johnny, while Paul spends all his resources on computers, and faster internet connection. Also, he has established quite a habit with prostitutes. I have never spent so much time with Paul, and just assumed he didn't have sex. To see him with men is something I will need to get used to. He's been taking hormones to make himself look and sound more feminine. I think it's amazing he's being himself, but a little part of me feels he's changing his identity to get out from under HSAC, since they have frozen a lot of his online bank accounts. We are, in accounting terms, 'in the red', meaning we are hemorrhaging money. I have a small circle of people I can borrow from, especially since Ruben hasn't returned my calls.

I feel a shadow crosses the sun. No rain or clouds are forecast today. It must be the bar boy checking to see if I want a drink. I open one eye and see a familiar bearded face. My heart almost jumps out of my chest. *Does he know Claire is dead and does he think I had something to do with it?*

"Ava. Looks like yah having a nice vacation; I think I'll join ya," my father says. He's wearing a ridiculous pair of floral swim trunks and matching shirt, left open, his stomach bulging over his shorts. His chest has fuzzy red hair all over. He drags an empty lounge chair between Paul and me. My father doesn't realize Paul is with me, or at least he pretends he doesn't notice.

"So, Ms. Ava, what are ya doin' in the Caribbean?" He pauses, but not long enough for me to respond. "Think, before you lie to me again. I wouldn't ask you the question if I didn't already know the answer."

I can't tell what he wants me to admit to.

"I had to get away…"

"Bullshit, fuckin' bullshit. You're a lying bitch, just like ya goddamn mothah." I have never heard my father raise his voice or talk in that tone before. I bite my bottom lip, fighting back the tears before I respond.

"Who, Claire? Or my foster mother, Mary. Which mother, Daddy. Please tell me, what bitch are you referring to?"

He sits there in shock, staring out at the ocean. I swing my legs around sitting sideways in the lounge chair and lean in to whisper in my father's ear.

"Your silence confirms Claire is my mother. Now, you are wondering how I know? It was my fake mother's graduation gift. She must have known the Irish were coming for her because she was killed afterwards."

It still stuns him but now he's sitting up facing in my direction.

"Ava—" he tries to explain.

I stop him because I don't want an apology; it won't help, and I don't need an explanation because it doesn't matter. What's done is done. The past only matters if it helps me move forward.

"Jimmy, you're not my biological father. I had a DNA test done."

I let him absorb the truth before continuing.

"I don't care that we are not related by blood, I still look to you as my father. Our relationship will not change as father and daughter. What will change is that I'm next up after Claire dies. I want you to get your ass back on the first plane to Boston, and you tell my dearest mother Claire that I'm coming for her position with the Mob."

With that, I get up from my chair, grab my hat and sandals and, without looking back, I begin my routine walk down the beach without a worry in the world.

Author's Note

Thank you for reading my first novel, In the Red. This is not the last you will hear from Ava and her criminal entourage. I've left you wondering what will become of Ava, but not to worry. I've already started writing the sequel, *In the Black*. The story will continue at the beach where Ava was last seen. For updates on the release date, please visit my website lisalibby.com, follow me on Instagram @ lisalibbyauthor.

As a new writer I appreciate you purchasing my book and supporting a new writer such as myself. When you have the opportunity please consider leaving a review on Amazon and recommending my book to your family and friends.

Thank you,
Lisa Libby